The Doomsday Machine:

Another
ASTOUNDING
ADVENTURE
of
HORATIO LYLE

Catherine Webb

www.atombooks.co.uk

ATOM

First published in Great Britain in 2007 by Atom
This paperback edition published in 2009 by Atom

A CIP catalogue record for this book
is available from the British Library.

ISBN 978-1-905654-02-4

Typeset in Fournier by M Rules
Printed and bound in Great Britain by
Clays Ltd, St Ives plc

Papers used by Atom are natural, renewable and
recyclable products sourced from well-managed forests and certified
in accordance with the rules of the Forest Stewardship Council.

Mixed Sources
Product group from well-managed
forests and other controlled sources
www.fsc.org Cert no. SGS-COC-004081
© 1996 Forest Stewardship Council
FSC

Atom
An imprint of
Little, Brown Book Group
100 Victoria Embankment
London EC4Y 0DY

An Hachette UK Company
www.hachette.co.uk

www.atombooks.co.uk

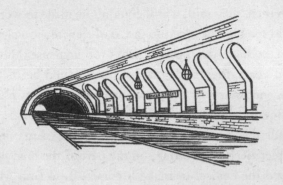

INTRODUCTION

Expense

To build the Machine, it took seven years, fifty-two scientists, nine eccentric inventors, three idiot geniuses let out of the asylum, two hundred and twenty-three labourers, forty-nine railwaymen with a grasp of steam technology, three barges of coal a day, ninety colliers to shovel it into the furnaces, several hundred thousand pounds levied from that year's import of opium into China, one man with a will sliced from silvery steel, and a gentleman with a thing for lightning storms. And the London sewers – that part came last, five years into the project, the final breakthrough that they hadn't even realized they needed, the moment when everyone at once sat up and thought, *yes*.

Even then, they said, it still couldn't be made to work – the scale was too big, the idea too grand, the enemy too clever, the expense too high, the forces at work too immense. Maybe in a hundred years, they said, maybe, there would be the understanding necessary or the tools available, able to chisel the two-mile construction site down to something smaller. Maybe, in a hundred years, men would understand the energy necessary to complete it. It took a risk, on the part of the man who had conceived the device, to make it come off, to find what was needed to turn the Machine into the monster it was meant to be.

But most of all, when the expense and the smoke and the heat and the metal, so much metal, was ignored, it took an *enemy*. In every glistening part of the Machine, in every cog and piston and giant arm fatter than an elephant's waist, in every bolt and screw, thousands of them gleaming in the firelight, was written the determination to win the war. Without an enemy, there was no need for the Machine. With so much feeling and anger built into its very rivets, even the coldest of observers watching its burning sides as it belched orange flame, began to speak of it as something alive. When it was only a few days from completion, work if anything seemed to sag – completed, it had only one purpose, and when that purpose was done, there would be no enemy, and therefore there would be no need for the Machine. It could rust with the rest of the weapons of this very special war. And also in those final few days, as the last coil was spun, one man, who had poured already a large part of his soul into the device, sat up and thought the forbidden thought – *Which* enemy?

This is the story of what happened next.

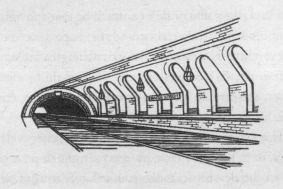

CHAPTER 1

Eyes

London, 1865

Somewhere in the eastern edges of Clerkenwell, a man is running. His feet splash in still, turgid puddles of oddly coloured liquid dripped from poorly dyed shirts hung out across the way, sending up droplets of thick water as he races down the street. He slips in the mud that has been loosened by the early spring showers, grabs hold of an old cart made entirely of splinters and mould left to rot in the middle of the road, swings himself round a corner and squints through the gloom for a light more than the sick orange glow from smelly tallow candles, seen under the doors of the houses. He hears footsteps behind, squelching on

3

the mud, and above, the rattle of something fast and light on the roof, glances up and for a moment sees a shape dance across the plank between two rooftops and down through a broken ceiling into a house ahead. He spots a doorway to his right, open, dropping down and smelling of rotting straw and sewage, and turns, and runs into it.

The running man flees down the stairwell, under a black iron lamp that hasn't burnt for years, into a tight street whose old cobbles are faintly visible underneath a thin coating of slime. He accelerates as his shoes slap loudly on the stones, as he hears ahead the sound of voices, sees a flash of light and prays this is it, escape, not believing he was so foolish as to get into this situation in the first place. He turns a corner and almost immediately runs into a shoulder that is pressed up against another and another and another and smells roasting nuts and lamp oil and sees cheap lace and neckties and hears, 'Hey-o, Billy, Billy get the doxy missus!' and, 'Two'penny, yours for two'penny, if you just got the glint . . .' and 'Haybag, haybag, I ain't never done nothing . . .'

He pushes his way into the crowd, turning sideways into it and ramming his shoulder through, stepping on shoes and moving even as voices shout, 'I was here first!' and one or two, more sympathetic, cry, 'Make way for the toff,' and are answered by hoots of laughter, and one or two more knowing say, 'It's a bobby!' and immediately open up space to let him through. The man is an odd sight in this crowd, and not just because of the way he moves, constantly turning his shoulder and feet to find the fastest way into the depth of the crowd, eyes forward and down. His coat is long and black, well cut but obviously neglected, with patches sewn on using the wrong colour thread; his pockets bulge; his shoes are practical but battered, turned pale brown from the mud spattered halfway up to his knees; his sandy-ginger hair is half-hidden by an old-fashioned broad-brimmed hat pulled low over his eyes; he wears no waistcoat but looks as if he should; nor does he have any gloves. He has long fingers stained with odd, faded colours, though not from tobacco. As he moves, he starts pulling off his coat, not diverting his eyes from where he steps, but working steadily towards the object of the crowd's attention: a set of double doors pulled wide open to let them into the heart of the nearby buzz. He elbows his way forward, slips a penny into the hand of the waiting doorman, a boy of no more than seven years of age with his cap out and an expression suggesting that if you didn't pay *this* doorman, your kneecaps would never see another day, and enters the heat of the hall.

He can hear distantly the sound of two voices straining above the babble of slang within the theatre's thin walls, muddling their way through a sketch that will soon lead to a rousing chorus of 'The Nutting Girl' – a tribute to London's best-loved ladies of repute – and other light classics. The heat is worse than the noise; it hits him full in the face and makes every capillary dilate in distress; it falls on him like a wave, making each moment more intensely hot than the last. Everywhere there are people, elbow to elbow: girls draped on the arm of their chosen lad, boys in groups shouting random abuse at another group across the hall, old men dragging their daughter off a rival's son while glowering within the fringe of their overgrown whiskers. Few actually pay attention to the man and woman on stage, in huge ginger wigs and quantities of cheap lace, who are desperately trying to muddle their way through a chorus of, 'Ah-hey-ho the haybale!' Those who are listening join in, each in their own key and with their own special version of the tune, determined to drown out any rivals who might believe *they* know better.

The fleeing man glances over his shoulder, and for a second thinks he sees a flash of green, and a black silk top hat horribly out of place, that even as he looks is knocked off by someone in the crowd with a cry of 'Toff, toff!' He ducks down into the crowd, bending forward so that his head is lower than the average shoulder and the world smells of armpit, and starts butting his way further into the mêlée, following the nearest flow of people past the downward staircase that leads into the pit in front of the stage, and on to the upper balcony, which creaks and heaves under the weight of bodies who have piled in there for the evening. Something white and sticky falls on his shoulder: hot wax dripping from the foul-smelling, smoky candles intermixed with the battered lamps hung round the edge of the hall.

As he moves forward, he methodically turns his coat, pulling the sleeves back in on themselves and out the other side, revealing underneath a pale grey fabric, sewn just like the black, and looking just as much like the outside of a coat as its lining, complete with bulging pockets. He starts pushing his arms back into the sleeves, almost kneeling down among the crowd to hide his actions, then straightens up, scrunching his hat down to a handful and ramming it inside his coat pocket in a further effort at disguise. He peers over the heads of the crowd, then looks down the short distance to the pit, where a fight, over what he couldn't guess, has broken out in one corner near the old man with his three-stringed fiddle. A hint of black coat somewhere on the edge of the crowd, really too finely cut to be in this hall? Perhaps – it is hard to tell in the dim light.

He edges to the far corner of the hall, where the shadows are deepest, and muscles his way into a patch of wall between an old soldier missing an ear, and his drinking companion, who is clinging on to the wall to stop it swaying around him. He shuffles down to keep his head low, folds his arms across his chest, tucks in his chin and prepares to wait out the evening amid the sweat of the hall. He claps when the audience claps, boos when they boo, swears fluently when they swear, roars with laughter when they laugh and somehow, by a strange twisting of his face and lilt of his voice, isn't the same toff who walked in a few minutes ago, but shrinks down into himself while throwing his voice out across the hall with every cry of 'Get off!' or lets a tear well in his eye with the sadness of a true war veteran when the man in the big waistcoat and huge moustache raises his hand and calls for a moment to remember the lost of the Crimea and Britain's noble undertaking. Only when he thinks no one is watching does the openness of his face cloud for a moment, as he scans the crowd in search of something out of place, and shrinks further into the darkness at some half-imagined shimmer of movement by the doors.

And while the man hides in the music hall, and watches, without any connection or awareness of circumstance, the thoughts of another are about to turn in his direction, and they go something like this . . .

'*Xiansheng?*'

'Berwick has gone. Run. They found his bed empty in the night.'

'I find it hard to see how.'

'Nevertheless. *They* helped him.'

'How could they know?'

'They have friends in high places; you know this. They were watching him for some months before the calamity at St Paul's.'

'Where has he gone?'

'I don't yet know.' A sigh, a letting out of long breath, that just happens to have casual words tangled up in it. 'He took the regulator.'

A moment's silence, while the full implication settles in. Then an overly contained, 'I will send my men.'

'They won't find him.'

'You underestimate our will, *xiansheng*. What are you thinking?'

'If Berwick felt himself to be in danger, where would he run?'

'The city is a good place to hide.'

'Who would he run to?'

A silence while the speakers in the room contemplate this question. Then, very quietly, one man says, 'Oh. I see what you might be thinking. Is it going to be a problem?'

'Maybe. Not yet. We'll see what he does first, we'll see if Berwick contacts him. There's still time.'

'I hope you're right, *xiansheng*.'

Some miles away from both the hiding man and those who contemplate him, a hand stained black with coal dust reaches out for a lever the height of a ten-year-old child and the thickness of a woman's wrist, and presses the brake off. Its owner looks up, awaiting a command.

'Well?' says a voice like the snap of a silk flag in a strong breeze.

'Without the regulator . . .' stumbles the owner of the blackened hand.

'The regulator is only needed for discharge, and by his own mathematics that is three days of pumping away! Do not concern yourself with the regulator.'

The man with the black-dusted hand, who is smarter than the owner of the commanding voice gives him credit for, thinks about this, then shrugs to himself and pushes all his weight against the lever, rocking it heavily forward. Somewhere a long way below the gantry on which he stands, something goes *thunk*. Something else gives off a long, painful hiss, something tall and metal screeches inside stiff gears, a furnace door slams, a shovel digs into coal, a fat coil of tightly wrapped cables, each one thicker than an arm, turns on an axis and locks into place between two metal points that gleam in dull orange light from the banks of burning coal a long way below, and, as slow and irresistible as an iceberg, the Machine starts to move.

It is bigger than the deck of the largest man o'war; it fills the space of an average cathedral; it burns more coal than twenty trains rushing from London to Edinburgh; it contains more metal than Brunel's greatest construction; it is hotter than the hottest music hall on a summer's night; it needs a hundred men to throw coal into its furnaces just to keep it powered up. Even to the man who created it, whose monster it is, it can have no other name than the Machine.

Although he didn't know it at the time, to the man hiding in the music hall, all these things were, in fact, related. If he had known that then, he might have been tempted to argue that by the same reasoning, everything in the universe was related, an endless pattern of inter-connectedness and general shared being, and so on and so forth, but frankly his attention was occupied with more practical matters. The fight in the corner of the pit was resolved by the fiddler smashing a small sandbag over the head of the nearest combatant. This in turn led to a general acceptance that nothing more in the show would be as impressive, and so the two singers, looking relieved, started winding it down. This was followed by a huge burst of rousing applause and a spontaneous chorus of five different versions of 'God Save the Queen', three of which weren't even that profane, and which led the hiding man to think that maybe this was a comparatively civilized hall after all and that perhaps when circumstances were different, he might come back again for a nice night out, maybe bring the children as an educational experience or nostalgia trip, depending on which child was watching.

As the crowd started to move, he took hold of an arm belonging to the drunk old soldier, who seemed too far gone even to notice the stepping of his own feet, and with a muttered, 'Evenin', pops,' started walking him towards the door, keeping his chin tucked down towards the old man's face as if at any moment the man might speak words of wisdom that he had to hear. 'Come on, grandpa, ain't your night, where's the patch, huh?'

With the old man supported firmly under the arm, he made it out into the night air on a tidal wave of heat, the darkness shockingly cold after the hall, and followed the main flow of the crowd along the street. The walk took him west, towards

Smithfield, and he was almost on the edge of the market there before the crowd started to thin out to just a few stragglers. He found an inn, the door half-open and the shutters drawn, and led the old man in, depositing him by the scarcely burning fire. The drunken man, oblivious, let his head loll and, within an instant of being settled, gave out a sound that was half a belch and half a snore.

Satisfied with his night's work so far, the man in the grey coat slipped to the door and peered outside. A single lamp hung down from a house bridging the end of the narrow street; at the other end, another faint light burnt by the doorway of a small church, its stones stained black with soot. Across the way was the high wall of a workhouse, all the lights long since out, and the gate chained shut for the evening. He listened for the sound of movement, and heard nothing more than the scuttle of a rat somewhere in the churchyard, the hiss of a cat that has seen its prey, and, in the distance, the shout of the butchers as they started to prepare their meat for the morning's market, and the bleating of a flock of sheep being herded through the arches of Smithfield for slaughter.

There was no sign of another person on the street.

The man let out a sigh, closed the inn door quietly behind him, and started walking, his feet barely making a sound now as he moved up the side of the road, hands in his pockets. He passed under the light and glanced round the corner, into more quiet streets, all darkened now. He took a moment to recover his bearings, glanced up out of habit to see if there were any stars – the clouds were too thick that night to tell – and looked down again, into a pair of bright green eyes, so bright he could see their emerald colour even though the owner stood just outside the light.

He didn't speak, didn't even have time for the surprise to show on his face, but dragged one hand out of his pocket and opened his fingers, hurling something small and silverish on to the floor. It shattered, the fragments of glass lost behind a sudden explosion of smoke and sparks that hissed and spat around his feet, obscuring him in a second. He turned and ran. Down the street, past the door of the inn, over the old rusted fence of the church, into the churchyard, bounding over graves and past ancient memorial slabs, over the fence on the other side – a longer drop than he expected; his feet almost went out from under him on the street as he landed – crouching low beneath the raised bank of the churchyard wall, turning and running again, down an alley that smelt of the sewers and old refuse, into a courtyard criss-crossed with empty washing lines, round the side of an old trough converted into a washer-woman's basin, searching for an alley at the other end, a flicker of light ahead, the sound of a voice calling, 'Two of the clock, two of the clock!' somewhere in the distance, and a policeman's whirling rattle. He chose a direction based on the sound and ran blindly into the darkness, feeling his way along a wall, across shut doors spiky with splinters, until the wall stopped and turned into an alley so tight he had to swivel sideways to edge through it, pressing his back against one wall and shuffling his way along it towards the darker patch of darkness at the end that suggested, dear God, perhaps another street.

He stepped out into it, looked left and right, and saw just a second too late a white-gloved fist swinging towards him. He turned his face in time for it to hit his shoulder, knocking him back; heard steps, and felt another hand grab his other arm, dragging it back, another hand somewhere across his face, leather-covered fingers scraping over his teeth and nose, pulling his head to one side. And there it was again, the flash of green eyes that he shouldn't be able to see were green, like the gleam of a cat's gaze in the night, before it darts away. Knowing too well what he might see, he closed his eyes as tight as he could even as he gave up fighting, feet scrabbling in vain for a foothold, slipping half to his knees, held up only by the hands that restrained him.

Silence settled. The only breathing he could hear was his own, fast and heavy. He took a deeper breath and held it, letting his ears adjust to the quiet in those few seconds, and heard other, softer breaths near by, from at least three or four people, and the sound of shoes on the cobbles. He let out his breath in a rush as fear and adrenaline took control of his heart again and made it hammer.

Gently, a voice said, a woman's voice like the sound of wind chimes, 'Open your eyes.' He squeezed his eyes shut even tighter and rammed his chin into his chest, bending his head down towards the ground. 'Please open your eyes,' said the voice. He didn't respond. 'You know, I could try my subtle womanly graces on you,' continued the voice easily, 'or I could cut off your little finger. Which would you rather?'

When he didn't answer, someone took his left hand, which was duly raised, turning his palm skywards. He blurted, still not opening his eyes, 'Subtle womanly graces, please! Any day!'

The fingers across his hand stopped moving, although the grip on his arm wasn't relaxed.

'Where is Berwick?' He could feel the warmth of the woman's breath in his ear as she whispered the question.

'Who what?'

'Little fingers are surprisingly useful; it's difficult to play an octave on the piano without your little finger. Where is Berwick?'

'Uh . . . south of Wensleydale?'

'Mr Berwick, Mr Andrew Berwick Esquire.'

'I think you've got the wrong man, ma'am.'

The fingers that had seized his hand let it go, then brushed his chin and gently pulled it up. 'Why do you close your eyes?' breathed the voice.

'Nervous reaction?' hazarded the man.

'Don't you want to see who I am?'

'No, not at all!'

'Why not?'

'You might . . . not want a living witness?' he suggested.

'To what crime? Here we are, pleasantly discussing an acquaintance of yours. Where is Berwick?'

'Never met the man.'

'He was your father's closest friend.'

'Children never pay attention to their parents; it's all part of learning about life!'

'Are you scared of being bewitched?'

'I'm superstitious, me, never open my eyes anytime I get mugged in case of the evil eye and the pox and . . . and . . . other bewitching things.'

'I thought you were a scientist.'

'Why'd you think that, miss?'

'The contents of your pockets are unusual for an ordinary working man.'

'I'm a physician's apprentice.'

'You're too old to be an apprentice.'

'A physician's life is one of constant learning, miss!'

'You're certainly a poor liar, whatever else you may be.'

'You catch me at a bad time.'

A foot hit somewhere behind his kneecap, not particularly hard, but enough to send him staggering, sliding awkwardly down on to one knee, head immediately pulled up from behind to look at what he guessed must be the darkness in which stood the woman with the wind-chime voice. She said, 'You are carrying a magnet inside your coat pocket, sir. And you're still afraid of us? Does it not make you wonder why, after all that you have done and all you have seen, we do not just kill you now? Don't you desire to know answers? Don't you want to know where Berwick is?'

The man hesitated. Slowly, he said, 'Why do you want Berwick?'

'He is building something; a machine. It is a terrible thing, this creation; he should not have started it, and he now realizes this. Others are looking for it, others will know that you know him, others will ask you these same questions that we ask, but they may not be so sparing of your little finger. So, I ask you again: where is he?'

'I don't know!'

'With your eyes shut, your imagination must run wild. You must be thinking, "What are these people going to do? What next?" It is a strange security and a strange danger, not being able to see — security in that the pain may be less without seeing what is done to you, like an amputee who didn't see the leg being removed and can't quite believe it's gone, who still thinks he can twiddle his toes. Or like the blind prisoner who knows that pain must come but doesn't know where from, and so imagines a thousand different ways of dying, a thousand different kinds of torment, until his mind is so wild with terror that the pain he merely thinks of becomes real, more real than anything that could be inflicted on him.

'Which are you, sir? Do you imagine a thousand horrors worse than anything you could survive? Or do you cherish the comfort of not needing to know; do you need to see to believe that you really are dead, that you really are dying, that you really have been hurt? Have you ever had occasion to find out?'

'I don't know where he is! I swear, I haven't seen him for years, I don't know what you want! *I don't know where Berwick is!*'

Silence. Then a sound of movement in the air, and the grip on his arms was relaxed. He flopped forward on to his hands and knees, still keeping his eyes tightly shut. There were footsteps moving quickly away.

Her voice overhead said, 'I believe you.' He heard an intake of breath, a hesitation; then, in a rush, almost an apology. 'You have to understand; the thing he is building will kill my people, without discrimination. They will set it off and never even know those who die, but they will rejoice in their deaths. It is blind, cold, effortless murder. Do you know all your enemies well enough to say that every one of them is evil, that every one of them must die? I choose to let you live, Horatio Lyle.'

Eyes

He opened his eyes, saw black leather shoes capped with shiny silver buckles, looked up at a huge black cloak and half-concealed white-gloved hands, thence to a fur-lined collar, to a chin the colour of almond, past a warm, lightly amused smile, to a pair of emerald green eyes, crinkled at the edges, and a face framed by tightly tied and plaited long black hair.

'Mister Lyle,' said the woman politely.

'Miss,' he mumbled.

'You have lovely eyes,' she said. Turning smartly, she marched off down the street, leaving Horatio Lyle alone in the night.

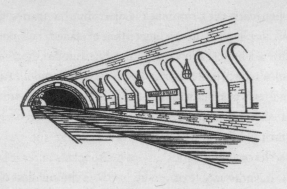

CHAPTER 2

Curiosity

A brief history of Teresa Hatch. It is brief of necessity, since at the time of her coming down to breakfast the morning after a man ran through the streets of Clerkenwell and a Machine began to move, Teresa Hatch was, in her own words, 'not so old and proper as how you shouldn't go and pay for all my things an' cook for me an' all'.

She was born, so she'd been told, in a workhouse in the Aldgate area, and raised to be respectful, God-fearing, dutiful and hard-working, until about the age of five, when she discovered that all of those characteristics put together didn't put bread on the table half so well as the ability to do a four-hundred-yard sprint with someone else's bread stuck under one arm. Upon which discovery she promptly departed by the nearest window from the orphanage where she'd been placed, wandered the streets for a while, fell in with a small but companionable group of snipes whose prime trick was distraction (she would fall down at the feet of a passing stranger and mumble incoherently while someone else did his pockets) and gradually worked her way up through the ranks so that by ten years of age she was widely respected as one of the most adept pickpockets and cat burglars in the East End, capable of crawling down the smallest chimney to grab the largest prize, always sought by the police, and never ever caught.

Except once; and indeed the one time she'd been caught, it hadn't been so much by the police, as by a special constable who always adopted a baffled expression when presented with a truncheon, and held it between the tips of his fingers as if it might explode. Considering his attachment to the use of chemicals that often did exactly that if you gave them so much as a dirty look, let alone picked them up, this was a character trait Tess always found odd. The gentleman's name was Horatio Lyle, and Tess had quickly struck up a mutually beneficial deal with him. He provided breakfast, a roof over her head, money, relative liberty and the occasional brush with death in unusual circumstances, and she picked any lock he wanted her to, held test tubes with pliers and a frightened expression, learnt the English alphabet and even, under the greatest of pressures, took baths.

Admittedly, on occasion in Lyle's company the brushes with death and adventure were a bit too real: in the few months she'd known him she had seen more things explode, and wielded more nitroglycerin than the average artillery officer, at a wide variety of monsters, demons, battling hordes and insane, occasionally indestructible psychopaths. But overall, the deal between Teresa Hatch and Horatio Lyle was a good one.

Except for this morning.

Tess had come downstairs, ready to be fed, at exactly that hour when it's too late for breakfast and too early for lunch, so that Mister Lyle would have to cook something huge and greasy just in between the two meals and comprising all Tess's favourite mid-morning foods, but Lyle wasn't cooking. He was not at the stove ready to fulfil his side of the bargain in bacon and eggs form. Instead he sat slumped in an old rocking chair, duly rocking, fingers steepled in front of his nose and heavy bags under his eyes. Under the chair was the fruit of their combined toil over the last couple of weeks – an object that Lyle called the 'High Velocity, Low Torsion Wind Bolt Delivery Device', Lyle having a somewhat exacting standard for the names of his inventions. Teresa, more accurately, described it as 'the big crossbow type thing what probably won't never be safe for no one to handle'. Scattered around the rest of the kitchen were bags of flour, sacks of sugar, preserved hams kept in the cool, bundles of herbs, stacks of cadmium and zinc blocks kept between clay sheets, pots of tubes and wire, ladles and saucepans and charcoal and bottles of silver nitrate, and all the other necessary paraphernalia of Lyle's profession, whatever it was Lyle's profession could be said to be.

Over the past few months Tess had found a role within Lyle's household as somewhere between lab assistant and self-appointed spiritual guide, at least in her own mind. This morning she squinted at him suspiciously, considered all the choices available and announced, 'You're smelly this morning, Mister Lyle.'

His eyes didn't glance up from the floor, where they had locked with a look of suspicion, as if surprised to find the tiles exactly where he'd left them the night before. His voice, however, was cordial enough. 'Good morning to you too, Teresa.'

'Ain't you slept none?'

'Not last night, no.'

'Ain't good for your health, Mister Lyle. You'll get all grey and old.'

'You show a touching care for my well-being.'

Tess hesitated, not sure what he meant but certain that it couldn't be good. Finally she said, 'Ain't we havin' breakfast this morning?'

'Breakfast?'

'The big – really big – meal what is vital for a healthy and happy day,' she added helpfully.

'Oh.' He looked distracted, worried. 'Haven't you had breakfast yet?'

Tess gave him the look that Popes down the ages must have given junior cardinals when asked if they'd found God already. He didn't seem to notice. Her confidence waned. 'Oi,' she said. 'Summat . . . bad happen?'

'Maybe.'

'Like . . . bathtub bad?'

'Perhaps.'

'Maybe we should have a holiday and see if it fixes itself!'

'Possibly.'

'You don't really mean that, do you, Mister Lyle? It's the way you ain't saying "yes" that gives me the clue. When you ain't saying "yes" what you really mean is "no".'

'Teresa, did I ever introduce you to Berwick?'

'Nope. Is he rich?'

The question seemed to take Lyle a little by surprise. 'Well, I suppose he's passably well-to-do.'

'Is he charitable with his money?' Tess's face was a picture of innocence.

'He's an old family friend, one of the first to really dabble in electricity and magnetism, an acquaintance of Faraday's, even. Unorthodox, but . . .'

'Not charitable?'

'I must admit the idea never crossed my mind.'

'But in askin' about Berwick you must have an ult . . . ulte . . . a nasty plan, right, 'cos there's got to be a *reason*. So I'm thinkin' as how all this you not sleeping and not cooking breakfast – not even for a poor hungry waif such as myself, for example – and how you're not cooking breakfast and this Berwick fella are all sorta tied up together, right?'

'Probab—' He saw her expression, and sighed. 'Yes.'

'I've been practising insight when no one's looking, Mister Lyle,' Tess confided smugly. 'Are you going to cook now?'

'Teresa,' said Lyle in a righteous voice, 'I find myself in a conundrum.'

'Oh dear. Is it itchy?'

He tried again. 'Perplexed. Bewildered. Bemused.' Tess's face remained optimistically empty. Lyle sighed and gave in. 'In a bit of a pickle.'

'Oh, right, yes, in a conunundrum! 'Course. Should've said.'

'I think I may be about to do something very, very stupid.'

'That ain't much like you, Mister Lyle.'

'Do you think you could say that without grinning, Teresa?'

'No.'

'Thank you for your devotion and respect. If I do this thing . . .'

'What thing?'

'Let me get to the end of a sentence and I'll tell you!'

'Oh. All right. You just keep goin' an' all. Don't let me put you off.'

'*If* I do this thing, it's quite possible that I'll be plunging myself, my friend and you into terrible and fraught danger, mystery and entrapment, daring-do and doubt, so on and so forth, you get the general idea – from which there may be no escape.'

'Uh-huh.'

'What do you mean, "uh-huh"?'

'Like how you does when you goes "perhaps". What thing?'

'But I mean really, where's the harm?'

'Hello, Mister Lyle? What thing?'

His gaze detached itself from the floor and met Teresa's. For a moment, she saw something unsettling within it. He said, 'I'm going to go and see Berwick.'

Elsewhere in the city, waiting in a hansom cab, a woman with white gloves is polishing a crossbow. There are a lot of things wrong with this picture. For a start, crossbows had gone out of fashion even in the most obscure of aristocratic sporting circles several decades ago. And any woman seen handling such an implement, at least if she was from a class that had enough money to care about such things, would be an automatic candidate for the asylum, with its black walls, ice baths, boiling furnaces and faint aroma of opium. To make matters worse, the crossbow that was being polished was of an odd design, all strange bends and tiny spiralling cogs, as if its designer had secretly wanted to build clocks instead and given up at the third stroke. The bolt that was being slotted with surprising ease into the bow was made of brass that shone dully in the lamplight by which the woman worked.

As she worked, she sang under her breath, an odd tune, wordless, whose notes see-sawed up and down like a bow drawn across a mountain top, seeing what tune could be scratched from stone. That said, she sang with a strong voice, and well enough to anyone who knew what kind of music she enjoyed and could recognize skill at it. As she sang, she oiled the cogs of the crossbow, and now and then glanced through the open window of the cab, watching a door down at the bottom of the street, and waited.

She watched a bobby in a dark blue cape walk down the pavement. Fat ginger whiskers stuck out from under his helmet like spilt paint overflowing from a tin. A woman with a little parasol, a collection of street snipes trying to get it off her, a plump vicar on his way to morning tea, a chimneysweep and his boy, and the bobby again, on the other side of the road, going back the way he'd come. From the recesses of the cab the woman watched him pass, waited, and a few minutes later, saw him pass again. Letting out a patient sigh, she laid the little crossbow on the floor and climbed out of the cab. She walked up to the bobby, tapped him on the shoulder, and smiled.

He turned, and looked straight into a pair of bright green eyes.

'Good morning, sir,' she said. 'I think it's time for you to leave now.'

And he did. Of course, that still left the girl with the hoop and stick and the gentleman in the vegetable garden hiding out behind a particularly large marrow, but at least one of them was on her side anyway and as for the other . . . well, if the enemy really thought that Lyle would leave through the front door after his encounter last night, they were gravely mistaken.

She sat back, smiled, and settled down to wait.

Horatio Lyle was, Tess had to admit, very good at what he did. Recent activity at Lyle's house had involved large parts of it being destroyed by fire, rampaging mobs and what Lyle always tactfully described as 'excitable exothermic reaction' and Tess translated as 'a really big bang'. All this had led to extensive refurbishment, during which Tess managed to blag her way into an even bigger bedroom. It had also led to reconstruction both in Lyle's house and, to Tess's surprise and the amazement of Lyle's neighbours, throughout the entire area.

Horatio Lyle had established himself as something of a charitable figure in his neighbourhood, which was on that socially ambiguous boundary between the criminal slums of Blackfriars where only the most intrepid bobbies went, and the more genteel, old-fashioned houses of the Strand. With money gleaned from previous family adventures, wise investment and the selling of occasionally crackpot ideas to the interested, he'd met the cost of repairing several nearby buildings. A Methodist chapel found its roof mended, a pickle manufactory had new windows installed, and a small workhouse was graced, from the roof right down to the ground, with an iron staircase which, though the owners weren't sure what purpose it served, did look immensely impressive. The Fountain pub, where rumour went that more politics were decided than in any palace in the country, was gifted with a new set of polished doors and a brass plate to put next to them. A group of ladies who walked every day up to the flower market next to the Royal Opera, to sell blooms mostly stolen from the graveyard behind the rectory, suddenly lived with solid roofs, and new washing lines to string end to end across the narrowing streets that bridged the recently covered ditches leading towards the river and Charing Cross.

There was a genuinely charitable streak in Lyle's nature. But it tended to be thwarted, as with most things, by how much time he had and who was trying to kill him at that particular instance. These left him little opportunity to find causes to defend other than his own skin, and very few people bothered appealing to him for cash, for fear that while they were in his presence something excitingly scientific might happen and they'd never get the chemical smell out of their clothes. That Lyle would go out of his way to act as a benefactor had therefore been a surprise to his neighbours. But only Tess, a few select workmen and some startled pigeons had the faintest idea of the world he had been creating above the streets, in which the repaired weathervane on a church could be a lighting conductor to a lab, the window in a workhouse could be opened at the twisting of a concealed handle, and the chimney so considerately swept and repaired could now fit not just the monkey-like apprentices to the chimneysweeps, but a fully grown man on his way to somewhere else.

Curiosity

On some nights, Tess had climbed up the ladder in Lyle's attic, on to his sloping, red-tiled roof. There she would sit, and listen to the city a long way below, and watch the lights on the river, and feel at home.

This morning, Lyle climbed the ladder on to his roof with Tess in tow and, cradled in his arms, a bundle consisting mostly of two huge drooping ears and a large nose. The bundle's name was Tate, and though scholars and zoologists could never quite believe it, he was Lyle's pet dog.

Lyle took a deep breath of smelly morning air and declared, 'Today, it will rain just after lunch.'

Tess looked up at a grey overcast sky, and shrugged.

Lyle looked annoyed. 'Do you want to know *why* it'll rain just after lunch?'

Tess considered her options. 'If I says . . . *no* . . . you'll be sulky all day, right?'

'On the contrary, I'll consider it merely sad that this is information you have chosen to neglect, a new insight into a world of . . .'

'All right then!' Tess bounded to the edge of the roof with reckless abandon, picking her way easily down the sloping tiles while Lyle turned green and even Tate's usually dour brown eyes widened at the sight of her. She peered into the street below and said, 'So why we going out this way?'

'I don't want to use the front door.'

'Why not?'

'It might be being watched.'

'Why? What you gone and done?'

'Nothing, nothing.'

'And you ain't gone and told me why you want to see this Berwick bloke so sudden!'

'I met some people last night who were . . . interested in his well-being. Their interest has piqued my interest. Or rather, I want to know why they're interested, and suspect that they are going to be interested in my interest and following it with as much interest as I follow theirs, while of course never forgetting our common . . . *interest*.'

'That were a very odd thing you just gone and said, Mister Lyle.'

'I trust it was sufficiently obscure for you to fail completely to comprehend it.'

'You're usin' big words to scare me, ain't you?'

'Absolutely. Come back from the edge.'

'I ain't going to fall.'

'Teresa,' declared Lyle firmly, 'a *Good* brush with death and adventure is a *Safe* brush with death and adventure, yes?'

'Yes, Mister Lyle.'

'A *Safe* brush with death and adventure involves being *Prepared*.'

'Yes, Mister Lyle.'

'It involves *Caution* and *Consideration*. It is, in short, all about steering clear of steep drops when you see any and never, ever pulling the big lever marked "Bang". I hope we understand each other.'

'So . . . we're goin' on an adventure?'

'Maybe.'

'Oh. All right.' She scampered up the roof again, balanced for a moment on the raised edge of the top, swung round to cling on

28

to a chimney, looked out across the city and beamed. 'If we're playin' at the how-we-mustn't-be-followed game again, can I choose the way we go?'

'Very well.'

The route chosen by Tess took them across the old tavern with its wharfside crane, admittedly now a good fifty yards from the nearest water, down a ladder into a vegetable garden, up over a wall into an alley running down to a watergate, and through the back door of the local bakery – which suddenly found itself short of three scones and a loaf – and out into the black, crammed and overshadowed streets that ducked and struggled under and past the railway lines of Charing Cross, where every other face was a grey shadow, blacked out under the stinking belches of smoke from the trains passing overhead and across the river. From there, a very out-of-breath Lyle hailed a hansom cab.

The residence of Mr Andrew Berwick Esquire, was in one of the wide, shiny streets north of Gray's Inn, defined by straight lines and relatively clean windows all the way up to that other patch of splotched off-green, Coram's Fields. The streets in most other directions around this enclosure of gentility largely consisted of tenements compressed together. This, and the fact that just a bit further up Gray's Inn Road the unwary traveller hit King's Cross, where the murders were almost as regular as the trains, was something the inhabitants tended to ignore.

Berwick was no exception. The maid who answered the door wore an immaculately white apron, and requested that Lyle and Tess use the iron scraper at the door to wipe their feet clean of manure and mud from the streets. Valiantly she merely winced when Tate snuffled his way into the house, nose down and eyes suspicious of the clean carpet that smelt of expensive soap scrubbed into it by hand.

Mr Berwick wasn't in, the maid politely informed them, but the housekeeper was available if they wanted to speak to her. With that, she led them into a small living room containing a large piano. The walls were lined top to bottom with books, at the sight of which Lyle's eyes lit up and Tess let out a patient little sigh.

'Oh, magnets,' exclaimed Lyle, his fingers tracing the edge of one cover. '"A Study of the Magnetic Properties of Brass Conducted by Mr J. Krebbers, a Gentleman",' he read. 'A timeless classic.'

'It is?'

'An exercise in perfect, scientific futility. Over the course of four hundred immaculately bound and printed pages, Mr J. Krebbers demonstrates with sweeping insight, experimental gusto and scrupulous method that there are no magnetic properties of brass whatsoever.'

'Oh.'

'At least, none worth talking about.'

'So . . . *so* . . .' began Tess cautiously, like a blind woman trying to work out what she's just stood in, 'exactly what were the point in . . .'

'Good morning, sir.'

The woman who stood in the door had a bosom that could have besieged a small castle, a nose like the rocky surface of an Alpine mountain, and hair tied up in a bun so tight it could have been used for playing the drums. Tess shuffled automatically behind Lyle's legs for protection, and Tate shuffled behind hers. Even Lyle, who usually refused to be intimidated by anything that wasn't actively waving a sharpened stick, found himself tugging at his collar in the face of the woman's expression. It wasn't that her look was particularly hostile. It simply regarded anyone it encountered in the same manner as it would a lump of wood – an inanimate object to be assessed, shaped, ignored or discarded according to its unique, lifeless properties.

'Are you the housekeeper?'

'I am, sir. And you are . . .?'

'Horatio Lyle,' said Lyle, hurrying forward, hand extended. Her eyes moved to his hand, then away, while her own hands remained tightly folded in front of her. Lyle deflated. 'Erm . . . I'm looking for Mr Berwick?'

'The master is in America.'

'I beg your pardon?'

'Business calls him abroad; I'm sure you understand, Mister Lyle.' Tess almost gave a start – even the housekeeper was ready with 'mister', as if she had instantly realized that in Lyle's voice there weren't quite enough good vowels to put him on the same level as other gentlemen of the town; never mind that he used long words and his coat was relatively clean.

'He didn't say anything?'

'No, sir, it was very sudden.'

'Will he be gone long?'

'Indefinitely.'

'But he left his books.'

The housekeeper's eyes darted to the shelf and back again, as if they'd never moved. But that had been enough for Tess to think, *ah*, and feel the start of a suspicious grin. Somewhere around Tess's ankles, Tate looked up through deep, lethargic brown eyes, suddenly more interested.

'He was unable to pack many books.'

'I'm sorry, what did you say your name was?'

'I didn't – Mrs Cozens.'

'Mrs Cozens, may I ask how long you've worked here?'

'Nine months, sir.' She was back on 'sir' now, her voice sharp and to the point.

'And how long has Mr Berwick been away?'

'Almost five months, sir. But I have had a letter informing me of his safe crossing – you may see it if you wish.'

'Thank you, I would like that.'

She didn't so much walk as glide out through the door – if there were feet under her voluminous black skirt, they were doing their best not to be noticed.

The second she was gone, Tess tugged at Lyle's coat. 'Oi!'

'Yes, Teresa?' said Lyle in a tone of infinite, martyred patience.

'Oi, why's she fibbin'?'

'Now let's not leap to conclusions about a highly suspicious and deeply implausible situation coming on top of bizarre co-incidence, shall we?'

While Tess tried to translate that into a language she understood, Mrs Cozens returned, an opened letter in her hand. Lyle took it and read. Tess fidgeted at his elbow until he lowered it to her height. As she read, her mouth silently moved with big words like 'the' and 'and'. The letter read:

Dear Mrs Cozens,

I am safely arrived in America, and settled well. My work is going well. I hope all things are good with you in Britain. I deeply miss the country of my birth but business has called me away. Please ensure that the house is kept in good condition during my absence, and forward the correspondence attached here to the relevant addresses.

Yours sincerely,
Berwick

Lyle quickly held the paper up to the light, then lowered it again with an innocent expression as if he hadn't taken even that small action. He looked up to find Mrs Cozens's eyes fixed firmly on him. 'You can see the letter is in his hand, Mister Lyle,' she said sharply.

'Could there be any reason to doubt that?' Lyle replied. He added, 'There was other correspondence with this?'

'Indeed.'

'To whom?'

'A few people to whom Mr Berwick owed money, tying up business affairs. I'm afraid I didn't keep a comprehensive list.'

'That's somewhat lax of you, Mrs Cozens.'

'I do my best, Mister Lyle.'

'Has anyone else been enquiring about Mr Berwick's location?'

'A few friends have called. I've told them what I've told you, sir.'

'Of course, of course. Naturally. Tell me, what has Mr Berwick been working on lately?'

'I believe he was attempting to develop a safer form of loom. He is very entrepreneurial.'

'A loom?'

'Indeed.'

'That hardly seems a useful employment of his skills. When last I heard, he was still absorbed in material properties.'

'I believe he found such study unsatisfactory.'

'He must have left a forwarding address, some other way of contacting him?'

'Yes, I can give it to you, if you wish.'

Lyle seemed taken aback, then smiled and shrugged. 'Where's the harm?' And in the same breath, 'I apologize for the trouble I've caused, and if my tone has in any way been inappropriate.'

'Not at all, sir. It was a pleasure.'

'Nevertheless, I do feel I have been less than cordial in my manner – please, accept this.'

He opened up his palm, and Tess's eyes widened at the sight of a big, shiny sovereign. An indignant squeak tried to crawl out and she put her hands over her mouth to trap it.

Mrs Cozens looked uneasy. 'Truly, sir, there's no need . . .'

'If you do not take it, Mrs Cozens, I shall be greatly offended,' said Lyle.

She looked him in the eye, and saw nothing out of keeping with the flat tone of his voice. Hesitantly, she closed her fingers around the sovereign and slipped it into a pocket. Lyle beamed, and said, 'Good day, Mrs Cozens. I trust you'll give my regards to your master when you see him. Tess, Tate.'

Tate shuffled after Lyle with a bored expression, and Tess followed. However, at the last moment, she hesitated, turned and executed an inelegant curtsey. 'Evenin', ma'am,' she said, holding out one small hand to be shaken. Taken aback, Mrs Cozens shook it and Tess's eyes lit up. Brushing within an inch of Mrs Cozens's wide skirts, she scampered after Lyle and out of the front door.

The three of them walked in silence down the street for a long minute, until they reached the gateway into Gray's Inn, with its stately buildings and throngs of lawyers. Entering the Inn, Lyle, not taking his eyes off the people passing back and forth, said quietly, 'All right, what did you find?'

'Don't know what you mean, sir,' said Tess sweetly.

'In Mrs Cozens's pocket.'

'I never!'

'Teresa, I would never give anyone a sovereign in your sight unless I was sure you were going to steal it off them within a minute.'

'You imp . . . impu . . . you sayin' as how I'm all thievin', like?'

'Yes.'

Tess hesitated. So long as it wasn't actually moving by itself, there was indeed very little in this life that Teresa Hatch wasn't prepared to steal. The cogs in her brain kept moving, and she reached a shocking conclusion.

'Hold on! You *used* me, you did! You gave her a sovereign so as how you know I'd go and pinch it an' all, without tellin' me! You went and were all sneaky!' Lyle beamed, Tess pouted. 'I think I liked you more when you was a soft mark, Mister Lyle.'

'The pockets, Teresa; what did you find in her pockets?'

'I found . . .' Tess rummaged in her own bulky jacket, 'a silver thimble, a roll of black thread, two copper buttons, an old bit of pencil and somethin' all metal.'

'And my sovereign, let's not forget that.'

'I think I must have gone and missed that.' Tess's face was a study of innocence.

'Teresa,' said Lyle in a strained voice. 'Surely with your free education, fine room and board, liberal weekly budget and healthy, full meals provided gratis every day to a menu usually of your own devising, you don't *need* to steal my sovereign, you don't *need* to pick the pockets of strangers. Surely you could just . . . *not* do these things?'

'I only do it for you, Mister Lyle, so as I can keep in practice an' all.'

Lyle sighed. 'What metal thing?'

Tess handed it over. It was the size of a small pencil-sharpener, dull, grey and cold. Lyle felt its weight in his hand. 'Ah.'

'Oh oh oh oh I know what "ah" means. "Ah" means as how you've just got a *clue*!'

'It's a magnet,' said Lyle.

'Oh.' Tess looked disappointed. 'An' that's a good thing?'

'Teresa, who do you know in this life that don't like magnets?'

'Um . . . people who like brass?'

'Think more adventuresome than that. Think brushes with death and disaster, think explosions, think epic toil across the morally confusing landscape, think St Paul's Cathedral and thunderstorms, think . . .'

'*Them?*' Tess had turned white. '*They* don't like magnets, do they? What've *They* got to do with anythin'?'

'Teresa,' sighed Lyle, 'it was *They* who wanted to know where Berwick is.'

Tess stopped dead in the middle of the street. 'Oh . . .' she whimpered. 'Oh, this is bad. Can we go on holiday? That's why you wanted to go out the secret way, ain't it? Can we, Mister Lyle, can we go on holiday? Somewhere a long way away? This ain't my kind of adventure at all.'

'Think of it as . . . as . . .' Lyle's voice trailed off.

'See! They cause nothing but trouble, with their wicked ways an' all! Let's go on holiday; you know it ain't going to be right . . .'

'The question is,' began Lyle in a distant voice, 'why would *she* be carrying a magnet? Is she afraid of *Them* too? But then why do they want to find Berwick?'

'Dunno, dunno, let's go . . .'

'Tess,' sighed Lyle, 'if *They* want to find him, he's got to be in trouble. He's an old family friend. I can't just . . . *not* find out. Not when there's so much I don't yet understand.'

'But he's in America!' wailed Tess.

'No, he's not.'

'How can you be so sure?'

'Did you look at the letter?'

'Yeesss . . .'

'Did you notice the watermark?'

'Erm. Not so as you'd say . . .'

'Chalfont Printers: an *English* paper company. Now, even if I did accept for an instant that Berwick would have gone anywhere without taking his books, would he really have thought, "Ah-ha, I must pack a sheet of English paper with me to send back to England from the uncivilized beyond"? He's in England – perhaps he wrote the letter himself, I don't know, I'm not familiar with his handwriting. Perhaps he was forced, who knows? But the paper is English.'

At length, in a weak voice, Tess said, 'There ain't nothin' I can say what will tell you how bad this is?'

He patted her on the shoulder. 'It's all right. I already know this can't be a good thing.'

'But you're gonna do it anyway?'

'I rather think I am.'

She let out a long sigh. 'So what now?'

'We go straight back to Berwick's house.'

'An' confront the evil housekeeper lady?'

'Not exactly.'

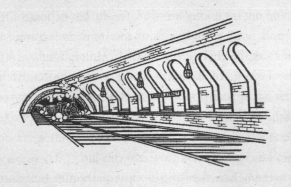

CHAPTER 3

Laundry

At the same time that Lyle, Tess and Tate were making their way into the mews behind Berwick's house, where old nags and new saddle horses nipped at hay bags drooping from low stone ceilings, and every other corner held manure filled with hungry worms, the Machine, rattling away with the sound of many steam locomotives racing along the same track, gave off the mechanical equivalent of a fart.

The invisible thing that accelerated at about three hundred thousand miles a second from the Machine's spinning heart therefore took approximately 0.00003 seconds to rise up from under the earth, ripple out in every direction and shimmer off beyond the limits of London. No one really noticed its passage, except for one clockmaker who found his delicate little iron springs unhappily straining for an instant in their frame, and one well-meaning scientist at the Royal Institute, who was surprised to find every one of his carbon bulbs, each the size of his own head, flaring up and popping into darkness as the unseen thing rippled through the room. Neither he nor the clockmaker even guessed at what the cause might be.

There was, however, someone who did. That someone, sitting in an armchair, reading a copy of the *Graphic*, looked up sharply as the thing passed by. His expression of astonishment didn't fade until he was distracted by a little *drip, drip, drip* sound. Unthinkingly, he reached to his nose and, with all the decorum of a custard-pie fight, wiped it on the back of his sleeve. White blood smeared the black velvet of his jacket, dripped from his nose and tasted salty in his mouth. He looked up and was surprised to see static rising across his vision and to hear a sloshing sound in his ears. With an embarrassed, 'Oh dear,' he tried to stand up, took one step and collapsed on the floor without another sound.

By the time all this had happened, the fading remnant of the thing risen up from the Machine had been to the moon and back twenty-seven and a half times, before dissolving out into insubstantiality.

Outside, it started to rain.

Horatio Lyle liked back doors. They encouraged the secret part of him that wanted to be a rebel; they made him feel reckless and dangerous. He also liked people who answered back doors more than those who answered the front, since they usually had other

things on their mind and couldn't be bothered to ask him relevant and embarrassing questions such as, 'Who are you, what's
that child doing, is that your dog, are you carrying any explosive
substances, do you have any identification, is there any danger
associated with talking to you?' and so on. What they said
instead, and what indeed the man who answered this door said,
was, 'You're selling something?'

'Whatcha wantin'?' said Tess quickly.

'We're not selling anything,' said Lyle, putting a firm hand on
Tess's shoulder. 'We're . . . do I know you?'

The man who'd opened the door and was wiping his inky
hands on a once-white apron said, 'I don't think so.'

'You're the butler, yes?'

'Yes.'

'Been here long?'

'A few weeks – what is this?'

'What's your name, sir?'

'Cartiledge; look, if you don't tell me what this is about I'm
afraid I'll have to ask you to leave.'

'Mr Cartiledge,' said Lyle brightly, holding out his hand.
'Special Constable Lyle.'

'What's a "Special Constable"?'

'The less-well-paid kind,' confided Lyle. 'Can I come in?'

'I should probably ask Mrs Cozens . . .'

'Mr Cartiledge, of all the things to do, that is the last.'

Cartiledge's eyes narrowed. 'She's not in some sort of trouble, is she?'

'Police business. I really couldn't say.'

And there it was, that look in the eye, that slight gleam of ambition that said here was a butler whose apron had been stepped on once too often. 'Perhaps we could talk in the kitchen?'

London rain takes one of two forms. Most commonly during the day, it drizzles so imperceptibly that it's like walking through a thin mist, droplets so small they won't even leave a gleam on the hairs on the back of your hand and which yet, inexplicably, manage to soak you through to the bone and leave a coldness in the air once it's stopped. The drizzle comes out of a constantly overcast sky that always promises more than it gives.

However, when it rains properly in London, it comes quickly, surprisingly, sometimes from an empty sky and only later do you notice how black the clouds are – in summer, when the temperature is high and getting higher from the chimneys belching smoke and the furnaces and clattering of the new looms down on the dockside and the new iron ships paddling up the Thames, there are thunderstorms and spontaneous downbursts that churn up the mud. The rest of the time, the rain is a clatterer. It comes without warning and clatters *tumtedetumtedetumtede* on the roofs and windows; it brings a clear, almost leafy smell from a cleaner place; it pocks holes in the river and races downhill to the very few, inevitably blocked drains that the city boasts. It turns noonday a dark, bruised colour, drives away all shadows and extinguishes all light except a pervasive greyness; and just thrums and thrums and thrums against the pavement, tracking huge stains down the soot-covered walls and making the heaps of rotting refuse steam in the yards behind the buildings.

And as it rains, the water of the Thames begins to rise. At

Richmond, it begins to slosh up the street, in Chelsea, it laps at the stairs up to the houses, and at Deptford, it slithers up the pipes into the two sewers – the old and the new – disturbing the rats, and a few things more besides.

This, as it turns out, is going to be very, very important.

Tess had found a small bag of roasted chestnuts and taken a seat by the fire to eat them. Lyle had found dried tea leaves and was busy straining them by the kettle on the stove, while one of the maids scampered back and forth into the rain to the black iron waterpipe just outside the back door to bring in more buckets.

At the table sat the cook, the butler, the stablehand, the upstairs maid and the cook's assistant, and they were bickering. Tess got the impression that bickering was something that happened a lot in this household; it had the quiet but fervent tone of a group of people who know that they're not going to win whatever their particular argument is, but are sure as hell not going to allow *her* to win instead! Lyle let them argue, fixated on the passage of water through the tea leaves into a small clay mug. Tess nibbled on her chestnuts, occasionally passing one to the expectant Tate, who knew where the next meal was coming from and always waited by her side for such an eventuality.

Only when Lyle was satisfied with the thin brownish liquid left at the bottom of his mug did he put down the drink and turn to the kitchen table with a resounding, 'I'm sorry, I missed that last thing.'

'I was just sayin',' said a huge woman in an off-white dress dotted with a mixture of flour, blood and chicken feathers, 'as how this is just the right time to buy eels!'

'Eels?' repeated Lyle, in the strained voice of a man who can't quite believe this is a conversation he's involved in.

'It's the season for them,' she said firmly. 'Any later and you have to cook them up in something special to give them any taste. But now, just give me an eel and whack it into a cold eel pie and I'll have the master drooling, you'll see.'

'Master ain't liking eels!' said someone else.

'He does!'

'He don't!'

'He does!'

'I'm tellin' you, he don't ever . . .'

'Perhaps he only likes in-season eels?' hazarded Lyle, before the argument could become violent.

Five pairs of disbelieving eyes turned in Lyle's general direction. Seeing that this was the way the feeling in the room was going, Tess glared at Lyle as well, to make it clear that she was on the side of the masses in this debate, whatever it was about. Tate took advantage of the pause to steal another chestnut from Tess's lap.

'What was you after again?' said the cook.

'He's here about Mrs Cozens,' hissed the butler in a conspiratorial voice.

'Oh, that bat! What's she gone and done?'

'Can't really say that, ma'am,' said Lyle in his best pompous voice. 'I just need to ask you some questions.'

'What about?'

'Mr Berwick – when did you last see him here?'

There was an embarrassed silence. Then the maid muttered, 'He's in America an' all.'

The silence stretched out so long Tess became aware of the sound of the upstairs grandfather clock ticking, and the fall of feet on the crackety floorboards above. Finally Lyle said, 'America?'

'That's right.' No one met his eye.

'Have you heard of Newgate exercise yard?' Five pairs of eyes gave nothing away. Lyle sighed like a patient man and in the same breath said, 'It's a space about five foot by five foot, where every day the prisoners of the Crown are allowed to march round and round in circles for an hour stretch, maximum, wearing masks so that they can't see the faces of the others and holding a piece of string for guidance. If they speak, they are punished. And then there's the oakum hall, where you have to sit working at getting rope from oakum until your fingers bleed, and then there's the treadmill which is rather self-explanatory, and the crank, where you wind and wind and wind a crank on a barrel for no good reason until you collapse from eventual exhaustion and then . . .'

'He ain't in America,' muttered the cook's assistant.

'No,' said Lyle kindly, 'I know he's not. So, where is he?'

'We don't know.'

'Why did you say he was in America?'

'He told us to!'

'Him, personally, he told you to lie?'

'It ain't a lie if your master tells you to tell it.'

'I wouldn't use that as a defence in court, if I were you. When was this?'

''Bout five months back.'

'Five months? My goodness – does he turn up here at all?'

'Sometimes.'

'Well,' Lyle's voice had taken on the tones of infinite patience, 'when was he *last* here?'

'What's this got to do with Mrs Cozens?'

'Your master has told you to lie and is pretending to be in America, a lie Mrs Cozens maintains with gusto. I think I'm entitled to a question or two, don't you? When was he last here?'

'Four days ago.'

'He doesn't stay the night here?'

'No, he stays where he works.'

'Where does he work?'

'Don't know!'

'What did he do here?'

'Looked at some books, ate some food, left clothes for washing, and left again! He gets paid really well.' The maid's eyes lit up.

'How do you know?'

'He gave us all a rise! And with him hardly here we need do nearly nothing; he's just throwing away the money!'

'What books did he look at?'

'Don't know. It's all just books, right?'

Lyle flinched. 'There's no such thing as *just* . . .' he began painfully, saw Tess's reproving expression and swallowed the words down again. 'Right,' he said. 'Yes. Well, perhaps. So he comes here every now and again . . . how regularly?'

'Every other week or so, you know? No predicting for sure when he's going to turn up.'

'And then leaves almost immediately?'

'Yes, that's about right.'

'And Mrs Cozens – she's new?'

'Hired in special to look after the house while he's gone. Don't think he interviewed her or anything, she just sort of . . . turned up.'

'Who does she talk to?'

'Sometimes this bloke in a top hat comes to talk to her.'

'The city is full of blokes in top hats,' scowled Lyle. '*Who? What name does he leave?*'

The butler sat up. 'Mr Augustus Havelock,' he said. 'The man's called Mr Augustus Havelock.'

In the silence, the tick of the upstairs grandfather clock became deafening. At length, in a voice rattling from a throat suddenly tight as a noose, Lyle said, 'Are you sure of that name?'

'Yes. Is he important?'

'He . . . has his moments. I need to see Berwick's room.'

'I ain't sure if that's . . .'

'Miss,' snapped Lyle, grey eyes suddenly burning, 'in my time, I have been hit by lightning and chased by madmen, I have built a machine that can fly above the city and fought a battle on the ice of a frozen river. If you could imagine half the things that frighten me, you would never be able to sit alone in a darkened room by yourself, and of all the things in this world that alarm me, Augustus Havelock is right up there, next to demons with glowing eyes, on the top of my list. If your master is mixed up with Augustus Havelock, and wanted by *Them* at the same time, then your salary had better be very, very good, because I swear all manner of trouble is just itching to come your way. Now show me his room!'

*

Tess had just one memory of Augustus Havelock, and even then, she couldn't put a face to it. It had been an encounter that felt an infinity ago, when the world was fuzzy and out of focus, and she woke up every day surprised to find that a week had gone by, not sure of when the next week would come, a time before the night she'd met Horatio Lyle, and everything had changed.

Even if there was no face, there was the voice still firmly in her mind, as sharp as the snap of a silk flag in a strong breeze, soft until the click of the sharper sounds, when she could hear the teeth in his mouth as sure as if he was a feeding piranha closing his jaws for the kill.

He had said, 'Miss Teresa Hatch. I'm informed you are a very, very good thief.'

She had said, 'I'm good, yep. Whatcha want, bigwig?'

He had said, 'For a start, respect. You may call me Mr Havelock. And I will pay you five pounds for the privilege.'

And for five pounds, she had called him Mr Havelock. For the same five pounds, she promised to do just one job for him, on a house on that strange class barrier between the slums of Blackfriars and the streets off the Strand, where the medieval buildings of Fleet Street decayed into rotting wooden sheds or were replaced by new brick houses, and where Mr Horatio Lyle patiently carried out his experiments, long into the night. For five pounds she would have run to Edinburgh and back and still had change from the expenses – but things were different now. Things had changed the night she went to earn her five pounds, and now she only remembered Augustus Havelock as a bad dream.

*

Horatio Lyle clearly remembered Augustus Havelock with more distinct feeling, apparent as he systematically tore Berwick's bedroom to pieces, dragging pillows off the bed, peering under the mattress, opening every drawer and even looking behind every book, running his fingers down their spines and scowling at every title on the shelf.

'Magnetism, magnetism, magnetism!' he chanted, turning from the bookshelf. 'Berwick, Havelock and bloody magnetism!'

'It might be all right?' hazarded Tess. 'I mean . . . like this bloke Havelock, he ain't done nothin' *evil* for a while, yes?'

'Apart from hiring you to break into my house?' suggested Lyle.

'Well, yes, but that were all his fault and nothin' to do with me!'

'Augustus Havelock is a *bad person*,' hissed Lyle. 'He's never doing anything but it's for something *bad*.'

'How'd you know him anyway?'

'Oh, we've met many times,' he rumbled, running his fingers round the edge of the wall in the forlorn hope it might not be as solid as it looked. 'He likes to say he's a scientist.'

'Well, that can't be so nasty!'

'He's a scientist who's stolen every idea he's had from better people, a scientist who bullies and threatens and buys his way into power. Everything he's ever done that's been in any sense original work has all been about power; *power* is the end of learning, he learns for wealth and ambition and studies for greed and personal gain and reads to use what he knows, to manipulate it and . . .'

'That don't sound bad.'

'Teresa, he will only study the ocean if he's sure there's buried treasure under it. He will only study the stars if he thinks he needs to navigate, he will only study the soil if he thinks it can be tilled to grow a cheaper kind of tobacco.'

'So?'

'He has never once looked at the stars and . . . and just *stopped*. He has never once thought that the moon is beautiful and that the sky at night is a marvel. He has never once looked at the ocean when the sun is coming up across it and thought it would make a picture. He has never once looked at the mathematics of a pine cone and seen an infinite regression of numbers, a dance of numbers in nature, and smiled to think that there is something more we do not understand, smiled to realize that there is more to learn, more to see, more to marvel at, he . . . he does not *marvel* at it. There is no beauty in the sun unless it is warming his crops, there is no miracle in the maths unless it is winding the spindle on the loom, there is no joy in the stars unless they are falling to earth to be counted and sold again. Everything he does is for himself. He is nothing but . . . coldness. Calculating, dispassionate coldness.'

'Is that why he . . . wanted stuff stolen from you? 'Cos you and him . . . are all grrry an' all?'

'Teresa, he wanted my plans for a . . .' Lyle froze. 'Oh my goodness.'

'What?'

'He told you to steal the papers in the study, didn't he? Top left shelf, behind the silver nitrate?'

'So? An' remember, it ain't my fault an' all an' how I'm all nice really an' you promised not to turn me in 'cos . . .'

'Teresa, those were preliminary designs for a capacitor bank.'

'A whatty?'

'A tool for storing charge, but I mean a lot of charge, I mean millions and millions and millions of coulombs of charge, billions – do you know what a billion is?'

'No. What's that?'

'It's a number with nine zeros after it.'

'An' . . . that's big?'

'All right, put it another way. If everyone in Britain and France and probably Italy too all came to London and stood shoulder to shoulder, they would fill every street of the city to the very, very edge, and there would be no space to move, no space to breathe, every house and every floor of every street in the city full of people, yes?'

'Yes?'

'Now take about eighty Londons full of all these people and put them all shoulder to shoulder and you have roughly a billion people.'

Tess thought about it. Finally she said, 'That's . . . big, right?'

'You're there.'

'So . . . this big, big number . . . what's it doin' exactly?'

'That was what the drawings were about. So much energy, all locked up in one place, ready to be discharged at any moment. They were only preliminary plans, of course, I don't think it could really have been built, the resource needs were too high, not to mention the gold, but . . .'

'Gold?'

'. . . but Berwick expressed interest in the designs too . . .'

'You said somethin' 'bout gold . . .'

'My God, what's he got himself involved with?'

'Dunno.'

'Thank you, Teresa.'

'Just tryin' to be helpful.'

'I've got to find him.'

'*Really?*' She saw his face and let out a pained little sigh. 'Right. 'Course. What we needs is a *clue*. Oh oh oh oh . . . maybe!'

'Maybe?' asked Lyle hopefully.

'Erm . . . no. I don't think it's going to work.'

'Fantastic.'

'How's about . . .'

'Yes?'

'Erm . . . uh . . . maybe Tatey-watey could track him down?'

Two pairs of sceptical eyes turned to Tate, who, aware of the attention fixed on him, rolled over with his paws in the air, ears sprawled out on either side of his head, and belly up, waiting to be scratched. Lyle said in a strained voice, 'I'm not sure if Tate appreciates his role in this investigation.'

'You're always sayin' how he's a bloodhound an' how he's really good at stuff an' all! Maybe he could just *smell* this Berwick fella and then we just follow Tatey-watey, because he's a good little Tatey, aren't you, yes you are, yes you *are* . . .'

'Through the rain?'

'Well, we'd have to wait, I suppose, 'til after. An' we'd need some kind of thing of this Berwick's.'

Lyle's eyebrows twitched for a moment, and Tess stabbed a triumphant finger in the air. 'Ah-ha!'

'Ah-ha?' he echoed, confused.

'You just looked all pen . . . pensi . . . thinkin', like! You reckon my idea ain't a bucket of pure!'

'Language!'

'What? I was bein' good!'

'Polite young ladies don't refer to buckets of pure in decent conversation,' he said primly.

'But . . . it's dog poo,' she said, in the voice of one trying to get her head round an important but difficult distinction. 'I didn't go and say how my idea ain't a bucket of dog poo, now did I?'

'You know, you're right.'

'See!'

'I want to see Berwick's clothes.'

They found them in the scullery, which was essentially a stone sink an easy totter from the outside pump. It was filled with all the equipment of a modern laundry room, such as a metal and wood scrubbing board, a bar of soap that dissolved into acidic little flakes and hissed with an ugly chemical smell on the faintest contact with water, and a pair of rollers set in an iron frame that Tess had always associated with crushed fingertips, designed to squelch the water out of even the thickest of fabrics. Lyle went straight for the dirtiest-looking clothes he could find and held them up, sniffing deeply. 'There!' he said triumphantly, a snort later. 'Tess, what do you smell?'

'Erm . . .' said Tess, leaning away from the clothes like a cat from off milk.

'Come on, come on, this whole smell thing was your idea, what do you smell?'

She took a cautious sniff and turned white. 'It's horrid!'

'I'd say . . .' Lyle took another long, luxurious sniff, which made Tess turn even paler. '. . . copper dust, eel pie, ammonia, pure ethyl alcohol, coal and raw sewage.'

'An' this makes you all happy?'

He rummaged in the jacket pockets, and his face split into a grin of delight. 'It gets better!' His hand came out, holding a small papery stub. 'A used single ticket, Baker Street to King's Cross.'

'A single ticket for what?'

'The Metropolitan train, Teresa. Raw sewage and an Underground ticket: only one place now to look for Berwick.'

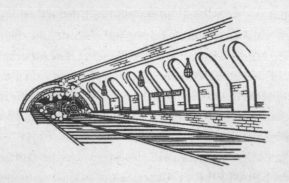

CHAPTER 4

Underground

Tess, although she had to admit she was growing less alarmed by
the whole science thing, didn't hold with these new-fangled ways
of travelling. She understood big, overland trains, giant snorting
things with gleaming green engines and giant wheels that gave off
belches of steam, and compartments and travel in general, and she
was even willing to come to terms with the iron steamers that were
starting to be seen everywhere, with their big paddles churning at
each side. But the new London Underground Metropolitan Line,
advertised as the first of its kind in the world, running Paddington
to Farringdon, unsettled her. The strange little steam engines that
pulled open-air carriages through the cut-and-cover tunnels
between the stations seemed insufficient for the task assigned to

them, and the smoke and steam billowed through the tunnels, making them suffocating and claustrophobic, despite the tremendous cheers of first-time travellers whenever they experienced the novelty of taking the steam engine underground, and the strange sensation of rising up into the light at King's Cross. Only in a confined space, however, did you begin to realize quite how much steam a steam train gave out.

'Technology!' proclaimed Lyle as they dropped down under the giant brick arches of Baker Street Station into the sooty blackness of the Underground. Along the platform, the dimness was broken up by a lamp under every other arch and above each low wooden bench. 'The new way to travel!'

'It's smelly,' said Tess.

'Teresa, in this city you can smell like horse manure, or you can smell like coal dust; it's your choice.'

'You went and said manure!'

'Well . . . yes . . .'

'An' you go an' are all . . . *adult* when I say pure,' she scowled. 'Typical.'

'Yes,' said Lyle in a strained voice, 'but when *I* talk about manure I use it in its scientific sense, to guide and direct the mind in a precise direction that more delicate language might not permit. When *you* say manure, you say it because it makes you giggle.'

Tess beamed. 'Yep!'

'Teresa, do you smell that?'

'I smell lotsa things, and it ain't good.'

'All right, let me rephrase. Teresa, can you please coax Tate out from underneath that bench?'

Tate was indeed hiding under a bench, eyes watering in distress, head tucked so far into his belly that he looked like a pair of paws surrounded by ears, with no other attached limbs to speak of. It took Tess less than a second to notice what was causing Tate so much dismay. The overwhelming stench of sewage rose up from a grate set in the floor at the end of the platform. It didn't even bother with the nose but went straight through the throat and settled on the lungs, making every breath oppressive; it seeped into the skin so that she could feel her own sweat crawling with the odour of it, as if the smell was static that snapped and rippled with her every movement, or a gauze veil draped in the air, that had to be physically pushed aside.

'Raw sewage and the Underground,' said Lyle, though even his customary brightness in the face of New and Interesting Revelations had diminished a little in the presence of the stench. 'All good so far.'

'*How?*'

'Teresa,' declared Lyle firmly, 'a *Good* brush with death and adventure is a . . .'

'. . . is a *Safe* brush with death and adventure, Mister Lyle,' chanted Tess dutifully. 'What we gonna do now?'

'Follow the smell.'

'Where?'

'Down there.'

His toe, being the only part of him sufficiently insensitive to move much closer to the smell, pointed straight at the grate, and downwards. In Tess's arms, Tate started to struggle and whimper. Tess stood rooted to the spot. 'You have got to be takin' the . . . I mean . . . got to be havin' a laugh, with all undue respect an' that.'

'I'll buy you a new pair of shoes?' hazarded Lyle, seeing that Tess was not about to be moved.

'What's that s'posed to do?'

'I'm told it's something you're supposed to say to young ladies of a certain age as an incentive,' he mumbled, the tips of his ears starting to turn a little pink. 'You say that you'll buy them shoes or . . . or a ribbon for their hair or . . . or a new set of lock picks or the latest efficiency of hydraulic piston or something . . .' Lyle's voice trailed off into silence, withered out of the air by the heat of Tess's glare. 'It was just a thought.'

'A ribbon for my hair?'

'It did seem like a silly idea at the time.'

'*Shoes?*'

'How about a new set of lock picks?'

'Mine work fine! Although . . . you never know when that acid stuff . . .'

'Hydrochloric acid?'

'That's the ducky! Never know when that might come in handy.'

Lyle patted her on the shoulder, a gesture that over the last few months had become a distracted habit. 'Maybe for Christmas, Teresa. In the mean time, I'm going down that grate and you are more than welcome to stay here, all by yourself, getting bored and impatient while I dance with death and clash with criminality, all by myself. Don't you worry your head about it; you just stay here.'

Tess let out a frustrated little sigh. She had a feeling that she was being used, again, but in the end what was she going to do that was any better? So, with a stamp of her foot she hissed through her teeth, 'An' whose goin' to cook me breakfast if you get all dead?'

'That's my girl,' said Lyle, leaning down to lift up the grate.

London's sewers were almost as new as London's Underground. But unlike the Metropolitan Line, which had been built to last, the tunnel that Lyle and Tess dropped into had not aged gracefully. Tate had refused to go within a foot of the grate, and Tess didn't blame him, trusting in his highly developed survival instinct, and increasingly regretting that she hadn't stayed above ground and cowered with him under the nearest bench. Thin, stagnant water, mixed with something else that Tess didn't want to contemplate, barely rippled around their feet. Where the tunnel curved up and away from the dark liquid with its oily, rotting sheen, Tess slid her fingers down a wall encrusted with a mixture of hard, rough, crystalline ridges and strangely warm, organic areas of total smoothness, where odd lichens seemed to have forced their way through the darkness out of the brickwork, their surfaces bubbling and fuming with strange bacterial explosions. Tess felt through the darkness for something less sinister and found Lyle's waist. 'I don't like it here!' she whimpered.

In the gloom, there was a faint *whu-phumph* sound, followed by a billowing of dull, smoky yellow light as Lyle struck a match almost as long as his upper arm. The match dripped shards of loose yellow phosphorus that hissed and faded under the surface of the almost-black-traced-with-yellow sludge beneath their feet.

'This isn't right,' muttered Lyle, holding up the light. 'Look at the brickwork – it's at least ten years old.'

'So?'

'Bazalgette's sewer opened more recently than that. Come on, Teresa.'

Tess picked her unhappy way after Lyle as he moved on down the tunnel. The light from the match held out in front of him turned his shape into a black silhouette, picked out against its faint yellow glow. Overhead, Tess heard the clattering as it slowed and the long *whheeeeee* sound of an engine letting off steam in the station, and the long piping of the stationmaster's whistle. She felt the brickwork hum as the wheels rattled overhead, a gentle *gu-dunk, gu-dunk, gu-dunk* as the train picked up speed, until she felt as if her brain was being shaken inside her skull.

They didn't have to walk very far. After five minutes the tunnel began to narrow, until Lyle was walking almost doubled over, and the walls were little more than a shoulder's-width apart. Every ten minutes or so Tess felt the world shake as a train thudded overhead. When Lyle's match guttered out, Tess was surprised to see that there was light in the tunnel anyway, a spot of greyness far ahead. The ground became more solid, finally condensing to produce a dull crunch underfoot. In the light that Lyle struck again Tess could clearly see the dull ochre-red of the walls, and the black of the filth-encrusted floor, trampled down by a tide of what were just distinguishable as footprints.

In silence they walked up the tunnel. As it got smaller, the heat became worse, although the smell didn't; it was as if the body could cope with only one overwhelming sensation at a time and had chosen to concentrate on the dry burning of the skin rather than the distress of the nose. The heat was too great to allow for sweat; it just burnt dry in an instant, dragged the life out of every breath and suffocated even smell. Eventually the tunnel stopped at a grate, which had a shiny new chain drawn across it and through a hook in the wall.

Beyond, by the thin grey daylight filtering down through a thousand seeming pinpricks set into the ceiling, was a room, all by itself in the middle of nowhere. It was high and domed, made of the same red brick as the rest of the passage, but its floor was clean, except for the odd dirty footprint, and covered over with grey stone slabs. On the far side, shadows lurked beneath a low arch, half-obscuring some long wooden tables and a number of chairs.

But the chairs had been violently overturned: indeed, the whole room had been smashed. Tess saw retort stands thrown down, the broken glass of test tubes and flasks, open burners, wrenched pipes and a forest of twisted wire scattered across the floor like a shrubbery of copper and steel, whose deadly torn points stood here and there at knee height.

Lyle muttered, 'We need to get into there.'

'Professional at work,' sang out Tess with false cheerfulness. She rummaged in her pocket for the little bundle of tools and hooks that were her only possession treated with real love; oiled and polished, they were always kept ready for who knew what circumstance. The lock was not the worst she had come up against — it too was new and relatively well oiled, making the little pieces inside it click more easily into place. She searched with one tool for the points of weakness, where the catches wanted to slide back, and with another eased them gently upwards, pinning them in place and twisting. The lock snapped open, and she pulled the chain free, triumphantly pushing at the gate.

'Wait!'

She stopped dead. There was no arguing with Lyle when his voice rang out that loudly in a tight space.

'Don't move.'

Tess stayed absolutely still. Lyle eased past her, his back against the wall. With the tip of the match he prodded at something just beyond the half-open grate: a wire, strung at one end to the opening gate, and disappearing at the other into the wall. 'What do you think?' His voice was now quiet and intense.

'Cut it,' hissed Tess.

Lyle threw the match past the grate into the gloom of the chamber, and pulled out a flick-knife the length of his middle finger. He slid it up and through the wire, which snapped back into the wall with a deep *boing*. Overhead, something thudded in the ceiling, sending down a cloud of dust. They waited, holding their breath, for the dust to settle. When it became apparent that nothing else was going to happen, Tess dared to breathe out again. 'Don't want visitors, you s'pose?'

So saying, she pushed the grate all the way open.

The thing in the ceiling that had gone *thunk* suddenly started to clamour. Somewhere overhead, a bell began to ring, and from down the tunnel there came a gentle whisper, like the last breath of an elephant, heard far off.

'Erm . . .' began Tess.

'Can't be good,' murmured Lyle. 'Quick, inside.'

They hurried in, Lyle picking his way straight to the nearest table. 'Right. Now.' His voice came unnaturally fast, and in the distance the elephant's breath grew to the sigh of a gentle breeze. 'Think! What's been going on here?'

Tess took in the shattered equipment, the broken glass, the torn wire, the overturned boxes and crates. 'Uh . . . science like how it shouldn't be done?'

'Teresa!' Lyle beamed at her.

'Wha'?'

'For a moment you actually sounded as though you had a decent grounding in laboratory procedure!' He saw her deliberately blank expression, and sighed. 'Never mind. All right, it's a laboratory, for studying . . . oh, look!' With an expression of delight he picked up an object that to Tess looked for all the world like a glass squid. 'I've been trying to get one of these for years!'

'What's that?'

'You use it for the crystallization of leached potassium nitrate from . . . certain waste products.'

Tess's eyes narrowed. 'What . . . *waste products*?'

'Well . . . you know . . .' The tips of Lyle's ears started going pink. 'Potassium nitrate is commonly found in . . . you know . . . places where waste has been allowed to settle . . . erm . . .'

Realization struck. 'It's poo again, ain't it? You get it from poo!'

'Now that is a gross oversimplification! Although I'll admit there are other products of a similar nature involved in the process . . .'

A distant clunking, the sound of something jarring in old stone, a faint noise like the humming of a trapped hornet in a jar, getting angrier, fast. Lyle's eyes swerved to the door, and Tess's followed. Quietly, he said, 'All right, a laboratory, studying what?'

'Uh . . .'

But Lyle's attention had already moved on, the strange contraption forgotten. 'Wires, coils – all right, coils, that's magnetic induction, what else? Chemicals? What do you smell? What chemicals have they been using? Potassium nitrate . . .'

· 'Dunno.'

'Black powder, explosives, that's what potassium nitrate's all about. Things that go bang.'

A distant sound like the rattling of many wheels across a rough cobbled street . . .

Tess waded in valiantly at Lyle's pent-up silence. 'Erm . . . ash. Ash! Burnt paper, erm . . . been a fire, but ain't much smoke, no soot, so . . .'

'Chemical fire, good – explosion?'

'Could be, there's marks in the wall like as how somethin' hit it fast . . .'

'Explosives and wires, bombs?'

A sound like the rumbling hungry stomach of a giant, getting closer, footfall of stone . . .

'Erm . . . distillation, purification, they've been makin' stuff, acid burn on the table, that means . . .'

'Acid burn, good! Electricity and chemicals, bomb-making. They've been making explosives.' Tess felt something cold slosh against her ankle and looked down to see cold, clear water rising around her feet, running quietly in from the door. A closer sound now, much, much closer, like snow falling down a mountain . . .

'Tess, get over here!'

No disobeying. She raced over to Lyle who was already look-ing around with the wide eyes of a man in search of a plan. 'All right, so Berwick was here,' he murmured, not taking his eyes off the grate through which the water was rushing. 'And he was making explosives. That's good, that's worth knowing, worth getting our feet soggy for.'

'Mister Lyle?' squeaked Tess. And now there was no mistak-ing the sound: the noise of water bouncing against brick, swirling down an ever-narrowing tunnel, rumbling closer and closer and closer and . . .

'It's all right,' muttered Lyle. 'It's *fine*.' He kicked over one of the large metal crates, spilling out its broken scientific equipment with an unusual disregard for the mass of breaking glass and the pooling chemicals. 'When it hits, just don't let go, all right?'

She nodded. A sound like the cracking of old bones dried in the sun, like the falling of every leaf off a tree all at once, like the splintering of a trunk, the feeling of wind rushing from the tunnel, pushed ahead of something that filled every inch of space and moved so fast even the air didn't have a chance to escape. Tess clung on to Lyle's waist as Lyle turned the box upside-down, so the open top was now the open bottom. Then, to Tess's astonishment, he put the entire thing over his head like a hat, so that the sides came down almost to his elbows.

Tess had just enough time to say, 'You look real stupid, Mister Ly—' before it hit.

She had never thought of water as frightening. Even when the Thames flooded in the marshes to the east of the city or lapped high up beneath the bridges so that ships had to wait for the tide to change before they could pass under them, water had just been something more or less contained, predictable as the slope of a hill.

However, when the water surged in from the tunnel, it came fast, so fast that it knocked the grate off its hinges, so fast it tore the legs off the tables: a wall of grey-greenness that battered the bricks in the wall and gleamed for just a second with a thousand diamonds of reflected light as it swallowed the broken glass and wires of the laboratory. Tess had never learnt to swim. She clung to Lyle for all she was worth and squeezed her eyes shut as the water hit, with a punch that knocked the breath out of her, lifted her feet from the floor, spun her round and round and burnt into her lungs and rumbled in her ears, so that she imagined it storming round her brain and rushing through her blood: a sickening whirlwind pulling at her skin and hair with a thousand hands, each more determined to be the one that finally ripped her apart. She felt the water spin her towards the ceiling and knew it was still rising, pushing up against the walls and carrying with it the detritus of the lab. Then she felt Lyle's head bounce against the ceiling and knew that her own head would follow just a second later. She took one last breath and waited for the water to roll into her nose and mouth and lungs while she held on to Lyle for dear life, however much of that was left. With her eyes tightly shut she felt Lyle's hand pulling at her and something metallic sliding against her shoulders. Cold water lapped at her chin.

The movement of water that had spun her subsided. She wondered if death was like this – not especially violent, just a gentle shutting down of signals, since she had no doubt that the torrent must still be raging around her. When Lyle's hand touched her shoulder, it was such a shockingly real gesture that instinctively she inhaled, and was astonished to find some air to breathe. Tess opened her eyes and saw utter darkness, and heard the sound of her own half-suffocated whimper and Lyle's rushed breath. She reached up and felt a tiny world composed of Lyle's face, and a lot of metal box, so tightly compressed around her that she couldn't even stretch out her arms to feel around the edges. The water still came no higher than her chin, and around her shoulders her hair loosely drifted. Lyle was treading water, the crown of his skull wedged against the top of the metal box he'd put over his head only a moment before. With arms outstretched, he was pressing his hands against the metal crate within which they now paddled, heads suspended in a bubble of trapped air. Tess considered this, together with the sound of Lyle breathing, a few inches from her, and said, 'What the bloody hell in God's name I mean really is goin' on?'

'I'll tell you,' Lyle's voice was unnaturally strained, 'if you just relax a little bit.'

Tess realized she was still clinging to Lyle's waist and loosened her grip. Lyle let out a long wheezing breath. 'Thank you.'

'Same question, an' I don't think as how you want me to go an' scream in a small space like this an' all! Where's the rushin' water thing and why we in a *box*?'

'Well, in order,' said Lyle, his voice reverberating oddly in the crowded darkness, 'no, please don't scream, for more reasons than just the noise – the rushing water thing is all around us although I suspect the worst is over; and we are in a box because it seemed like a solid watertight surface and because I have an inherently practical grasp of the fact that air when compressed within an area of fixed volume by water rushing into a large room will have no way to escape, assuming the pressure from the water below is equal to the pressure of the air compressed inside the . . .'

'You're scared, ain't you, Mister Lyle?'

'Now what on earth gives you that impression?'

'Way as how when you get scared an' all you talk science in that really squeaky voice, an' how you don't breathe an' stuff.'

'In this case, not breathing is a very apt response to our situation, Teresa.'

'You had to go an' say it, right?'

'I think we might have enough time left for me to finish my explanation of pressure and hydrodynamics . . .'

'Must you?'

'There is an alternative . . . but you aren't going to like it.'

'More than I like bein' trapped in a little bubble of running-out air made of, not to be too prissy about it, a big metal box on your head, sir? I dunno as how that may be the case, Mister Lyle.'

'Now, Teresa,' said Lyle, 'we have to swim.'

The difficult part, Tess discovered, was getting the bubble of air from the top of the ceiling, where it had drifted along with her and Lyle, to the mouth of the tunnel without letting it escape. If the box overturned while they struggled to drag the bubble downwards, as Lyle pointed out, then their conversation about whose fault the rush of gas from the box into the water above would be, of necessity, one of the shortest arguments they'd ever had.

It was surprisingly heavy work, and Tess was made no happier by Lyle's assurance that it wasn't actually going to get lighter the more they worked at it, because even though they were breathing in, dammit, they were also breathing out too. Eventually Lyle had to take a gulp of air and turn upside-down in the water to drag the crate and its bubble downwards. Even that operation caused bubbles to ripple out from the base of their air pocket, pulling at the crate which Tess clung on to with dear life to preserve those precious breaths, while the water rose closer towards her mouth and nose.

When they reached the tunnel, it was easier: the bubble simply bumped along the ceiling, with Lyle paddling along. They had no idea where they were, so every few yards Lyle would swim outside the bubble, feeling his way along the walls. The darkness inside the bubble destroyed all sense of direction, all awareness of time, so that after a while Tess began to wonder if they were in the tunnel at all, or simply swimming round and round inside the room, unable to find a way out, until they finally used up all the air and sank down, lost in the dark.

After a while, it wasn't just her imagination playing tricks: she could feel the difficulty in every breath, and the rising temperature inside the bubble, until finally Lyle said, 'It'll be all right, Tess.'

'Oh, that's bad, that's bad, that means you're scared!' cried Tess.

'We're nearly there.'

'How d'you know? There's nothin' but dark!'

'I promise, we'll be safe. Just keep breathing, all right? I'll be back in a moment.'

69

Before she could swear as only an East End orphanage could teach a girl to unburden herself, there was a sound of splashing as Lyle ducked out from under the box. Tess kept paddling along; without sound or sight, time became measured only by small, fast breaths. She thought, *It'd be stupid to cry it'd be so stupid to cry I ain't goin' to cry I ain't I ain't I ain't so there!*

Something moved by her ankle and she exclaimed. Something else bumped against her middle, and a moment later, she heard another breath under the box, dragging down a gulp of tight, hot air. 'Found something,' wheezed Lyle. 'It's just a few yards away, but you're going to have to come with me, do you understand?'

'No! Mister Lyle, no, I don't wanna, please . . .'

'The ladder's just there, we can swim up it, you simply need to take a deep breath. Do you understand? Tess?'

She nodded mutely, and then realized how pointless a gesture that was in the dark. 'All right.'

'We just need to go under the box. Are you ready?'

'Yes, Mister Lyle.'

'Take my hand.'

She felt his hand, cold from the water, slip into hers.

'Take a deep breath.'

She drew the deepest she could, her muscles aching from the strain of trying to find something, anything, breathable in the tiny bubble of their world, and ducked out from under the crate. Cold water crawled up her nose, and burnt in her eyes. She almost shouted at sensing it, nearly let out the breath she'd just taken. Then Lyle started swimming, and she followed, clinging on to his wrist with both hands, half-paddling, half-walking along the bottom of the flooded tunnel. She felt her shoulder bang against something hard and metallic, and suddenly up seemed the place to go, blissful up. Lyle was already pushing her, and there was light somewhere up there, criss-crossed by a grate, and distorted by the faintest shimmering of the water's surface. She climbed the ladder with her arms and kicked with her feet, not knowing what she was doing but drawn by that light, letting her own natural buoyancy propel her forward.

The grate opened without resistance and there was air above it, and a large puddle. Tess climbed out into the puddle and fell on to solid ground. She had time for two very deep breaths before the laughter took her, hysterical and giddy, shaking every soaked limb as she lay and looked up at the dim light of Baker Street Station and laughed. She wondered where Tate was, and then Lyle appeared, a hand at a time, heaving himself over the edge of the shaft, crawling into the puddle of water spread around its opening and sprawling on his front. With his head turned to one side, he heaved in lungfuls of air, not even bothering to pull his feet out of the shaft until he had oxygen back in his blood.

Only when he felt that the world wasn't trying to dance the polka in his vicinity did he bother to roll over and wheeze, 'Tess?'

'Yes, Mister Lyle?'

'Are you all right?'

'Yes, Mister Lyle.'

'Sure?'

'Yes, Mister Lyle.'

'Have you seen Tate anywhere?'

'No. He's bugge . . . he ain't here, Mister Lyle.'

Lyle groaned. 'Tate!'

From the end of the platform there came a growl. Lyle heaved himself up, and saw Tate, sitting sulkily by a pair of shoes. With a frown, Lyle looked at the shoes, black and highly polished; thence at a pair of black pinstriped trousers below a black waistcoat with a silver fob watch, above which a pale face and a head of thin dark hair were crowned by a silk top hat.

The face gave a benign smile.

'Horatio Lyle,' it said. 'Are you busy?'

Lyle stared past the top hat to the two other men standing a few respectful paces behind. They wore plain working clothes, and in each right-hand jacket pocket there was a suspicious-looking bulge over which their hands hovered, ready to move at any moment.

'Augustus Havelock,' Lyle said wearily. 'Fancy seeing you here.'

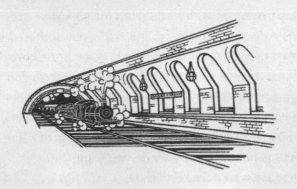

CHAPTER 5

Acquaintances

Near the duck-thronged ponds of Regent's Park there stood a small gazebo, where on a Sunday when the weather was good the ladies and gentlemen of the neighbourhood sometimes met for tea. More often it was used as a meeting place for illicit lovers fearful of being seen by their families and friends, sometimes in the name of true love, sometimes for quick money.

Today, on a cold spring afternoon with the rain belting down outside, it housed a dripping Lyle and a surprisingly dry Augustus Havelock. At the nearby roadside Tess and Tate cowered in the company of the two men with the bulging pockets, who had explained in a few short grunts that they did not share Tess's sense of humour. Somewhere the sun was probably getting on with setting, but the pervasive greyness of the afternoon gave no sign that it had even bothered to rise, and only a deepening darkness on one edge of the horizon suggested that there was anything the city might wish goodnight.

Augustus Havelock sat in silence, hands folded, on a bench, while Lyle wrung out his coat and the rest of his clothes dripped busily on to the gazebo's polished floor. At length Lyle snapped, 'All right, get on with it. What do you want?'

'There is no need for bad manners, Horatio.'

'My day is not going well,' Lyle retorted. 'And your own presence serves to convince me that it won't get much better. Now, we could wait here, dancing round the essentials while I catch a chill, or we could have a conversation. So let's get on with it.'

'You always were crude, Horatio Lyle. It's a family trait.'

'If you want me, I'll be on holiday,' growled Lyle. Throwing his sodden coat over his arm, he made as if to stride out into the rain.

'Horatio.' Havelock's voice was a low, warning rumble. 'What were you doing in those tunnels?'

'What are *you* doing with Andrew Berwick?'

'I don't know him.'

'You're lying. You know him perfectly well; you visit his house regularly, you are interested in the same areas of science that he is; probably too closely interested for anyone's comfort. What do you want with him?'

'And you were in those tunnels because you found a ticket for the Underground line in Berwick's pocket, and decided to follow your instincts below ground?'

'There was more in question than that; but yes, you've got the essentials. Where is he? Where is Berwick?'

74

A half-laugh, almost a hiccup, escaped Havelock's lips. 'You think I know?'

'Shall we answer every question with a question?'

'No. Sooner or later one of us will have to come up with a statement. I feel you should set the trend here, in view of my shortening patience for this game. What were you doing in those tunnels?'

'I'm sorry, is there something down there I shouldn't see?'

'From the fact that you triggered the sluice by entering the laboratory, I'd say that you knew perfectly well there is something you shouldn't have seen. Does that thrill you, Horatio Lyle? Do you taste the spice of adventure?'

'Berwick was a friend. I will find where he is.'

'I hardly see how, and I doubt very much that he would wish to be found by you anyway.'

'I have no interest in talking to you, Augustus Havelock.' Lyle turned to go.

'If you walk away from me, Horatio Lyle, you will walk into your own destruction – and that of your friends,' said Havelock quietly. Lyle stopped in the doorway of the gazebo.

'You know that I am not . . . *crude* in such things. I am not talking about simple, childish devices, the tricks of fools. I will not send thugs to your house, I will not cause you actual physical harm; these things are nothing. Even having you crippled is nothing; it will make you fight all the harder, and the only way I believe I can truly cripple you is to stop your mind, that which makes the essence of you, not the flesh and bones – and that is no pain at all, to stop, to be nothing; that is simple. These things are never so simple.'

Lyle turned, head on one side, watching Havelock. He wore a look of dull expectation, almost a smile. 'Go on,' he said quietly.

'Teresa Hatch,' said Havelock, voice as low and level as the drumming of the rain. 'Did you know that she was once mine? That I paid her to break into your home? Yes, of course you do – you would have found out immediately, am I correct?'

'I knew.'

'She told you, I imagine. For . . . what . . . a shilling? Maybe even a sovereign? She is quick to sell her loyalties.'

'Get to the point, Havelock.'

'I bear her no malice for her failure to fulfil her part of the bargain; the sum offered was small and the task was menial. She is nothing more than a tool, Horatio Lyle.

'And Thomas Edward Elwick, your companion? His disappearance would be only a little harder to effect than hers. There would be some outcry when he vanished in the night; his parents would shout and rail. Perhaps, thanks to the prestige of his family, there would even be something in the newspapers.

'Can you protect them for ever, Lyle? I will only come when you can no longer stay awake, I will let you sit up and sit up and watch and wait, knowing that I know them. I will let you waste away because you don't dare leave their doors, waiting for them to vanish, for something to change in the night; I can be patient. The torture will be entirely of your own devising – expectation, because you *know* I am capable of what I threaten. And when you do sleep, when it is too much for you to watch and protect them any longer, I will be there.

'I can destroy everything that makes you you. I can have the police turn you away, never a case passed on to you; I can pay even the postman and the paper boy to steer away so that you have nothing, nothing to solve, no wrongs to right, so you are just another man in another house too big for him, alone, getting old, an old grey man with an old grey life. I will watch your experiments burn away to nothing, I will see the ink of your papers run before they hit the press, I will follow everyone who dares speak to you; in the night, something will change for them too, and you will always know it. You will know that when your friend's friend is found in the river, it was you, for you, because of you. I will see to it that you endure while everything else changes, alone and watching. You know I am capable of it. So. I'm going to let you walk away, Lyle. And you are going to stop looking for Berwick. Let this be the one sacrifice in your life, the one letting go of a case. Is this not fair?'

Lyle waited, to see if there was more. Then he smiled and nodded. 'I understand,' he said. 'You don't want me to find him; I understand. But what you're building down there . . . electricity and bombs, chemicals and wire – that you're so determined to protect! How do I walk away, knowing what you might do with that? And more; so much more, I have to know. If I walk away from this case now, then who's to say I won't walk away for ever, and just keep walking, never looking back and stopping to think that perhaps there is something wrong, and that *here* is a place to do something *right*.

'And you probably know this. That's what the nice gentlemen with the revolvers are for, yes? I admit, you have every advantage – I'm stuck out on the edge of things, not sure which way to turn. But, I conclude .... someone has to try. So, Augustus

Havelock, here I am, walking away, for just so long as it takes to work out what you're doing, when I'll stop you. Good afternoon.'

Lyle turned and stepped out into the rain. It ran down his face and under his collar, as if it had a chance of making him even wetter than he was, and pooled at his feet.

'Horatio.' Havelock's voice could have announced a funeral. 'You can't stop it.'

'What are you going to do? Shoot me in a public place? Hope the rain washes away the blood? You're smarter than that, Augustus.'

'I can hurt *them*. I will always come for them before I come for you, Horatio Lyle.'

Lyle nodded at nothing in particular, and announced in a voice a million miles away, 'If you so much as touch the children, I will destroy you. Nothing subtle, just you, alone in the dark. You know I can. Good day to you.'

He touched his forehead politely, and walked off into the rain.

Night across London, in early spring. There is a smell that comes after rain, that for a moment is clean, as if somehow the drops of water falling from the sky had melted around the dirt drifting in the air, and dragged it all underground, to be washed out to sea along the farther reaches of the Thames. Combined with a cold wind that twists the rising greeny-grey smog and makes it billow like the vapours from a genie's lamp, the night is as shocking as a cold plunge after a Turkish bath, and no less unpleasant.

There are people following Horatio Lyle through the city. No point in counting them now; even he knows it's inevitable. Suffice it to say, more than one interested party has caught his scent. To shake them off, he is going straight to Hammersmith Bridge.

Thomas Edward Elwick was bored. Bored bored bored bored bored. Agonizingly bored, excruciatingly bored. Boredom of this calibre became after a while a physical pain, a realization that every bone in his body weighed a ton, that he hadn't eaten in what felt like an eternity, that his stomach was a churning hollow under his ribs, that his neck was stiff, that his knees creaked, that his arms ached, that even his ears itched. Perhaps this was how it always felt to be a perfectly normal youth, but until now he'd just been too distracted with other, more interesting things for him to notice the pain of his own existence. It took a sermon from Mr Barker to make him realize how badly painted the ceiling was, how the carpet was scuffed around the edges, how the wooden floors needed polishing, how the candle on the left of the mantelpiece dribbled wax faster than the candle on the right, how the painting of Lord Elwick, one of many portraits of one of many noble lords, was slightly crooked above the fireplace, how loud the gentle clicker-clacker of his sister's domino set was upstairs, and he was *bored*!

He knew that Mr Barker was a well-meaning man. He reminded himself of it as the aspiring parson, so desperate for his father's patronage, turned each page of the large, leather-bound family Bible, and announced, 'Ah, now this passage I find particularly poignant . . .' or, 'I would trouble you with the reminder that . . .'

Thomas also knew he should be grateful for a good, religious upbringing, that he should pay strict attention, focus on every word and cherish the opportunity of coming closer to God. But after the first three hours of Mr Barker's company, the inspiration was fading. When he heard the doorbell ring, despite the proximity of the sound he immediately thought he had imagined it, his mind playing tricks in its desperation. Only when the maid appeared in the doorway with the words, 'Mister Horatio L—'

. . . and Lyle burst into the room, 'Thomas! Queen and Country are calling you!' – did Thomas jerk into full, intensified awareness.

He knew his parents knew *of* Horatio Lyle. Lyle had, after all, been there following that violent night at St Paul's Cathedral, clapping politely in the crowd while all praise was heaped on Thomas's head for an act of heroism that Thomas had mostly chosen to forget. Lyle was known about town anyway, as a man with money who didn't seem to notice that he had money, and who did not live in the manner to which he could be accustomed but instead skulked around the dirtier streets and spent his day with machines, something of which, it had to be said, Lord and Lady Elwick did not approve. When asked, Thomas had said he was visiting his Latin tutor, or dining at the house of a distant cousin, until his parents had come to accept that once a week Thomas would slip away, and sail down the river to Blackfriars Bridge. They never knew quite what he did there, but just assumed that it was all right. Various servants were complicit in the truth; but never until this moment had Horatio Lyle and Lord and Lady Elwick come face to face.

Already, Thomas could see that it would go wrong. Mr Barker

was on his feet; in the doorway, so was his father, in wide-eyed confusion. 'Who the deuce—' Lord Elwick began, and it was going to go wrong, so terribly, wrong . . .

'Horatio Lyle,' said Lyle, hastening forward, one hand outstretched. And now Thomas noticed how Lyle's clothes were soaked through, and Tess's too – and there was Tess, an East End thief, standing in his father's door and, oh God . . .

'A pleasure to meet you, my lord. Thomas speaks of you so often.' Lyle's voice cut through the nausea that rooted Thomas to the spot. 'Might I have a word in private with your son?'

'What? Why?'

'Urgent matters of state, my lord.'

'Why should you need to discuss state matters with my son – and who are you anyway?'

'I said, I am Horatio Lyle.'

'Should that name mean anything to me? I am, you should be aware, a man of extensive authority and reputation within the government and House of Lords, and I have *never* in all my days encountered such –'

'My lord' – and there it was, an edge to Lyle's voice, a roughness as the words escaped his gritted teeth; and there it was again, in the tension in Lyle's left hand, clenched into a fist; and in the way Tess shrank back in the doorway. Even Tate, usually quite ready to jump on to the furniture, looked cowed. Thomas recognized it immediately: a shimmer of unease in Lyle's face, his eyes, his voice, that no amount of babble could disguise.

'My lord,' Lyle repeated, 'what exactly do you know of me?'

'You are Horatio Lyle, a man of some wealth, I suppose, albeit based on industry, and an occasional tutor to my son.'

'Ah – good – yes, a tutor! What exactly has Thomas said I tutor him in?'

'What do you mean?'

'What exactly has Thomas told you?'

'What are you implying?'

'My lord, this will be a very short conversation if neither of us is prepared to answer the other's questions and, believe me, I've already played that game today with a man far, far worse than any peer of the realm, so please answer me.'

To Thomas's surprise, and Lord Elwick's too, the older man replied. 'Geography.'

'I *see*.' Lyle's eyes flickered to Thomas, whose skin by now was the colour of cold milk. 'My lord, might I have a word in private?'

Thomas and Tess sat alone in a hall full of marble and chandeliers, while Tess continued to drip.

'Hello, Miss Teresa.'

'Hello, bigwig.'

Because conversation lagged, Thomas added, 'Hello, Tate.'

Tate raised a thoughtful eye in Thomas's direction, found himself uninspired, and went on duly smelling of wet dog at Tess's feet. Thomas knew it would be appropriate to have Tate removed for this sin, but inappropriate to acknowledge the smell if the lady didn't, and wondered what to do under such straining circumstances.

'Is there something wrong?' he asked finally.

'Whatcha mean?'

He couldn't help but notice how Tess's voice snapped, and

how she didn't even try to meet his eyes. 'Well, I've known you for about six months, Miss Teresa, and Mister Lyle the same, and you've never once come here or even asked where I live. And then you just . . . turn up. Without any warning. Or . . . anything. Is something the matter?'

'Mister Lyle says as how it ain't safe to go to his house.'

'Isn't safe?'

'Nope.'

'Why not?'

''Cos there's this bigwig bloke with a gun who knows this other bloke called Berwick what we think was workin' in this lab thing underground that got all flooded an' *They* want to know where he is and Mister Lyle says as how we had to go and lose any followers what we were bein' followed by in the fog and then come straight here 'cos you'll be safe 'cos of how you're a bigwig an' they won't dare attack a house like yours with all its people an' all.'

'Attack?!'

She shrugged. 'Like I said, he don't think as how it'll happen.'

'I see. It sounds . . . a little chaotic.'

Tess met his eyes, and for the first time he saw fear. 'Bigwig,' she said, her voice little above a whisper, 'I seen magic an' people with glowin' green eyes and statues move and dragons an' all that since I met Mister Lyle, an' it ain't scared me nothin'. But I also met this Havelock bloke, an' he scares me.'

'Havelock? Who's Havelock?'

'He paid me to break into Mister Lyle's house, he did.'

'Miss Teresa! Are you saying that you would accept such a commission for . . .'

'I dunnit, bigwig. That's how I went and met Mister Lyle. An' I ain't never given another thought to this Havelock bloke since. But I seen his face, Thomas. I heard his voice, I know what he . . . how he thinks an' all, seen bullies like him out in the streets before. But I ain't never seen Mister Lyle so frightened as he is now. An' that scares me more than any monster.'

In Lord Elwick's study, Horatio Lyle stood. The older man sat down behind a polished leather-topped desk and poured himself a glass of port, without offering one to Lyle.

'Mister Horatio Lyle,' he said at length. 'Forgive me if I dispense with polite necessities, now we are out of the lady's company.'

'Polite necessities?' echoed Lyle faintly. 'Those were polite necessities?'

'You may find me a little . . . abrupt.'

'Oh no, not at all!' Lyle tried to keep the sarcasm out of his voice; and Lord Elwick probably wouldn't have noticed anyway.

'But I am led to enquire,' went on his lordship in a voice like the brushing of two passing icebergs, 'what exactly you are doing here?'

'There's really nowhere else to go.'

'Please explain that remark.'

'It's complicated.'

'See if your mental powers of explanation can rise to the occasion, Mister Lyle.'

Lyle half-smiled a bitter smile, and said, 'My lord, may I be frank with you?'

'I would demand nothing less.'

'I'm here to see your son, my lord.'

'Why are you here to see my son, Mister Lyle?'

'Because once a week, every week, he sneaks to my house near Blackfriars, and I teach him about machines. Because I know he comes from a home with a hundred staff waiting on your every wish; because I know that Lord Elwick's son cannot disappear and not be noticed; because I need somewhere safe to stay and, most of all, because I need to warn him. I . . . there are those who may try to harm him.'

'Harm him? Why?' Lord Elwick's fine features were white, but his voice didn't waver above a flat calm.

'I would not presume, my lord, to intrude, but that . . .'

'Harm him *why*?' The tone didn't change, but the voice filled the room; it hummed through the panelling and rattled the window panes.

Lyle met Lord Elwick's eyes, and saw nothing but burning anger, although his face was ice. 'Because of me, my lord. Because it is known to some who are my enemies, that Thomas is my friend. They may try to hurt him, to hurt me.'

'Why?'

'Did I not just explain that?'

'Why are they going to hurt you, and why would they assume you have any sort of relationship beyond a passing one with *my* son?'

'Because I teach him!'

'What do you teach him?'

'What do you mean?'

'What do you teach him, Mister Lyle? I know full well that once a week he departs for the city, and once a week he does so claiming to visit a teacher or a relative or attend a concert or a sermon or a lecture or some such device – does he visit you? What do you teach him, what do you tell him, who are *you* to have put *him* in danger?!' Lord Elwick was on his feet, and now his face was purple. 'How *dare* you?!'

'Science.' Lyle's voice was cold and unmoving. 'I teach him science.'

'Is that it?'

'That's the part I think you'll understand, my lord.'

'He has no need for science!'

'He has more need than anyone I've ever met.'

'I do not need a stranger to tell me about my son! Why did he lie? Why did he not mention you?'

'Perhaps because you *do* need a stranger to tell you about your son, my lord.'

'Do not push me, Mister Lyle!'

'I'm sorry; there's no nice way to tackle this. Believe me, I tried when first I came through that door; but you just wouldn't let me, would you? So I'll get to the point.' Lyle sought a good way to begin, and failing, gave a shrug and dived in.

'Your son has flown, in his own machine – has he told you that? He has built a flying machine from bamboo and canvas, launched it off Hampstead Heath, flown across the city, so high and so fast you'd think he could touch the moon, called it Icarus, after the boy who flew too close to the sun until his wings melted in its heat. And he made it work; he did the maths, he calculated the pressure, he worked out the speed. He has . . . such a passion for it, an astonishing brilliance. Perhaps he has not told you because he is afraid, because science is not what the Elwicks do.

In his own way, I suspect that is his attempt to be a good, dutiful, son. That means he doesn't admit to his interests – it is not what you expect of him. Not that this is important, it's not what I'm trying to say . . .' Lyle hesitated, then said, 'Put it like this. Forget the science, forget the maths; what matters is that he does what he thinks is right – studies what he thinks is important, does what he believes will make things better.

'It was by accident that he met me, and I suspect he'd do what he does regardless. His connection with me . . . is nothing. Just a nudge along the way. But I *do* care for your son, and I think it would be a tragedy and a loss if he were not to study and do what he does. And now a man who is . . . how can I put it? Without scruple. A man without scruple is going to try to use your son against me, and I am scared sick that I won't be able to protect him, and I *need* to warn him that this might happen. Is that enough, my lord? Is that what you needed to hear?'

Lord Elwick had sunk back down into his chair. Now he murmured, 'But . . . he is *my* son.'

'Yes, my lord. And he is my friend. Between us, he should be all right, don't you agree?'

'Thomas?'

Lady Elwick stood in the doorway. Thomas got to his feet. Tess stood too. Instinctively, in the presence of someone obviously a lady, she attempted a little curtsey, and almost stood on Tate's ear.

Lady Elwick was pale. 'Thomas,' she said softly, 'your father is asking for you, and . . . you, young lady.'

Tess tried not to feel like a walking, soaking refuse heap in contrast with Lady Elwick. Thomas moved stiffly towards the study door, his face empty. Tess followed and Tate slouched after her.

At the door, Lady Elwick put a hand on Thomas's shoulder. 'It's all right,' she said softly. 'I know what you do. The servants told me. And it's all right.' She smiled weakly when he froze, and nudged him forward. 'Go and speak to your father.'

He walked into the study, not registering his surroundings, unaware of his own movement or Tess shuffling behind him. His father sat at the desk; Lyle stood in the window and peered round the curtain at the street outside, seemingly oblivious of anything else. Thomas felt like the most lonely person in the world.

His father cleared his throat.

'Thomas.'

'Yes, Father?'

'Mister Lyle informs me that . . .' his voice trailed off, then started up again. 'There are some things you have not been telling me, Thomas.'

'No, Father.' His voice was barely a whisper.

'Now, before I make my mind up about this situation, I need to hear you tell me, just once, why you do these things. Why you . . . wilfully endanger yourself, why you court trouble, linger where you know there will be risk, why you . . . why you . . . no, I will not ask why you do not tell me, the answer to that is too easy: what father would permit knowingly the things you do? But I need to understand why you so readily accept that this man' – a glower in the direction of Lyle's impassive back in the window – 'can risk his life and yours, why you can just let

88

that happen and not blame him, not run from this . . . strange
world you seem to inhabit. I need to hear you tell me why.'

Thomas looked behind him at the shivering Tess, then down
at Tate, and across to the window, where Lyle was watching him
over his shoulder, face closed, saying not a word. He turned back
and saw his father, shorter in real life than the portraits on the
wall suggested, whiskers sticking out either side of his face, back
slightly hunched with age, dressed in fine evening wear that,
being designed for a younger man, just made Lord Elwick look
older. For almost the first time in his life, he found he knew
exactly what to say.

'Because it's right, Father. What we do is the right thing to do.
And someone has to do it. You can't just . . . walk away from
something like that. You told me . . . that it's my *duty* to do right.
You said that I had to do right by my family, my servants, the
people who would look up to me – you said that because I
was . . .' he hesitated for a moment, glancing up at Lyle, who
showed no reaction, '. . . because I was born to privilege, it was
my duty to follow a code and do the best I can for those who
were born beneath me, who trusted me not to mislead or abuse
them. More – not just *not* to mislead, but to try to do something
so that they would be better, that I could make a difference
because of who I am! If you say that it is a duty to be a gentleman, and that duty means I should be understanding and kind
towards my family and my servants, does it mean I should ignore
everyone else? I can't make everything better – but I can't not
try.'

He stopped, feeling the blood standing out on his skin, trem-
bling at the end of his fingers, and looked at Lord Elwick.

His father's face seemed to empty, smoothing out as every muscle unknotted itself and as he let out a long sigh that seemed to start at his strained shoulders and flow all the way down to his fingertips. 'In that case,' said Lord Elwick, and his voice no longer rang with imperious command, but was gentle and real, 'you have my blessing, Thomas. Mister Lyle?'

Horatio Lyle looked up and smiled faintly. 'My lord?'

'You and your . . . companions . . . may stay here for as long as it takes you to resolve this situation. I will ensure that there are guards outside your friend's door, and my son's – no harm can come to them. I will help you make right whatever it is that is wrong, I give you my word.'

Lyle bowed. 'Thank you, my lord.'

And so Tess goes to her room, a larger one than she has ever seen before, where a steaming bath awaits her, and hot food has been brought in on a tray. The window is twice her height, and the carpet is so thick she thinks it'll reach to her knees. The bed is so big she could roll in it like an ant across a dune and, at her door, a footman keeps guard with a poker, lest any stranger should venture upstairs.

In the kitchen of the Elwick house, Tate lolls in a basket lined with an old eiderdown, while the women servants coo over him and brush his coat and scratch him behind his ears and tickle under his chin and rub his belly, until even Tate has to admit he's having a very pleasant evening, before rolling over in front of the stove, kept warm all night and all day, to sleep in a dry, peaceful bed.

In the living room, Thomas Edward Elwick stands opposite

Horatio Lyle, who is gently steaming in the blasting heat of the fireplace, and says, 'Mister Lyle?'

'I'm sorry about this, Thomas.'

'About what?'

'Coming here in this way. I know it's not what you wanted.'

'It's all right.'

'I should explain. Havelock . . .'

'Miss Teresa explained.'

'Did she?' Lyle raises an eyebrow, then shrugs. 'Well then. Havelock. He means the threats he makes, Thomas. I know this from experience.'

'How do you know him?'

'Oh,' Lyle smiles uneasily and turns to dry another side of his clothing in the warmth of the fire. 'You can't help but notice men like Havelock, particularly when they're climbing to the top. I will do what I can to make amends for this situation, Thomas.'

'There's no need, Mister Lyle.'

'I think there probably is.'

'No! There isn't.' Thomas smiles, and finds he means it. 'I chose this, Mister Lyle. I chose to help when we first met; so did Miss Teresa. It's for the best.'

Lyle seems to deflate a little in the firelight. 'You're getting old, lad.'

'Only in a good way, Mister Lyle.'

Lyle pats Thomas absently on the shoulder. 'Yes,' he says. 'You may be right.'

Later, upstairs, Lady Elwick kisses her son goodnight on the cheek. Lord Elwick stands uncomfortably in the doorway, before moving forward and patting his son on the shoulder and saying, 'Sleep well,' in a stiff voice, and wondering if his son isn't too old after all to be tucked in. Afterwards Thomas crosses his bedroom, pulls open the bottom drawer by his desk, lifts up its false bottom, and takes out some papers. Numbers and pictures and lines of force and letters and ideas race across the paper in thick, scrawly lines. Having considered them by the light of the candle, he doesn't put them back, but leaves them on the floor like an artist's greatest work, to be admired by anyone who might now decide to look. At various places outside his door wait a valet with a sabre, the head groom with a shovel, three footmen with candlesticks, and one of the gardeners with a crowbar, just in case someone should even *think* about approaching his room at night.

At the back of the house, above a rear parlour, Horatio Lyle yawns, scratches at the dry shirt and pants the second undergardener lent him, being the only person in the household whose clothing seemed to fit, and which smell slightly of loam. He turns the handle of the door to his small, gloomy room, and steps inside.

Three things meet his senses. The first is the smell of smoke, sharp, from the wick of a candle just extinguished. Second is the faint sound of something moving through the air, silk rippling. Third is a flash of green, implausibly bright in the darkness – no, two flashes of green, a pair of eyes rising out of nowhere, locking themselves into his. They are the only things there to focus on, the only things to see, and thus the only things he looks at, to find he cannot look away. He opens his mouth to call out, and a hand is over his mouth. Something, someone, slams him back against the wall, and there are the eyes, filling his world. The hand over his mouth is small and neat and has the strength of a blacksmith's, and wears a black silk glove. And a soft voice like the distant sound of wind chimes whispers, 'Don't speak, don't move, Mister Lyle. They put guards on every door except yours – you didn't expect someone to come for you. Just relax.'

He tries to look away, sees emerald and the colour of spring leaves with the sun overhead and . . . *and* . . .

'You did not need to lose your followers by the bridge, Mister Lyle. When everything else is taken from you, where are you going to come, except here? I only had to wait.'

. . . just needs to close his eyes and fight, kick, struggle, raise a fist, bite, anything except look and sink and drown in warm greenness and . . .

'No magnet, Mister Lyle. You left it in your coat on the end of the bed. No iron either. Time to fall asleep.'

. . . *no no no no no NO NO NO* . . .

'Just fall asleep, Horatio Lyle. I promise you'll be all right.'

. . . *please no . . . please* . . .

And finally, Horatio Lyle closes his eyes, and lets his head loll, and obeys. He falls asleep in the Tseiqin's arms, without a word or a sound, while she carries him to the window.

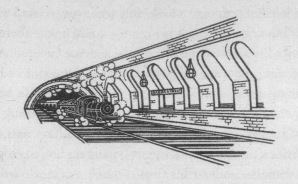

CHAPTER 6

Strangers

Flashes of a journey, nothing more. Frozen glimpses. A carriage window, green eyes opposite, a moment. Hyde Park – sleep, Mister Lyle, just sleep. Park Lane – a glimmer of street lamp and lamplighter with his ladder; sleep, Mister Lyle, you have nothing to fear. A nightmare; the mansions of Mayfair – wake cold and sweating, did they come and there they are, a waking nightmare, dream made real, green eyes, black silk hand reaching out and brushing eyelids shut again; you must trust us, Mister Lyle, sleep until we ask for you. Sleep.

This time, he was ready for the awakening. Rather than open his eyes, he lay still and waited for every other sense to report in, to confirm by the ache in his shoulders that this was not a dream.

Lyle didn't dare to move or look, although every second wilfully blind was an agony, not knowing what could be out there.

Smell of wood burning in a fireplace, some coal too. A taste of lavender on the air, and soot as well, a chimney that hadn't been swept for a while. The feel of padding and silk beneath him, the undergardener's warm, dry clothes still itching at the back of his neck, and a new itch, rope around his wrists, thick, almost like a piece of ship's rigging, wedging his fists together and making the ends of his fingers numb. A crackle from the fireplace, and somewhere, near by, laboured breathing – not threatening, but wheezing: a long-drawn-out whistle on the way in, that rattled on the way out. With every other sense describing all it could, he did what he'd dreaded to do, and opened his eyes.

The room was a bedchamber and, more to the point, his kind of place. The walls were lined with books, and above the fireplace hung a painting that caught Lyle's eye and didn't let it go. From the corner of the room, somewhere behind the sofa on which Lyle had been ungracefully deposited, the voice with the wheeze spoke, with a sound like sandpaper across rough stone: 'Turner.'

'I beg your pardon?'

'The painting. Turner.' The voice managed to imply without so much as changing tone that if Lyle didn't know exactly what this meant and who Turner was, then he was clearly an idiot.

Lyle eased himself up, waiting for the blood to settle in his head and his thoughts to pick up speed. At length he risked standing. He turned, his back to the fire, and looked in the direction of the voice.

In a giant bed there was a man. He was old, of that there was no doubt, but somehow his face seemed to have aged unevenly. His skin was lined and leathery. But his hair was such a pure white that its colour didn't look like a consequence of aging, and his eyes sparkled bright green. He was sitting up in the bed, wearing a long nightrobe and an undignified nightcap with a bobble on it, and seemed oblivious of the rattle of his own breath. Around him stood or sat a group of five or six other people of various indeterminate ages, all with the same bright green eyes. Their silence suggested deference to the old man in the bed.

Finding that he felt neither hypnotized nor threatened, Lyle looked at the man and murmured, 'Who are you?'

'At present I go by the name of Joseph Turner. I like that artist's work, although perhaps you think it is arrogance to steal his name? I am also known, among my own kind, as Old Man White. You may call me whichever you think more appropriate.'

'You're Tseiqin.'

'And for you to notice, we only had to hypnotize you and carry you halfway across the city.'

'I'm sorry; it was more an exclamation of surprise than a question.'

'In that case, you are welcome. We are Tseiqin.' Old Man White put his head on one side and, smiling faintly, said, 'Does that alarm you?'

Lyle's laugh came too fast for him to control it: fear overrode all other instincts. He felt his ears burn red. 'Yes, God damn it,' he choked.

'Why?'

'Angel-demon people with hypnotic green eyes, white blood and an allergy for all things magnetic? And me, here among you? I can't imagine how it might end well.'

'We haven't hurt you.'

'*Well* . . .' Lyle raised his bound wrists accusingly.

Old Man White shrugged. 'You are Horatio Lyle. You destroyed the Fuyun Plate in a blast of lightning; you fought Selene, who was once one of us, tooth and claw; you were there when her blade was shattered into a thousand pieces; you build machines that hurt us – unintentionally, perhaps. But the iron is in your blood; you can't help what you are. You can't help but uproot the land that we loved, to build your new, strange, iron world. That does not make you any less dangerous.'

'As I said, it can't end well.'

'Mister Lyle, you miss the point. You have encountered the full wrath of my people, and survived. This is something few humans have achieved. Are you surprised that there are some here who fear you?'

'You're scared of *me*?'

'Indeed.'

'Really? In that case I'll just be going, wouldn't want to cause trouble, always dangerous, me . . . please?'

Old Man White looked sceptical. '*How* you survived, Mister Lyle, always strikes me as something of a mystery. Please come here.'

Too late, Lyle tried to look away. But there were the eyes, already filling his mind. He'd let his guard down and *damn damn damn* . . . He felt his legs jerk, moving him forward; he bit his lip until he tasted blood as he tried to fight it – and perhaps, for an instant, there was resistance, that taste of iron on his tongue, the tang of salt. For a second he stopped, tried to twist his head away, to shut his eyes and . . .

'Please, Mister Lyle.'

The voice and the eyes were overwhelming; he could feel his vision narrowing to a pinprick of green and heard the sound of the fire receding. There was no arguing with that voice. He staggered like a drunkard the last few paces across the room, the other Tseiqin moving out of his way. He could feel their eyes on the back of his neck as they watched him obey, kneel down at the bedside, shuddering and drawing in deep breaths. At last Lyle found himself released from the Tseiqin's influence. His muscles ached from the strain of trying to resist. A long, cold hand, almost as white as the old man's hair, reached out and pulled Lyle's chin up until he stared into those green eyes once more. Lyle nearly whimpered. *Of all the ways to die . . .*

. . . I'm so sorry . . .

'Tell me. What do you know of the Machine?'

'What Machine?'

The green eyes narrowed; filled his world again. 'Tell me, Horatio Lyle. Did Augustus Havelock ask you to build the Machine?'

'No.'

'Do you know what it is?'

'No.'

'Very good. Do you know where Berwick is?'

'No.'

'Do you know what the Machine is?'

'*No.*'

98

'Why did you go to the Elwick house? Tell me the truth.'

He felt the words rising and tried to bite down on them, but it was like trying to give up breathing. 'Scared!' he blurted. 'Havelock will hurt them, he will, I know he will, he'll hurt them and I can't stop him, had to get Tess to safety, had to make sure Thomas was all right, had to keep them safe and . . .'

'You've been threatened?'

Another half-bitten-off choke of laughter scratched Lyle's throat. 'There are smarter questions,' he mumbled, 'considering the circumstances.'

To his surprise, Old Man White smiled. Lyle felt the greenness withdraw its power, and the world swam gradually back into focus. He let his head knock against the edge of the bed while he dragged in shuddering breaths and tried to will his heartbeat out of his ears.

At length he demanded, 'What do you *want*?'

'Do you . . . hate me, Horatio Lyle?'

'You abduct me in the middle of the night and play games with my mind . . . I admit, I have had more and better reasons to like a man.'

'I apologize for that.'

'Well then, that's all right, isn't it?! Just tell me, please, what the wicked scheme is now and get on with it. No games, no mysterious questions, please; let's simply establish the new depth of depravity and adjust our moral senses accordingly.'

'You think *we* are wicked?'

'The precedents are not encouraging.'

'But you would condemn us all? You have met Lord Moncorvo, Lady Lacebark, you have seen . . . terrible things,

99

yes. They have threatened you, hurt you and the ones you love, and for *their* sins you would say that we are all evil? Have I hurt you, Mister Lyle, despite provocation? Have I raised my voice, have I told you that you must die for being what you are, have I called you my enemy? Will you really say that all the Tseiqin are wicked, for what has been done by the few you have met?'

Lyle opened his mouth to say, 'Well, yes, all things considered the allergy to iron doesn't make you the happiest of housemates in this new world, and the fact that there really were a *lot* of you who stormed into my house, trashed most of it, murdered your way to my doorstep and pushed me off the top of a cathedral in a thunderstorm, doesn't bode well for the collective mass, so go dip your head in quicksand, dammit!' Instead he found himself mute, with nothing at all worth saying.

Old Man White seemed to see this, because he smiled and let out a more relaxed, rattling breath. 'We are not all what you think, Mister Lyle. I admit that I find the touch of iron . . . repulsive; the presence of magnetism causes me pain. And there are those among your kind who are doing terrible things to each other, to my people, to the whole world, blasting whole mountains in search of more and more iron to fuel their machines, until nothing is left but rust and soot. However, I cannot but feel that ignorance, the ignorance of your species, is not a good enough cause to condemn them all to die. I am in no hurry to be a lord, a god over your kind. I love the places outside the city; I flinch when I think of what your kind has done to them. But I also love Mozart and Beethoven and Turner and puppet shows and the buildings you make and your jokes about the Scots. Our time was centuries ago; your people are very, very young compared to ours. It is your time, your world, and has been for hundreds of years. I accept this. Perhaps, with all this considered, you can understand why there are some of us who aren't in such a hurry to cut off your little finger, Mister Lyle.'

Lyle's gaze moved instinctively from Old Man White to another pair of green eyes, belonging to the only woman in the room. She smiled sweetly, head on one side, with silent laughter in her look. 'I'm sorry,' he said, taking his time with each word, in case the next one brought disaster, 'I'm just trying to clarify this. You . . . are claiming not to be evil killers intent on the destruction or enslavement of the human race.'

'That's right.'

'You are, in fact, claiming to be *nice* Tseiqin.' The words dripped like acid off Lyle's tongue. 'Concerned Tseiqin, human-liking Tseiqin, Tseiqin who, in short, would never use their demonic powers – not that we should go into that sort of thing right now, not demons at the moment, thank you – but that you are basically sweet and loving people, accepting of humankind with a paternal twist of sad, ironic appreciation of all humanity's bumbling mistakes. Have I got the gist?'

'I still detect scepticism in your tone, Mister Lyle.'

'Well, I am building up to the big wheel-locker of a question.'

'Indeed?'

Lyle's voice had the heightened squeak of a scared man trying to remain in control. 'If all this is the case, then why oh why oh why did you decide to *kidnap* me! And on that matter, why didn't you help me when your bloody people decided to muck around with the Fuyun Plate and a lot of voltage? Why didn't you say something when Lucan Sasso was remoulding London in a not entirely pleasant image? Why don't you *do* something?!'

'It is your time, Mister Lyle. It is humanity's time to do what humanity can; we do not intervene.'

'Well, that's just a bucket of dung!' shouted Lyle. 'I mean, for goodness' sake, what do you expect? Of course we're going to get things wrong; of course there's going to be stupid bloody people doing stupid bloody things. And you just stand by, shaking your head and tutting? What in the name of all that may or may not be sacred do you expect to achieve?'

Old Man White didn't raise his voice, but the words stopped Lyle dead. 'Mister Lyle, we are effectively at war with our own people. We wish to help you; we cannot. I fear that for now you will have to accept that.'

Lyle shook his head, as if trying to move the words on from his ears and into his brain, waiting for them to settle like snowflakes and freeze into place. When he spoke again, it was very slowly, eyes fixed on some distant spot visible only to him. 'In that case, what am I doing here?'

'Ah.' Old Man White drew a deep breath that evidently scratched and banged all the way down into his lungs. 'That is more complicated.'

And here is the Machine.

The colliers have been piling coal into it now for two days without pause, working in tight shifts of four hours at the furnace, one hour's sleep, one hour's food, and another four hours carrying the coals again. The temperature on the floor is so high that the boots of some workers have started sticking to the ground, and some of the younger boys, employed in watching the pressure gauges and crawling under the belly of the Machine to make sure the connections are holding, have started to faint. Water has become each worker's most precious commodity, every sip a decadence: tiny wettings of the lips in the hope that this will be enough to last until the next ration.

Above the furnace, and beyond the generators hissing and hooting, belching steam as the giant magnets spin and spin inside the coils and the pistons pump for all they're worth, trailing thick, black grease, is the bank. To a stranger, it looks like a forest of coffin-sized tubes standing up from the ground, each one encased in thin, unpainted plaster, and some of them starting to smoke. At the foot of each coffin-like structure protrude two one-arm's thicknesses of cabling, each running away in a different direction – one joins a river of wire headed towards the spinning coils, one veers away in another direction, through a hole in a wall composed almost entirely of wire and cable looped together, into an unseen darkness. There are nearly two hundred of these coffin-like structures across the floor, each being connected and disconnected one at a time to the spinning coils around the furnaces. At each new connection, the breakers snap with fat blue sparks. After approximately two days of firing the fuel and powering the generator, this part of the Machine's working is nearly over, and the bank is almost charged.

If there was one thing that Harry Lyle had taught his son, Horatio of the same name, it was always to keep an open mind. The only exception was for an obviously idiotic proposition. In this case, so Horatio had been taught, he had a choice between an almost holy duty to enlighten the ignorant, or backing away with a nod and a smile, depending on which idiot was expressing the idea, and whether they were armed. As old Mrs Milly Lyle had pointed out, if the proposition were truly idiotic and there was nowhere to run, then all you could do was smile.

Horatio Lyle sat, drinking tea at the end of Old Man White's bed, and tried to keep an open mind.

'Do you know a man called Augustus Havelock?' asked Old Man White.

'He does,' said the Tseiqin woman, flashing Lyle another cheerful and rather wicked smile. 'They're not good friends.'

'What do you know of Havelock?' persisted Old Man White.

'He's somehow involved with Berwick.'

'How do you know this?'

Lyle said, sharper than he meant to, 'Sweeping and insightful detective work.'

'Delightful.'

'There was a laboratory – Berwick was there.'

'Where's this laboratory?'

'At this exact moment, underneath a lot of water.'

'I see.'

'Havelock was there too – after, I mean.'

'"After"?' repeated Old Man White, with a raised eyebrow and an unsympathetic face.

'After the large quantity of water happened,' Lyle explained in a voice that brooked no further argument.

'What did he want?'

'He told me to stop investigating Berwick.'

'I see – and he threatened the children?'

Lyle suddenly felt overwhelmingly tired. 'Yes.'

'Which is why you went to Lord Elwick's house.' It wasn't a question.

'Yes.'

'This is good, Mister Lyle. It is good because it suggests you are an enemy of our enemy, which should perhaps sway you our way even if our situation does not. It is also good because it suggests you are getting closer to Berwick. There is now something more that you need to know.'

'Astound me.'

'Your friend, Mr Berwick, was, until a few days ago, working for Augustus Havelock.'

'I see.'

'You don't seem very surprised.'

'Let me guess – he's been working for Havelock for . . . five months? Give or take?'

'How do you know?'

'You've got the glowing green eyes, why don't you tell me?'

'Do not trespass on our good nature too far, Mister Lyle; the matter at stake is urgent.' There was an edge to Old Man White's voice. This, and a ripple of movement among the Tseiqin around the room, brought full awareness back to Lyle. His skin tingled once more with the sense of danger.

'His house – the servants said he was barely in for the last five months, just briefly appearing and going again. And his housekeeper – Mrs Cozens – has been there for five months and was as shifty a character as you could find. You say he's been working for Havelock?'

'Indeed – building a machine.'

'What kind of machine?'

'We are not sure. The science of it . . . eludes us. We know that Havelock has been attempting to build it for nearly three years; that it is costly; that he has powerful supporters, and that it is designed to destroy us.'

'Right.' Lyle rubbed his eyes.

'Is that the extent of your reaction, Mister Lyle? It is *the Machine*; it is a monster, it will kill us all! Every Tseiqin will die!'

'How? How does it work?'

'We do not know.'

'How do you know it exists?'

'Two ways. Firstly, because we have felt its effects. Last night, a . . . a thing happened, that we cannot explain.'

'A "thing"?' Lyle's voice dripped the polite scorn of a scientific man faced with the ignorance of others.

'We do not know how to put it into your scientific terms, Mister Lyle. What I do know is that one moment I was well, and the next I felt as though I had bathed in iron filings; the thing nearly tore me to pieces. It was sensed across the whole city; every Tseiqin, every one of us, felt it, a blast like the splitting of the earth.'

'Did you see anything?'

'No. As it came and went, there was no sign of its passage.'

'Magnetism?'

'I don't understand.'

'Erm . . . magnetic, waves . . . fields . . . look, magnetism is a force that can act over a wide area, that's why it's a magnetic *field*, it can exert itself through any material, you just need . . . well, a big enough magnet, I suppose, or a really, really, *really* big electrical bang. Electricity, magnetism, it's all tied together, they operate simultaneously. You don't need to hold a magnet to feel the force it exerts, it can act over an area . . . you're not really interested, are you?'

'We understand the basic principles of science.'

'Yes,' said Lyle, straining to be tactful in the face of ignorance, 'but if you're talking about a . . . a wave of magnetism, I suppose, as the only thing I know of that really hurts you . . . people . . . then you're talking about some very, very advanced science – the kind understood by almost no one but Berwick.'

'You accept, then, that Berwick is involved in the construction of this Machine?'

'It's possible,' he admitted.

'You accept that this Machine is real?'

'I accept its possibility.'

'I see you're determined to keep an open mind.' Old Man White smiled, a gleam in those bright, bright green eyes. 'That's what I respect the most about you, Horatio Lyle. It is the only thing that sets you apart from Havelock.'

'Oh, you *are* the essence of good manners and tactful sentiment, aren't you?' muttered Lyle. 'If this is all true, where's Berwick now?'

'He ran.'

'He did what?'

'He has vanished, he has disappeared, there was . . .' Old Man White stopped dead in the middle of the sentence.

'There was what?'

'Some of our more . . . aggressive . . . brethren, reasoning that Berwick was the key to the project, attempted to remove him.'

Lyle gave a sickly grin. 'That's what scholarly people might call a euphemism, isn't it? "Removed" is a tactful way of saying, "Tried to kill him with knives and relished the task," right?'

'He survived their attempt, if that's what concerns you.'

'Let's not go into what concerns me right now; the night isn't long enough. What then?'

'He vanished, shortly after the . . . attempt. We don't know where, and by the actions of your friend, Mr Havelock, neither does he. He is the key, Lyle, to finishing the Machine, he is the grease that oils its gears, he is the one who can make it work, and now no one knows where he is.'

'How do you know this? You said there were two things that proved the Machine's existence – what's the other?'

'Simply, we had a spy inside the Machine's construction.'

'What?'

'Obviously not at the location itself. The tools you people use to make your devices – iron and steel – are painful to us; we could not venture too close. This was a spy at the Machine's highest level of conception; one who was aware of the personnel, the leaders involved – it was he who found out about Berwick's involvement, who prophesied that Berwick was the final piece, the one who could complete the device, that Berwick was the key to making the Machine work. Unfortunately, before he could inform us of anything else regarding the Machine, he was . . . removed from his position.'

'So you *had* a spy, and don't any more?'

'That is correct.'

'And the spy told you about Berwick?'

'Not directly, but through contacts we found out about the spy's discovery.'

'It's sickeningly complicated, isn't it?' muttered Lyle.

'Quite. Doubtless the spy knows more than he has passed on, either to us or to those Tseiqin whom you categorized as "angel-demon people". Unfortunately, he is at present beyond our capacity to communicate with.'

'You mean you've lost him.'

'No, no, we know exactly where he is.'

Lyle hissed in frustration. 'All right, where is he?'

'In a cell composed entirely of iron walls, bound with iron chains down an iron corridor constantly guarded by soldiers carrying magnets, underneath Pentonville Prison.'

There was a long silence. Feeling that something was expected of him, Lyle said, 'That can't be good.'

'It is certainly not conducive to our efforts.'

'I think I begin to see where this is leading.'

'Doubtless the spy has useful intelligence.'

'Doubtless.'

'And as I'm sure you can understand, the Machine is a monstrosity.'

'I'm still divided as to that.'

'You would have us all die?'

'I'm not convinced of your nicer nature, Mr White, sir.'

'Then it is because you are convinced of the more wicked nature of Augustus Havelock that you will help us.' Statement: no room for saying no, nor any question that this would even cross Lyle's mind.

'If anyone can help you find Berwick, this man will – he who had knowledge of the Machine's most intricate workings and who has made the greatest efforts to stop it.'

'Let me get this clear. Berwick was building the Machine.'

'Yes.'

'Then, for reasons unknown, he fled.'

'Yes.'

'And now everyone's looking for him – your lot, presumably, to kill him, to stop the Machine being built . . .'

'That is not everyone's wish –'

'And looking for Havelock, so that Berwick can finish the Machine.'

'Yes.'

'And no one knows where he's gone or why.'

'Correct.'

'But you had a spy involved in the Machine, who knows a lot about it, who may be able to help find Berwick and – assuming that's a good thing – stop the Machine?'

'Yes.'

'But who is at this moment under hefty guard somewhere beneath Pentonville Prison.'

'All of this is correct.'

'Where you can't get at him.'

'Yes.'

Lyle's rictus grin could have been put in place by a sadistic sculptor. 'And I just bet you want me to try.'

'Yes. I think that sums it up.'

'I'll consider it.'

'You'll *consider* it?' Even Old Man White couldn't keep the incredulity out of his voice.

'Yes. That's the best I can offer, I'm afraid.'

'Mister Lyle, the Machine will kill us all!'

'*May* kill *you* all, let's not be reckless with those plural pronouns, shall we?'

'Berwick was your friend!'

'Yes, but remember, I still don't have the smallest proof of anything you've said. And now I want to go home.'

'Mister Lyle, there is not much time!'

'What will you do? Play games with my mind? Compel me to help you? Change my thoughts, manipulate my brain, wipe all memories from me? How does that make you worth saving? I'm going home, Mr White, and maybe, just maybe, I'll help you. But if I do, it's *my* choice, my decision, my free will, the outcome of my own untarnished thought. Give me that, and I'll help.'

For a moment, just a moment, he thought Mr White would say no; saw his face contract as he contemplated his options. Then the Tseiqin's features relaxed, and he smiled, not so much at Lyle, but at a realization just dawning. He nodded, more at the carpet than anything else, as if appreciating it for the first time. 'Very well, Mister Lyle,' he said. 'And may I say, it is a pleasure to have come to know you at last.'

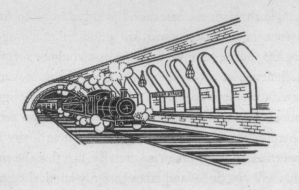

CHAPTER 7

Choices

There were Tseiqin, and then there were Tseiqin. Some liked humans, some thought they were the scourge of the earth; some didn't particularly mind iron so long as it kept a safe distance away from them and wasn't particularly magnetic, and even then it would probably bring them out in a rash; some found the merest thought of going within five miles of the city painful, a crawl across their skin. Some liked Beethoven, some liked the populist delights of a Punch and Judy show, some despised both as impure cultural art forms and longed for the plangent twang of the nose flute – no way round it, there were Tseiqin and there were Tseiqin. And then there was Lin Zi.

And Lin Zi was . . . *different*. The fact that she walked

unashamed through the streets of London in a top hat and black trousers a little too short for her, sporting a long black coat that flapped around her knees – this would be forgivable. After all, actresses and other creatures of the night were also rumoured to commit such travesties. Her obvious foreignness, her dark almond skin and laughing green eyes, would also have been pardonable, maybe even an object of curiosity as the masses turned to stare. Likewise even the fact that she enjoyed reading the newspapers and talked angrily about the generals in the Crimea and their 'stupid incompetent mindless excuse for tactics', emphasizing every word with sweeping, ungraceful gestures – that too could have been excused, as an eccentricity allowable in the very rich; say, a female of the land-owning class.

There was, however, one problem which brought all others to light, and turned Lin Zi's eccentricities into embarrassments, and it was this: she revelled in them. She would say appalling things about Queen Victoria ('that short woman') in the presence of peers of the realm just to see the monocle drop; she walked through the dirtiest streets of the city, hopping over the corpses of rats and beaming at everyone she passed, her oriental face offering a friendly grin that inspired xenophobic anxiety in all those who beheld it. It was rumoured, indeed, that she had contacts among the Chartists and wrote angry letters to parliament about pocket boroughs, signed, 'a concerned gentlewoman'. Even among the more radical Tseiqin who knew her it was whispered that, somehow in Lin's young life, she had taken the cause of human-protectionism too far, and gone just a little native. However, since 'native' society didn't know where to put Lin or her mighty laugh, this conclusion was probably misplaced: Lin Zi drifted between worlds, enjoying every second of confusion she sowed in her wake.

This evening – now headed more towards morning – was no exception.

'You all right, Mister Lyle?'

Lyle shifted uneasily in the carriage taking him back to Hammersmith. 'Fine,' he mumbled.

'You look uncomfortable.'

'Just a little stiff.'

'Have you considered exercises?'

'Beg pardon?'

'Can you put your elbows on the floor?'

'What, now?'

'Can you?'

'Here?'

'Yes!'

'Possibly, why?'

'With your legs straight, I mean.'

'Why would I want to do that?'

'It's an exercise.'

Lyle's face was a picture of bemusement. '*Why?*'

'Gets stiffness out of joints.'

'Putting my elbows on the floor gets stiffness *out* of joints? What if I get stuck?'

'You wouldn't. Go on, can you?'

'Right now?'

'I'd be impressed. Keeping your balance would be a start.'

'I'm sorry, who are you?'

'Lin Zi. Don't try and get the intonation right, you'll end up embarrassing yourself.'

'The intonation?'

'It's not just Lin Zi,' explained Lin patiently. 'It's *Lin* Zds-ur!'

'Zds-ur?'

'That's how it's meant to be pronounced. You need to feel the end of your tongue buzzing . . .' Lin stuck her tongue out to prove the point, 'as if you'sh got thish bee on your tongue, yesh?'

'Aren't you the woman who threatened to cut my little finger off if I didn't tell you where Berwick was?' Lyle hazarded.

'You remembered!' exclaimed Lin. 'It's so nice to be recognized for my work.'

'Oh my,' muttered Lyle.

'Oh my, what?'

'This must be how Tess feels all the time.'

'Which one's Tess?'

'What do you mean, "Which one's Tess"?'

'Which one of your little friends?'

'I would have thought it was . . .' Lyle's eyes narrowed suspiciously. 'You're not from around here, are you?'

Lin beamed. 'I knew Old Man was right when he said you were sharper than a bag of raisins!'

'Razors.'

'What?'

'Razors,' said Lyle in a strained little voice. 'Not raisins. I'm sharper than a bag of razors.'

'I know what I meant. Which one is it?'

'What?' Lyle could feel himself sweating with the effort of keeping up with Lin's conversation.

'Which one of your friends is Tess?'

'Tess is the girl.'

'Tess. And the other is . . .'

'Thomas.'

'And the boy?'

'Thomas is the boy.'

'Oh. And the dog?'

'Tate.'

'That's a lot of "T"s.'

'That's hardly my fault!'

'I'm just saying.'

'You're not like other Tseiqin, are you?'

'See, there with the "T"s again — although arguably only because of your ignorant and incompetent transliteration system.'

'That's *definitely* not my fault.'

'I'm not.'

'Sorry?'

'I'm not like other Tseiqin.'

'This is a very demanding conversation for three o'clock in the morning,' whimpered Lyle, putting his head in his hands.

'Really? What's hard?'

'You're . . . very awake,' he sighed.

'So?'

'Well, I'm not!'

'If you like, I know a way to send you to . . .'

'No, no! No mind games, no sending to sleep!'

'I was just offering . . .'

'Stay well clear of my head, thank you kindly!'

'No need to get huffy about it.'

Something about her voice caught Lyle's attention. He looked up, trying to put his finger on it, and said finally, '"Huffy"?'

'I was just offering . . .'

'I haven't heard anyone use "huffy" for years.'

Lin fidgeted uneasily. 'Well,' she muttered, 'I like these words, yes? I find such human things quaintly pleasing.'

'My pa used to use it.'

'It's a good word,' she admitted. 'I doubt it's in Dr Johnson's dictionary, though.'

'Probably not.' He thought for about a moment, then added distantly, '"Blockhead" is, though.'

'What are you implying?' demanded Lin indignantly.

'Nothing at all, honestly! It's just such a good word, it should be used more often.'

'Members of parliament,' agreed Lin in a tone of disgust. 'Blockheads. And may I say, I think it's shocking that women aren't allowed to vote.'

'Neither are most men,' pointed out Lyle.

'That's beside the point! When you hear these people campaigning for another Reform Act, do they ever mention women? Do they ever stand up and say, "Incidentally, the fairer sex has a good head on its shoulders and a strong grasp of the necessities of life, I wonder if we should extend the franchise to them?" Can you explain to me why this idea is not even contemplated except occasionally by the wives of vicars during their ministrations in Manchester?'

'Erm . . .'

'The "weaker" sex, they say, unable to understand politics,

not to be burdened, a woman's place is in the home, a man's is in the world at large, gathering the goods. Even those among the Whigs who claim to be radicals blanch at the prospect of introducing even the slightest amendment that extends beyond the realm of local, church-hall governance! Well, I tell you . . .'

'How are you so awake?' wailed Lyle.

'I'm the product of several thousand years of what Mr Darwin would dub "special evolution", I think,' explained Lin. 'You're just a monkey in a pair of shoes.'

'I think you've missed the essential point of Darwin's work . . .' he began feebly.

'Where do you stand on the issue of the female franchise?'

'The female franchise?'

'Yes!'

'Erm . . .'

'You didn't think about it, did you?'

'Well, I . . .'

'That is half the problem of the attitude of men these days! If only they bothered to notice their womenfolk, to consider the contribution that they make to society, then perhaps they would realize that . . .'

'If I said I was in favour of the female vote, would you be satisfied?'

'I would suspect you of saying it to silence me,' she muttered, 'but I suppose from the likes of you, it is enough.'

'The likes of me?'

'Can you vote?'

'Well, yes, but only just . . .'

'Will you let my people die, Mister Lyle?'

'What?'

'Don't think about it, just go straight for an answer!'

'I . . . I suppose . . .'

'Will you? Let Havelock just stamp us all out in the blink of an eye, because he can? I've never met this man, so why is he trying to kill me?'

'I imagine that if I was put to the test . . .'

'Would you stand by, turn a blind eye, Mister Lyle?'

'No.' Lyle was surprised to hear himself speak, and surprised too at how calm he sounded.

Lin smiled and sat back. 'No,' she said, 'I didn't think you would.' She thought about it, then smiled brightly, a dazzle of white in the darkness of the carriage. 'Good! Yes, that's excellent! I think it will make this whole relationship a lot easier.'

'Right.' Lyle half-turned his head away to watch the long line of deeper darkness outside that was the edge of Hyde Park, but the part of him that was still awake drew his eyes back to meet the full force of Lin's smile. '"Relationship"?' he heard himself say in a voice like a coffin hitting the floor.

'Yes. Me and you.'

'What "relationship"?'

'You're not going to get to see my ankles, Mister Lyle, if that's what concerns you.'

'It isn't. What "relationship"?'

'I'm to make sure that . . . that no one can hurt you, Mister Lyle,' said Lin, deliberately emphasizing every patronizing word.

'*You?*'

'I'm very good at plucking chickens,' she added hastily.

'*What?*' Lyle wasn't sure whether to shout or moan, and ended up making a sound somewhere in between.

'I just thought I should make my qualifications clear. And I'm absurdly good at getting information – won't that be useful?'

'I don't need protection!'

'Well then, I'm going to protect your pets!'

'My pets?'

'The two children and the dog.'

'I'm sorry, I don't think I'm making myself clear . . .'

'No, you are; fear not,' said Lin cheerfully. 'What you fail to understand is that no matter what you say on this matter, I don't care. This, I find, is the marvellous liberty of being a potentially lethal Tseiqin with the power to move the minds of men at will!'

'You are a comfort.'

'And you have lovely eyes. Now be grateful for what you've got.'

Lyle scowled, and shrank back into the darkness of the carriage.

Breakfast in the Elwick family was a prosaic affair. The food provided was not prosaic, however – the chef and his staff were up from six a.m. preparing the gammon cuts and freshly baked breads and honey sweets to be delivered still warm to the Elwick family's table. But the actual business of eating, with its home-made blackberry and strawberry and raspberry jams, its marmalades and its morning papers and its fresh butters and clotted creams and coffees and sausages and bacons and hams and potted meats and mushrooms and eggs and breads – this ceremony was one usually conducted in the most rigorous, the most complete of silences.

This morning was different. As usual, Lord Elwick had his newspaper and, as usual, Lady Elwick ate as fast as glacial drift up a hillside, lifting slivers of gammon from her plate that were so thin, from a sideways aspect it appeared as if her fork had nothing on it. By eating at just the right pace, the moment her plate was cleared her husband finished reading the newspapers, and they could have the morning Conversation. On most days the Conversation went like this:

'The weather should be fine today, dear.'

'Yes, dear.'

'I hear Withers broke a plate last night. Shall I dock his pay?'

'Withers is an awful man. One last chance.'

'Lady Brunswick is having another one of her dinners tonight.'

'Those dinners are awful.'

'I thought I'd wear the green.'

'Very well, dear. Thomas?'

'Yes, sir?'

'I want to hear the names of all the Roman Emperors from Augustus down to Vespasian before we go out tonight, and their genealogy and contribution to culture.'

'Yes, sir.'

And that would be it. Always the meal ended with Thomas being given an instruction on how to spend the day, after which Lady Elwick would excuse herself. In her absence, Lord Elwick would secretly turn to the society pages of his newpaper, and smile a tight smile to read about who married whom last week.

Today, what marked things out as different was the arrival of Tess.

Thomas had observed Tess in many situations: he'd seen her climbing across rooftops, he'd seen her chasing/being chased by various monsters, he'd seen her trying to smooth-talk her way into posh clubs and trying to get out again by the nearest suitable window, he had seen her building explosives on the back of a falling aircraft. But he had never seen her looking like *this*. Someone, probably his former nurse, had tied her hair up with ribbons and scrubbed under her nails and washed every one of her clothes, and probably sat up all night drying them by the fire. For the first time in her life, Tess had submitted to a radical change in how she looked. And indeed, she took every chance to stare at herself in astonishment whenever she passed a large piece of reflective silverware or a mirror. The transformed Tess, the face that had emerged from somewhere inside all that hair, made her gape.

However, if she was open-mouthed with surprise before entering the breakfast room, she could have swallowed an orange whole, thereafter. 'What's that!' she squeaked, bouncing into the room, her eyes goggling at the table piled with food.

'Good morning, Miss Teresa,' Thomas mumbled.

Lady Elwick managed a, 'Miss', from somewhere behind her napkin, and Lord Elwick forced a twitch that might have been a smile. Tess exploded across the table – in thirty seconds she had a plate piled so high, she had to rest her chin on the topmost bread roll to stop it falling off, and the edges overflowed with bacon and sausages. Sitting down next to Thomas, she dug into her booty with a combination of fork and fingers, spraying crumbs with each exclamation of 'Ohohohoh, I want some of that too!' and, as she reached for an apple, knocking fruit in every direction off the work of art that was the fruit bowl.

Even Lady Elwick, who from infancy had been taught not to stare, found her eyes straying from the work of finicking through her breakfast. Lord Elwick showed almost an opposite reaction, edging the newspaper closer to his face to obscure the sight of Tess's table manners until it almost shook against his nose.

Thomas smiled at Tess and tried not to cry.

From the door came an embarrassed, 'Am I late?' as Lyle shuffled in.

And that would have been all right, except that with him was a woman, dressed in black clothes that didn't quite fit, sporting a long cane and a top hat, and smiling at them from behind a pair of glowing green eyes.

Tess leapt to her feet, as if looking for a window to jump through. Thomas found his hand tightening around a fruit knife, before the realization that it was only solid silver and not nearly magnetic enough sent a shudder right through him.

In the silence that followed, it was, surprisingly, Lady Elwick who took control.

'Not at all, Mister Lyle,' she stammered. 'Although we hadn't known that we should expect another guest.'

'It's one of *them*!' hissed Tess, who had backed so far away she was almost in the fireplace. 'It's gone an' bewitched Mister Lyle!'

'Teresa, I am not bewitched.'

'He's not,' agreed the woman next to him. 'Although I do suspect his heart palpitates that little bit faster in my presence.'

Lyle forced a smile. 'My lord, my lady, Tess, Thomas – this is Miss Lin Zi.'

'We need iron!' squeaked Tess. 'You go an' unbewitch him right now, all right? Else I'll . . . I'll run away!'

'Who is this young woman?' Lord Elwick had to force the words out, so rigid was the expression of distaste on his face.

To Thomas's horror, Lin Zi was across the room in an instant and holding out her hand to his father. 'Miss Lin Zi. Don't try the intonation, it won't help.'

Lord Elwick regarded the proffered hand as if it was covered in warts. 'I don't believe we've met. Why are you here?'

'Ah, yes. What happened is that I broke into your house last night – which was pitifully easy to do. Then I sneaked around until I found Lyle's room, hid inside, kidnapped him – admittedly, Miss Thomas –'

'. . . Teresa,' said Lyle quickly.

'Of course, whichever one you are,' went on Lin, not missing a beat as she nodded at the cowering Tess, '. . . admittedly by bewitching him – and took Mister Lyle to see a friend. As an upshot of this, I am now resolved to assist Mister Lyle in his brave and noble attempt to break into Pentonville Prison.'

In the silence, you could have heard a mouse sneeze.

Lyle gave an apologetic smile and a half-shrug. 'That's about the truth of it.'

At length Thomas said, 'Mister Lyle? Are you sure you are feeling quite well?'

'Give me a magnet and I'll prove it.'

'Is this a joke?' Lord Elwick's lips didn't seem to move,

although his voice boomed off the high walls of the room and made even Lady Elwick wince.

'No,' began Lin, 'although I can see the humorous aspects . . .'

'*Is this a joke?*'

'Mister Lyle, are you sure I can't smooth things over?' asked Lin, half-turning to him.

'No!' Lyle scuttled forward and spoke very hastily. 'My lord, I apologize; there's a lot that needs explaining.'

'*Do you think to mock me?* You come here without warning, in the middle of the night; you tell me my son is in danger, my only son; you bring strangers into my house, you bring strangers to my table; you speak of kidnap and prison and breaking the law. You dare to impose your madness on my house, on my home, on –'

'Father!' Thomas was surprised to hear his own voice snap out across the table. To everyone's astonishment including his own, Lord Elwick fell silent. Thomas stood up, fists clenched. 'Father, we know nothing. You know *nothing*. Until we understand more, let us behave towards this lady with good manners and decorum.'

Lord Elwick's mouth hung open like the jaws of a whale. Lin beamed, Lyle gaped, Tess cowered. 'I am sorry,' Thomas heard a voice say that might have been his own in ten years' time, 'but I now need to conduct important business with my friends.'

Lord Elwick sat, incapable of reply, his mouth slack. Lady Elwick murmured, 'Is this really what you want, Thomas?'

'Yes. Please, Mother, this is what I want.'

'Very well. We shall leave you to discuss your business. My lord?'

'Is this how it is to be, Thomas?'

Lord Elwick looked tired, Thomas realized. His shoulders drooped, his chin hung lower, his liver-spotted hands lay limp on the table. His grey eyes, always pale, seemed lighter than Thomas had perceived them whenever their look had reinforced some bellowed order.

'Later, I shall be able to explain.' Thomas felt his confidence suddenly draining.

'I . . . would like that.' Lord Elwick rose, took his wife's arm and half-bowed to Lin Zi. 'Madam, I apologize for speaking in haste. Please, feel free to help yourself to whatever you must.'

Lin bowed back. 'My lord, you are a kind man and a good father.'

Thomas felt himself go cold with anticipation. He scrutinized his father for any trace of . . . *otherness*, daring the woman with green eyes to have touched Lord Elwick's mind, to have interfered in his thoughts, to have even considered manipulating his father like *they* had: the Tseiqin; *them*; evil and cruel and . . .

Lord Elwick gave a smile, and there was nothing stiff or artificial in it. He bowed once more, and with his wife, left the room.

Thomas found himself letting out a breath that had been sitting in his lungs like lead. His eyes wandered across the table, seeking nothing in particular. From the fireplace, Tess hissed, 'Bigwig?'

'Yes, Miss Teresa?'

'Do summat about the evil lady!'

Thomas glanced at Lin and Lyle. 'Mister Lyle, are you bewitched?'

'Nope,' replied Lyle.

'Why ain't you bewitched, Mister Lyle?' shrilled Tess from the corner.

'I can answer that!' said Lin. 'It's because we need Mister Lyle conscious and self-aware in order to break into a place full of iron where our power would never work, and which indeed has been designed for that effect. Thus, bewitching him would serve no purpose!' She saw the children's horrified expressions. In a darker tone she added, 'Oh yes, and because bewitching him wouldn't be *nice*.'

Lyle opened his arms, a smile straining his features. 'See? What better answer could you hope for?'

Tess was unhappy. She was unhappy for a lot of reasons: because Thomas was sitting in a silence even thicker than his usual cloud of abstraction; because breakfast was getting cold and she found that eating and concentrating all at once was surprisingly diffi-cult, what with all that bacon . . . *bacon* . . . and eggs and ham and sausage and bread and buns and jams and . . .

Why else was she unhappy? She was unhappy because no one had commented on how pretty her hair looked; because Mister Lyle appeared tired and was talking in that low, flat voice he used when what he was saying was bad and he couldn't care any more; and because sitting opposite her and licking jam out of the pot from one long, dainty finger, was a Tseiqin.

Then Mister Lyle said the one thing that could make it worse. 'The Tseiqin really do want us to break into Pentonville Prison.'

Tess managed not to choke on a fingerful of jam. Thomas made a noise as if he'd just swallowed a spider. Curled up by the fireplace, Tate sneezed.

'What?' squeaked Tess. 'I don't know what part of what you just gone and said scares me more, Mister Lyle.'

'You're confident that you're not even a little bewitched, sir?' hazarded Thomas.

'Look, bring me a magnet and I'll bloody prove it!' snapped Lyle. He looked and sounded like what he was: a man who hadn't been getting enough sleep. 'I'm not even sure I'm going to do this damn thing for the Tseiqin!'

'Horatio,' sighed Lin, 'do we need to go into morality again?'

'Morality?' Thomas's voice was so high, Tess almost worried that he'd sat on something sharp. 'Since when did the Tseiqin care about *morality*? You kidnapped Mister Lyle; you want to hurt us; he came here because of you!'

'Well, actually . . .' began Lyle, a little sheepishly.

'*What?*' Thomas was surprised at his own voice. So was Lyle, who leant back as if trying to get a better look at his friend.

Lyle said, 'It's not the Tseiqin who've caused this latest trouble. Not unless you're going to take it right back to first principles, which is dubious and, I feel, futile.' He took in Thomas's expression, then Tess, back to gobbling her way through the fruit bowl, and Tate, who wagged his tail in the manner of a creature also aware of the food at the table. Lyle sighed. 'It's Havelock – *Havelock* is the one threatening you, Thomas. Havelock is the one who was involved with Berwick, Havelock is the one who knew about that damn laboratory underneath Baker Street. It's *Havelock*.'

'Who?' Thomas was amazed at himself, at how much he sounded like his father, the rich, indignant tones of aristocratic good breeding rolling off his tongue like magma down the side of a volcano. 'Who is this Havelock, and why are you afraid of him?'

'Oh, he *bad*,' offered Tess through a mouthful of fruit.

'He is a gentleman who has dedicated his life to the cause of technology,' said Lin. 'He seeks to build a new world out of iron and cogs; he attempts to spread the power of machinery.'

'And why's that bad?' asked Thomas.

She met his eyes. Instinctively Thomas recoiled, then found he couldn't look away. But it wasn't the same compulsion as when he had looked before into a Tseiqin's eyes. There was none of that sinking loss, the sense of drowning, or of suffocating with a mouth full of dry dirt. It was something more honest than that. In a voice like wind chimes, she said, 'Because he does not consider others when he builds. He creates only for himself, and sees in machines only power, not wonder.'

Thomas hesitated, the sharp reply dying on his lips, and a little 'Oh' escaping him instead.

'The Tseiqin do *claim*,' Lyle's quiet voice oozed scepticism, 'that Havelock is building a machine designed to kill all Tseiqin in the city, all at once.'

Tess raised a hand. 'Not to be too blunt about this, present company excepted, Mister Lyle, but ain't the Tseiqin sort of . . . *evil*? As in how they've got evil schemes and do evil things an' all?'

'It's true,' admitted Lyle, glancing at the now impassive Lin, 'that their record to date hasn't been . . . comforting. But there is something in what they say: Berwick's work seems to have been in the areas of magnetism and explosives – I don't know how in the world he intends to combine these two ideas. I don't even know if it's possible to create any machine –'

'Not *a* machine, Mister Lyle, *the* Machine.'

'It's just the way she speaks what makes it seem scary, right, Mister Lyle?'

Lyle drew the long breath of a man attempting a valid scientific point and finding himself thwarted at every turn, '. . . *if it's even possible*, as I was saying, to construct any machine capable of carrying out the purpose which the Tseiqin have described. But . . .'

'But?' Tess scowled and waited for the bad news.

'*But* . . . Berwick is still somewhere out there, and he's involved somehow. He's still my friend, I still wish to know what's happened to him, and there is . . . *something*. Something wrong happening.'

'How can you be sure, sir?' asked Thomas.

'Wherever Havelock goes, there's always something wrong,' groaned Lyle. 'It's one of the few certainties I have in this life.'

They all considered this. Eventually Lin said brightly, 'All right, humans!' Three pairs of disbelieving eyes turned to her. Thomas was openly gaping. She waved her hands, with the gesture of someone who is having trouble communicating. 'People! Companions! Darwinian equals in the evolutionary processes! Citizens of Her Majesty's Empire! You lot! Now that you've done your reasoning, worked things out and so on, all very commendable, et cetera, how exactly are you going to get into the Model Prison, and out again with one of England's most wanted criminals?'

'Who said anything about *leaving* with him,' exclaimed Lyle, 'when all we need is a conversation?'

Lin hesitated. 'You know, Mister Lyle, I personally find you a charming specimen, but I doubt whether this gentleman will be so inclined to talk to you.'

'I am *not* breaking anyone out of prison! I am not creating a riot, I am not . . . going to break the law; excuse me, miss, but I have scruples. All I want is a decent conversation.'

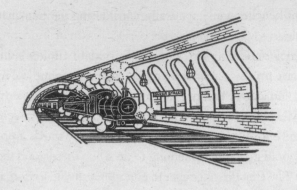

CHAPTER 8

Prison

Pentonville Prison. Situated at the top of the Caledonian Road, near the railway lines sprawling out from King's Cross Station, it was, to Victoria's London, unique. Here, Her Majesty's Government had tried to build something that had a *function*; that was self-sustaining and viable. Something that wasn't, in short, converted from the cells of the Old Bailey or the ramshackle remnants of some medieval palace with thick walls; something embodying an intention, a design, meant for just one purpose and that purpose to be fulfilled to the hilt. Situated behind high brick walls, everything about the prison – cells, courtyards, narrow corridors, iron doors, and halls where the condemned could spend their days picking oakum along silent rows of benches while, naturally, considering the reformation of their souls — was intended as the perfect fusion of function, form, efficiency and economy. For no more than fifteen shillings a week, the prisoner in his solitary cell could contemplate his misdeeds and consider how he might best return something to society, while such hearty, healthy activities as the crank and the treadmill, forever clocking up a futile total towards a pointless goal, would give him something to do when these good thoughts failed. The first prisoner ever to enter Pentonville Prison, twenty years before, would have been dazzled by the whiteness of the walls, the relative security of the cells, more than just iron bars set into a rotten wall, but solid in their construction, the open structure in its heart so that the warders could watch the prisoners at all times, without the prisoner necessarily being aware of it, and the smell of nothing more than whitewash and boiling cabbage.

Without a doubt, the prison was cleaner, brighter and better laid out than the half-converted old palaces and courtrooms that had housed more rats than inmates and where light had hardly ever entered. Moreover, the Model Prison was not just a holding point before transportation: it was a place of reform, where the condemned would learn new skills and trades so that they might re-enter society as useful citizens. And if indeed there was any one thing that characterized Pentonville Prison, it was the silence. From quarter to six every morning with the ringing of the morning bell to wake them, to the evening lockdown, the silence buzzed like a bee trapped in the ear, a constant, conscious awareness, the total straining of the senses every hour of every day to hear the tiniest noise, the scratching of a rat's claws on the floor, the dripping of the pump in the courtyard, broken only by the call of, 'Three D! Step quick, Three D! Two A, the Chaplain wants a word about those tracts he lent you . . . One C, scrub those floors!' Those shouts, echoing through the wings of the prison splayed like a strange five-pointed cross in the creeping suburb of north-east London, came as relief, a blissful reminder in the loneliness of the high-ceilinged, empty cells, that life somehow went on, that the prisoner alone hadn't fallen deaf from lack of hearing, or dumb from the inability to speak.

At night, the quiet was broken only by the wagon come from the courts with a new load of prisoners, or going to the docks with the next batch to be sent overseas or put on the hulks just offshore, or the distant rattle of a late goods train from the north, the whistle as it went somewhere *else*, somewhere far, far away from these thick walls and lifeless corridors. And sometimes, for those who were near the bottom floors and swore that the door at the back of the warder's office couldn't lead outside, the way the maps claimed they did, there was said to be the sound of someone whispering very quietly to himself, in the darkness:

'Let me out let me out let me out let me out *let me out let me out let me out Let Me Out Let Me Out Let Me Out I'll See You Burn For All You Have Done!*'

Then the clang of a staff on iron, and no more from the darkness far beneath.

In a police lodging house in the heart of Soho, a man had just fallen out of his hammock where he had been happily reading a book of cheap poetry purchased from one of the tattlers on Drury Lane. He fell with a bang and a shriek.

'You want me to do *what*?'

'Charles, don't be difficult,' said Horatio Lyle, brushing the policeman's uniform down and helping him to his feet.

'You know this is . . .'

'. . . more than your job's worth, yes, yes, I know. But think of all the times I've helped you!'

'Such as when?' Constable Charles – poor, unfortunate Constable Charles had been lured to join the Metropolitan Police from the Welsh hills and coal mines south of Abergavenny as much by the uniform's shiny buttons as by the promise of justice for all. He was not equipped to deal with Horatio Lyle in full placatory mode, and certainly not when at the same time Tate was quietly chewing on the leg of his regulation blue trousers.

'The Old Bailey,' said Lyle reasonably. 'I helped you then.'

'It was *your* fault they attacked it in the first place!'

'All right – St Paul's Cathedral.'

'*You* were dangling off the bloody roof while *I* was getting shot at.'

'Charles, I want you to consider the process of being struck by lightning for the greater good as more of a moral reflection on my character than the unfortunate consequence of being in a high place during a storm.'

'What?'

'Wha'?' added Tess helpfully.

Thomas, feeling that Lyle needed support, said quickly, 'I think Mister Lyle is referring to his presence on the highest point in London during a thunderstorm as an act of heroism rather than a rash venture into the realms of experimental meteorology . . .'

'Thank you, Thomas,' said Lyle and, in the same breath, 'Come on, you know it's got to be for a good reason.'

'Horatio,' Charles replied, 'there's only one reason for a man – even one such as yourself, who's supposed to be committed to the fighting of crime . . .'

'I'm not sure how I feel about "supposed", but go on.'

'. . . to want to get into Pentonville Prison!'

'And what would that be?'

'To get someone else *out* of Pentonville Prison!'

'I said nothing about *out*. I just want to have a conversation.'

'Are you going to lose me my job, Horatio Lyle?'

Lyle patted Charles gently on the shoulder. 'I know someone who can put in a very, very good word for you with the Commissioner.'

'Really? Who?' snapped Charles suspiciously.

'A young woman with a . . . a *knack* for persuasive argument.'

From the corner, a woman waved cheerfully. She had bright green eyes and outlandish clothes, and was probably grounds enough for dismissal, just by being there. Charles sagged. 'Just for once, Horatio, couldn't you be like an ordinary bobby?'

A moment, as the sun sets behind a billowing cloud of grey-brown smog, its bottom edge not so much disappearing behind the horizon as dissolving behind the vapours that ripple away to a burning bronze haze. Thomas Edward Elwick stands alone at the bottom of Caledonian Road, and looks north, and thinks.

And any creature with the power or the inclination to pick up even the slightest trace of his thoughts would have heard something like this:

. . . evil . . . so evil . . . why do they do this? They never mean well, they never do . . . all things end badly when they are here, all things . . .

. . . so sorry . . .

. . . had to be told, he had to know, couldn't live, grow like that, couldn't keep it from him, had to know, had to be told, he had to find out, my father . . .

. . . so sorry . . .

. . . duty! My duty, the lands, the name, the honour, the estate; an example, set an example, marry and grow old and do duty . . .

. . . and do the right thing . . .

. . . don't look away . . .

. . . the right thing for the right reason . . .

With that conclusion, Thomas Edward Elwick straightens up, pulls on his best pair of white gloves, tilts his hat straight on his head, and prepares to go out into the world, and do his duty. The right thing, for all the right possible reasons.

And as the sun dissolves on the western horizon, and the servants hide in terror round the corner of the kitchen door, Teresa Hatch sings a quiet tuneless, rhymeless, little song as she plays with the saucepans, and it goes like this:

'Three parts saltpetre and stir, stir, stir early in the mornin' . . . dash of phosphorus just for spice and let it hiss, mind the fumes and . . . where'd the mag . . . magnes . . . where's the thing what has the metal what goes all black in the air? Carbon carbon carbon smoke! Potassium chloride stir two three and sugar for the fuel and just a pinch of sodium bicarbonate and stir vigorously, *poof*! Oh damn, too much smoke, too much . . . where's the window gone?'

'Tess, what the hell is going on here?' Lyle's voice in the thickening gloom.

'Nothin', nothin', just . . . checking the recipe is right.'

'Mister Lyle, is your cooking always like this?' Lin's curious tones, mingled with a cough.

'No, Miss Lin, it is not bloody always like this! Well, except when Thomas cooks . . . but even then.'

'What exactly are you trying to make?'

'Smoke, miss.'

'I would never have guessed.'

'If you would never have guessed in *that* way,' growls Lyle, 'why did you bother asking?'

'Tell me,' says Lin, running one hand down a list of handwritten recipe books, only some of which are for food, 'what other kind of devices can you make?'

In his basket in the corner, Tate chews idly on his Special Bone, the only bone in the world that he'll ever chew on until next week's leg of lamb, thank you kindly, the bone which he will take to bed with him and sleep with his paws stretched warily across, just in case any fool should dare come in the middle of the night and try to take it from him. He ignores the billows of smoke as Tess flaps them out of the window, rubbing his nose against the tip of the bolt projecting from the crossbow-like device next to the doggy basket, and contemplates bones come from dinosaurs.

*

Some time and a few miles later, Horatio Lyle looked up, past a volume of wig and the scowl of two bailiffs, into the face of the judge, a man so conscientious in his job he goes to all the hangings he sentences, even when it's raining. Lyle said:

'Erm . . . I dunnit.'

'You done what?' boomed the judge. 'I do not appreciate being summoned on such irregular business!'

Constable Charles edged forward. 'This is . . . uh . . . John Smith —' a frown on the judge's face like a cliff face — 'John "Slasher" Smith, notorious uh . . . cattle rustler.'

'A cattle rustler?' demanded the judge, one eyebrow raised.

'That's right.'

'Thank you so much,' muttered Lyle.

'I thought the suspect was from Dulwich!'

'Ah, yes, well, I branched out, didn't I?' said Lyle hastily. 'City bred I may be, but cattle! Cattle cattle cattle! I mean . . . cattle! I just find myself looking at cattle and thinking . . . I mean . . . I think . . . cattle cattle cattle! Oh, and cows — cows are like cattle, aren't they? So, yes, there I am, in a field, I suppose, that's where you get cattle and I just think . . . cattle . . . they're just so . . . so . . .' he deflated, 'rustleable.'

There was a stunned silence in the small room, the antechamber to the court. 'Look, I said I dunnit, can't we get on with this, I've got a schedule to meet?'

'Do you *want* to go to prison, young man?'

Lyle hesitated, not entirely sure how to answer. 'Uh . . . *no?*' he suggested, hoping it was the right reply.

'Do you appreciate the gravity of your crime?'

A look of incredulity passed across Lyle's face, although he quickly tried to suppress it behind a more pained expression of tortured consideration and moral self-scrutiny. 'Cattle rustling?' he squeaked.

'The livelihoods you may have ruined?'

'Uh . . .'

'The souls you may have destroyed – have you not considered the corruption of your own being, the words our Saviour shall say to you at Judgement Day?'

'Can't say it crossed my mind. But,' Lyle clasped his hands in supplication, despite the ferocity of the judge's glare, 'should you feel as how I must answer my crimes, m'lord, dear m'lord, I'd be such a model prisoner, I would, if only I had a chance in a model prison, a prison where I could contemplate my sins, like . . .'

'Are there any witnesses?'

'Witnesses?' Charles nearly choked.

'Witnesses? Oh yes, witnesses, there's . . .' began Lyle.

'Silence!' Lyle found himself instinctively hanging his head in the face of fifty years of practised legal bark. 'Who is the witness?'

'A young . . . woman . . .' Charles's face would have been well camouflaged in a strawberry bush. 'And a couple of . . .' his last word was unintelligible.

'A couple of what?'

'*Children.*'

'Children? What kind of children?'

And from the door a voice that didn't need fifty years of legal training in order to bark, a voice that had learnt the art of projecting itself pompously across rooms and ballrooms and battlefields through the simple process of genetic inheritance, rang out. 'Not *children*, sir! I am Thomas Edward Elwick, and I demand the respect due to one of my position!'

And the judge, even if in his youth he'd harboured notions of fighting for the poor against the rich and the weak against the strong, was nothing if not shrewd. He looked up into the face of Thomas Edward Elwick, which was radiating aristocratic rudeness and good breeding, and found himself saying, 'My lord! This is an honour!'

Thomas smiled a tight little smile. 'The honour, your lordship,' he replied, executing a bow with just a hint of Italian flourish that in other circles would have been mocking, 'is all mine.'

Lastly, Old Man White sat, waiting.

Someone said, 'Do you think he'll do it?'

'Hm?'

'Are you all right, sir?'

'Oh yes, fine, fine. What was the question?'

'Do you think he'll do it? Will Lyle get into the prison?'

'Oh, I think so,' said Old Man White. 'Yes. I'd be very surprised if he didn't.'

'And let *him* out? What if we'd told him that –'

'I doubt he'd have gone in,' sighed Old Man White. 'Mister Lyle is, I feel, morally naive enough to risk breaking into the prison for what he believes to be a good cause. But if he knew exactly *who* he is breaking in for, I suspect even his sense of righteousness would have been somewhat underwhelmed.' Old Man White sighed. 'I feel like a cigar. Good for the health, steadies the head, clears out the lungs.'

'So I'm told, sir.'

'Yes. Maybe a quick cigar before bedtime. Although perhaps it would be more appropriate to wait and see how Mister Lyle reacts once he gets inside. Dammit, a cigar now. One here or there can't hurt, can it?'

Darkness outside Pentonville Prison was a patchy affair, not entirely sure of itself, but putting in a good attempt. Away from the pools of light from the few lamps on the street, the darkness was heavy as syrup, almost impeding movement as it stealthily followed behind the warders' steps. Tonight, poor Bob Steerwell was on duty, marching round and round the outside of the tall prison walls, as much to keep warm as in obedience to his superior's command. He didn't bother to notice which wall he was marching round now: the darkness and the brick and the silence were the same wherever he went. After a while there was no meaning even to the regular chiming of the new church bell down on the Holloway Road, a street growing fatter with every year as it wound its way towards Archway and the tunnel out of the city. Two, three bells – didn't particularly matter.

Bob Steerwell rounded another corner of the wall and contemplated bread and dripping, and marvelled that even his missus' bean soup, a thin grey concoction, was beginning to look attractive as he continued on patrol.

'Oi, mister!'

A girl, clearly one of the local street children, was standing a few paces off. In each hand she held a bag almost the same size as she was. She smiled an uneasy smile.

'You lost, missy?' asked Bob, reasonably enough.

The girl's grin widened and turned just a little nasty. Bob felt a tap on his shoulder and half-turned, to look into a pair of bright green, world-filling, darkness-vanquishing eyes. He heard a voice like wind chimes, like breeze across a forest floor, picking up the dry leaves as it moved; like the sound the first raindrop must have made, falling from the first cloud when the earth was new. 'Good evening, Mr Policeman, sir. Don't you think you should go and check the bottom of the road for a bit, to see if it's clear?'

'The . . . bottom of the road?' he heard himself say. Or perhaps it wasn't him, perhaps it was some other consciousness that made his lips move. It was very hard to tell, hard to look away, hard to blink, hard to breathe.

'Yes. Maybe down at King's Cross, perhaps there's something for you to do? I'd hate to think of you catching cold up here, not tonight.'

'I suppose . . .'

A long hand in a white silk glove patted him on the shoulder. 'Good man,' murmured Lin Zi. 'I knew you'd be co-operative.'

Bob Steerwell staggered like a drunkard into the fog.

Tess watched him go, then turned to Lin with a worried frown. 'Not as how I'm not thinkin' this is a useful trick what you got goin', miss,' she began.

'But?' suggested Lin.

'But . . . you sure you ain't just a *little* evil?'

'You said we needed to remove the policeman. I removed the policeman. What appears to be the problem?'

'Nothin', nothin'! Just . . . a bit unortho . . . unorthod . . . just a bit weird seein' you do it an' all.'

'You don't trust me?'

Tess gaped at the question. ''Course not! Don't be daft!'

Lin sighed patiently. 'So much for breaking down the cultural boundaries. Would you like a biscuit?'

Tess hesitated.

'It's got raisins in it.'

'It ain't poison?'

Lin looked surprised. 'No. At least, I don't think so. I did once make the mistake of using a bakery where they adulterated the flour with chalk, which I thought was cheeky, but I'm confident that this is the whole thing, the complete and utter biscuit. *Unless*,' she said suddenly, so loudly that Tess jumped, 'you mean, *I'd* poison the biscuit in order to kill people with it!'

'Uh . . . yes. That's what the poison thing is usually about.'

'Oh, nononono! Absolutely not! Why waste the time with poison when you can just talk people into walking off a cliff?'

Tess retreated into the darkness. 'Maybe I'll just . . . go without, miss.'

'Was it something I said?'

Horatio Lyle had seen all kinds. He'd seen prisons built one rotten, rusted bar at a time from ancient fortresses whose lower floors flooded each winter with stagnant water from the Thames, through which even the rats didn't dare waddle. He'd seen prisons built in towers where the stairs were so rickety that even the warders tiptoed up and down them, for fear of collapse. He'd seen debtors' prisons, cages full of the destitute and their families, visited only by the local pastors; he'd seen the hulks somewhere off the Norfolk coast, chained to the sea floor and melting away, a plank at a time, where a diet of eel and potato was rowed out every week by the local smith and his boy; he'd seen the prison ships to Australia; the murderer's chair where men would sit all day, every day, under a hood; the ice baths of the asylums; the gallows being tested on a cold foggy morning ready for the day's load – Horatio Lyle thought he'd witnessed it all.

Tonight, however, he was discovering that he'd been wrong.

Certainly, the place was an improvement to the first four senses. The usual prison smell – one of rotting teeth, mouldering clothes, rat-nibbled bread, blocked pipes and overflowing excrement – was absent. Indeed, the only strong odour was a faintly unpleasant one of cleaning products, scrubbed with hard brushes into the floor and, as it seemed, into the rough white walls themselves. There was also the musty smell of the basement, drawn up through metal vents that theoretically helped cool the place in summer and brought warmth up from the furnaces in winter. So far, so good. His skin, when he cautiously prodded the mattress on the bed at one end of the high white cell, didn't immediately burn with the migration of a small nation of fleas, and the blanket didn't carry the lingering smell of dead skin or the suspicious stains of nameless bodily fluids that Lyle associated with life and, more commonly, death in Her Majesty's prisons. There was no direct sign of anything in the room, animal, mineral or vegetable, that there should not have been. Although there was no other source of light in the cell, the copper basin in the wall gleamed from the moonlight above the fog that occasionally washed through the courtyard in billows like rumpled grey silk. The air tasted unusually clean for

London, a layer of purity just above the ever-present haze of smoke.

Lyle lay on the bed of his cell for cattle-rustlers in Pentonville Prison, and tried to work out what it was about the place that unsettled him so. There was, of course, the fact that he was *inside* and, more to the point, inside *not looking out*. True, he was reasonably sure that no prison could hold him without an armed guard on his door every hour of the day. If that wasn't comfort enough, there absolutely wasn't a prison which could hold Tess. And Tess was . . . well . . . she was Tess. She'd get him out sooner or later, if everything went wrong, because if she didn't there'd be no one to pay her pocket money (*although she could just steal it from his desk . . .*), or make her breakfast (*which she could just buy with the money . . .*), or warm her bath (*the biggest source of argument between the two of them . . .*) or just . . . generally . . . *be there*. Lyle contemplated all of this and found it only a little comforting.

What else was wrong?

He closed his eyes and listened. And he heard . . . nothing. Could fog make a sound? Or was the gentle hissing in his ears like the sound you heard with a conch pressed to your ear: just the effect of the air itself moving in and out, disturbed minutely by every breath you took, the illusion of hearing the sea far off, no more than the buzzing of blood moving near the eardrum? Nothing.

Nothing, after a while, had a texture all of its own. The mind played tricks, moved nothing backward and forward like the swish of the waves, in time to the pumping of the heart, nothing becoming nothing more than the circulation of blood around the skull, each breath getting louder and louder as he tried to silence it — or perhaps getting quieter and quieter and the ears simply getting more acute in their awareness of nothing, the mind filling in the blanks. The cell itself was a bit too tall and too long for him alone; he'd seen prisons where there would have been twenty people pressed into a space like this. The ceiling was just high enough to conceal where the darkness began or ended; the wall was a little too cold against his back; the door was too far away — although, stretched out on the floor, he would have been able to touch it with his fingertips while his toes pressed against the opposite wall.

All Her Majesty's other prisons had far too much character. They stank of various levels in hell, burnt in summer and freezing in winter, and men went there to die from every imaginable disease. This one killed in a different way: not through the obvious, painful explosions of sickness and decay promised by traditional places — the Fleet, Newgate and the hulks — but a quiet, tactful death, a smothering with non-sense, with non-life, with non-anything; perfect physical well-being while everything else became as white and pale as the walls around it.

And though Horatio Lyle knew, *knew* as rationally as he *knew* that there couldn't be angel-demon people who could control others' minds, as he *knew* that magic wasn't real and that gravity would *always* make the apple fall, though he knew that he would get out and wouldn't be there for long, there was no keeping out the little, irrational, terrifying thought that perhaps he'd made a mistake, and there would be no carriage waiting just outside the gates and no rope ladder and no distraction while he could sneak down, and no sliding the bar back across the door, and that would be it: he'd be stuck there, dying that quiet death each day all the days of his life.

He curled up tighter into the blanket and half-closed his eyes, and tried to think happy thoughts, from his new cell inside the Model Prison.

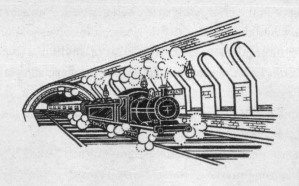

CHAPTER 9

Smoke

This was what Teresa Hatch was *good* at.

Thomas had wanted to use a grappling hook and rope. But to Teresa that was messy; it smacked of sloppy practice and, the worst of all things in a life of crime, reckless adventurism.

'Bigwig,' she announced in tones no less reproving for their voices being hushed, so close to the prison walls.

'Yes, Miss Teresa?'

'I don't know as how anyone's never told you before, but a *Good* brush with death an' adventurin' type things is a *Safe* brush with death an' adventurin', right?'

'Yes, Miss Teresa.'

'It means bein' all properly kitted up, makin' sure you got

your fence in the clear, your mark well greased, your team all in the know and the bobbies off the scent; it involves plannin' an' consideration an' above all, steerin' clear of anythin' a stupid pad what thinks he's the sharpest thing in the rookery can play with 'cos of how it's got the glint, right?'

'I think so, Miss Teresa.' Thomas was sweating with the effort of simultaneous translation.

'Oh, an' never, ever press the thing marked "Bang".'

'What thing marked "Bang", Miss Teresa?'

'Well, that's what I thought, but were I tactless enough to say it? No, 'cos I'm a well-bred young lady person. But who, I mean really, labels anything "Bang"?'

'Perhaps it's a metaphor?'

'Oi – no big words while I'm at work, Teresa's rule of . . . workin'. Got the gear?'

'If you can call it gear . . .'

'Who's the professional here?'

'I'm not sure if this is an area of employment in which you can seek such respectability, Miss Teresa.'

Teresa gave the martyred sigh of all uniquely skilled people being thwarted by amateurs, and looked over her stash of essential supplies for the night's work. Three large boxes, the fuse wires just visible over the edge, which Lin was setting neatly in the middle of the street, some distance from the carriage; a crossbow, all cogs and gears and springs, which Mister Lyle had proudly informed her could be loaded by 'a one-armed gnome with the muscular integrity of a banking clerk', the sack of goodies and a lot of rope for Mister Lyle, and of course, the thing that brought such disapproval from Thomas – the ladder.

As far as Thomas was concerned, if you had to commit crime at all, you should at least do it in style.

Tess beamed. It was a very, very good ladder. She was even thinking of giving it a name. They set to work.

A sound in the night?

Perhaps. It's hard to tell, so hard. The mind plays tricks in the darkness; no sense can be trusted in silence as thick as this. Even mountains have more noises and support more evidence of life: the movement of insects or the pressure of an owl's wings. But inside, tonight, it's so difficult to know, while the fog below smothers even the meowing of the prison's rat-hunting cat, with its one and a half twitching ears.

Perhaps . . .

The gentle thump of a wooden ladder being laid carefully against a wall, some way below?

Perhaps . . . soft-soled shoes on an uneven surface, perhaps . . . the tiniest movement of something light, no bigger than a child, perhaps . . . the thump of something coming to land in the courtyard below, the flop of rope, perhaps . . . no way to judge, nothing against which to compare the volume of sound except the beating of the heart.

When the distant church struck two a.m., it seemed so loud that Lyle nearly fell out of his bed. On the floor, he reassembled himself, gathered up a little dignity for the invisible audience that could so easily be waiting in that unloving darkness, and lifted one foot. He had, naturally, been searched, but what he was looking for was easy enough to hide. The small bundle of matches were tucked away just inside his shoe. He pulled one out, struck it easily off the wall and held it up to the high window. He repeated this three times over five-minute intervals, and sat back to wait.

A sound? Perhaps . . .

Something mechanical. Many cogs and springs greased tightly together, bending, turning, so efficient that a one-armed gnome with the muscular integrity of a banking clerk could operate them, perhaps? So hard, imagination knows what's coming, difficult to place it.

And a definite sound, so close and so loud Lyle thinks that the entire prison must hear it, must wake to it, but then once it's come and gone in a second, he's not so sure, perhaps he imagined it, the strange half-dislocation of thought and imagination as if he'd just woken up and spoke, not entirely confident if this was a dream or not.

The church bell struck two thirty, somewhere in the distance. A goods train from the north rattled by. An empty goods train from the south clattered northwards. The fog made whatever no-noise the fog made; the church bell struck a quarter to three. Lyle began considering plan B, and contemplated the effect of temperature on volume at a fixed pressure, and pressure on volume at a fixed temperature and all variations around a theme, to keep himself distracted from thoughts of doom.

When the knock came, he hadn't heard anything approaching and at first thought it was the warden come to demand what in God's name was going on now, or else. When it came again, it was, however, accompanied by a little voice from the small window set in the upper part of Lyle's cell. 'Oi! Is this the right evil criminal person?'

Lyle hastened to the window, jumping up on tiptoes to try and get the tip of his nose at the approximate height of the speaker. 'Tess!'

A shadow, darker than the darkness outside, dangled outside his window and exclaimed brightly, 'Hello, Mister Lyle!'

'Shush, shush!'

'Sorry.' Tess's voice dropped to a dramatic whisper. 'Hello, Mister Lyle!'

'Are you all right there?'

'You mean, apart from how I'm attached to a rope what's attached to, all due respect, a bloody ballista bolt from your really-nasty-should-never-be-fired-playin'-around-with-too-many-cogs-an'-frankly-, if I might say so, not-gettin'-out-enough machine, embedded in a bloody crumbly-looking wall, attached to a *prison* at height?'

'Language!'

'*Please.*'

'All right otherwise?'

'Fine.'

'Is Thomas down there?'

'Bigwig's scared of heights,' sang out Teresa, bouncing on the rope outside Lyle's window with an abandon that made even Lyle a little green. 'You'll be wantin' equipment for escapin' an' all then, Mister Lyle?'

'If it wouldn't inconvenience you.'

'You just sit tight an' let Teresa, as usual, save the day, don't you worry about nothin', Mister Lyle.'

There was a rustling sound outside the small pane of glass and bars, and a little tight squeaking. Over the squeaking came

Tess's conversational voice. 'You know, that machine of yours what you said as how anyone could fire it an' it'd be secure an' everythin' . . .'

'Yes?'

'I was thinkin' – isn't someone goin' to go an' notice as to how there's a bolt with . . . with . . .'

'Explosive expanding hooking implements?' suggested Lyle hopefully.

'I was thinkin' really big pointy bits, but if you want . . . stuck in the prison wall?'

'*Well*, ideally it'd crumble in sunlight . . .' began Lyle with forced brightness as the squeaking sound went on at the glass.

'It *crumbles*?' Tess's voice was a shrill, bat-killing squeak.

'No, no, I said *ideally*!'

'Oh. Right.' The squeaking continued at a nonchalant pace.

'But since it doesn't, and since it should be embedded at least a foot and a half into solid stone considering the explosive force of the stored tension in the gears and taking into account deceleration due to gravity of around tenish metres per second per se—'

'Since it don't?' sang out Tess, quick to sense any kind of information heading her way and cut it off before it could get the wrong idea.

'Oh. Well, yes, since it don't . . . uh, doesn't . . . don't . . . look, it's just going to have to stay there and confuse a lot of people, all right?'

'You don't think as how that might be inc . . . incrim . . . risky an' traceable evidence an' all? Should anyone start askin' questions?'

'Teresa, would you say I was the kind of man wilfully to break criminals out of prison?'

'No!'

'Then why should anyone ask?'

'Oh. All right, fair enough. Hold on, stand back, I think I'm done here.'

Lyle hastened back, away from the window. With a final little tortured squeak, a circle of glass slightly larger than the spread area of Tess's hand popped out of the pane and tipped forward. Lyle grabbed at it before it could smash, with an inelegant cry of, 'Whoops!', and looked up to see Tess's face peering in through the small hole above. She waved, rocking back and forth on the rope to which she was attached, suspended several floors above the ground and some yards below the bolt that had embedded itself in the building like a needle in a pincushion. 'Hello!' she hissed in another overdramatic whisper.

'Hello. Have you got everything?'

'Oh – no, I think I left it.'

'You *what*?'

'Don't be such a mark, Mister Lyle, 'course I got it. You think I'd come all the way up here an' all without it?'

'Teresa, now is not the time,' said Lyle with a scowl.

Grinning, Tess wiggled a small bundle through the bars. It got about halfway through and then promptly seemed to take on a life of its own, bending inside its tight cloth wrapping so that a part of it attached itself very firmly to one of the iron bars near the hole. With great effort, Lyle hopped up and dragged it off only by the weight of his own body, pulling it free with a sharp *clack*. After that came three larger packets wrapped mostly in brown paper and string, with a little line of fuse trailing from one end of each. Tess said cheerfully, 'So, when'll you be wantin' distraction?'

'Three a.m., stick to the time.' A look of sudden guilt passed across Lyle's face. 'Oh dear, this is a long way past your bedtime, Teresa. Don't get used to it!'

'You sure three's long enough?'

'Teresa . . .' growled Lyle in a warning voice.

'Just sayin', concern an' that.'

'Stick to the church bells,' he repeated firmly.

'All right! 'Byeee!'

With a final cheerful wave, Tess dropped from sight. She didn't so much climb down the rope as lessen her grip at a strategic point. She whizzed down in a cloud of hair and flapping clothes, repressing the instinct to go 'Wheee!' and landing without a sound in a courtyard a long way below, lost in the fog.

Inside the cell Horatio Lyle, refusing to be rushed, methodically unwrapped his bundle of goods. Lock picks, hooks, magnets, mirrors, suspicious tubes and glassy spheres clinked under his fingertips.

Lyle chose a long hook and slotted a mirror on to it, took another hook and walked up to the door. He walked up to the viewing hatch, and smiled with an undeniable edge of smugness as one of his magnets stuck to the iron sheet with a resolute thump. He drew the magnet across, and the hatch went with it, opening up easily to reveal the corridor outside. He dropped the magnet into his pocket, stuck the mirror out on the hook and turned it until he could see the large iron bolt running across the door on the outside. Standing on tiptoe, he eased an arm out, the other hook in his hand, until the end of the hook caught on the bolt. In the mostly-darkness, lit only by the unreliable moonlight coming through the small window, it was as much an act of luck and touch as an exercise in matching the eye to workings of the hand. When the bolt came loose, it was with a *thunk* and a reluctant, badly oiled rattle that made his heart race in time to each uneven slide of the bolt. He counted to thirty to still his heart and wait for retribution to come – and when it didn't he knelt by the lock on the inside of the door, and drew out Tess's finest lock picks, the ones she had chosen specially from a wide collection, with the words, 'Big doors . . . well, big doors need good tools, Mister Lyle . . .' With a long sucking in of breath, Lyle set to work at the lock.

It was heavy work, rather than subtle – the springs inside the lock were few and crude, but stiff, and Lyle kept half-expecting his tools to fracture with the strain of it. The release of pressure when the lock finally went was, he thought for a moment, the pick snapping. Only the outward swing of the door at his careful push gave him grounds to breathe again. He rolled up his tools quickly and stepped into the darkness of the corridor. If anything lived or breathed, it hid it well.

Lyle began the long, careful plod towards the centre of the prison.

Nothing ever happened on the Caledonian Road to give it distinction. Sometimes the English going to Scotland or the Scots coming to England rattled down the Caledonian Road, sometimes the odd red lady was caught selling her wares towards the place where the railway terminated at King's Cross. Sometimes barges blocked each other on the canal, but these days there was less traffic on the waterway as it was so much easier to send freight by train. The hoot of the locomotive's whistle and the distant church bells were the only distraction, or the occasional wagon carrying prison inmates towards Portsmouth and a different kind of confinement.

Theoretically, Lyle was a copper through and through. Once the criminal was caught, justice was justice, and if justice chose to put away the guilty in a prison like Pentonville, then all well and good. The law might not be a marvel, it might not work exceptionally well; but it was the *law*, universal and impartial, and everyone had to stick to it, otherwise what was the point?

Tonight, however, it was secretly glad to be able to bring something different to the top of the Caledonian Road.

Voices outside the prison? Perhaps one or two inmates of Block Four are awake at three bells of the church, perhaps they have noticed something thud into the wall, perhaps that strange sense of hearing that develops in the absence of all other sound detects . . . somewhere down in the fog . . .

'I said *that* one!'

'You said *left*, Miss Teresa!'

'Yes, there!'

'Miss Teresa, we've had this problem before. Left is *that* way!'

'Oh. Are you sure?'

'Yes! I am completely and utterly confident that you said *that* fuse! *There!*'

'Oh well, too late now . . .'

And the three boxes placed in the middle of the Caledonian

Road, give a fizzle and a hiss, and promptly explode. They explode *upwards*, and they explode like fireworks. From the warden's office to the outer gate to the topmost cell to the lower kitchens, the walls and ceilings of the prison light up an explosion of green, white, blue, red and sodium orange with the reflected light from the rockets. The noise fills every cell, rattles every window pane with the shrieks of the screamers climbing up and the hiss of the candles and spitting of sparks as they fizzle gently out on their way back into the fog and the boom of the big bangers as they reach the top of their flight and rupture outwards. And as they explode, they shower sparks that glow like dying fireflies as they fall, and they spew smoke that settles above the fog, in the fog, blending with the fog, the lights from the explosions somehow made out-of-focus by the haze, the grey smoke distinguishable by a sharper, sweeter smell as it begins to settle.

Inside the prison, Horatio Lyle looked up and smiled as the first bangs shook through the floor, and the first doors started clanging and the first voices started shouting. With intricate care he drew out the three paper-wrapped packages from his bundle of goods, struck a match off the wall and set the fuses burning. He threw the first down one corridor, tossed the second into another and, with a gleeful sense of satisfaction, chucked the final one into the main hall where the stretched-out wings of the prison joined. He counted to five, and heard the *hiss-bang* of the first package igniting, and grinned as from each corridor and hallway thick billows of smoke started to roll across the floor.

*

It took ten minutes for the panic to set in satisfactorily. Thomas was surprised by that: he had expected the reaction to be prompt. But then, in the fog and the smoke and the darkness, his own hand in front of his face had taken on a strange, drained, featureless aspect, a fuzzy outline in the dark – and such a complete darkness as he had never experienced. What little moonlight there had been from above was now lost; there was nothing even to cast a deeper shadow. Somehow the busyness behind his eyes, when he closed them, was brighter than the utter black of the smothered night outside. At least behind his eyelids imagination could fill in sparks and colours where there was nothing else. But outside, with everything smelling of smoke and the acrid whiff of gunpowder residue, the rising sounds of shouting and bells ringing in the prison, left all too little space for imagination.

He called out, his voice muffled in the darkness, 'Tess?'

A little voice somewhere in the night – up, down, it all had lost meaning – replied, 'Bigwig?'

'I can't see anything.'

'That were the whole point, bigwig. Just keep talkin' some, all right?'

'I can see well enough.' The voice came from close by Thomas's ear and made him jump. He peered into the night and even though the darkness smothered all sense, he could still *feel* her bright green eyes looking at him. 'It's a beautiful night,' murmured Lin Zi.

Somewhere in the dark Thomas could hear rising voices, a strange, far-off cacophony of orders and commands. A bell started ringing, a loud, insistent peal, cutting across the babble of voices.

'What's going on?' hissed Tess's voice off to his right.

'I imagine,' said Lin, 'they're calling out the guard.'

'And that's a good thing?'

'Panic, confusion – yes, I think it may be good, if used right.'

'An' how's that, then?'

You could hear the smile in Lin's voice. 'I may go and say hello.'

Even with his eyes streaming from the smoke, Lyle strode through the prison with the confident look of a man who belongs here and knows it and you'd better not question it any time soon, thank you very much. He could hear voices and bells ringing and doors banging and feet running, but with visibility down to a yard or two in every direction and more smoke gushing every second from the paper cylinders he'd thrown into the hallways, he didn't care. Whenever he saw another figure moving, he pressed himself into the shadows and waited for it to pass. The noise was a relief: every shout, every bang, every reverberation gave a reference point for where there was life and activity, something to avoid. It was far better to know that someone was awake and out there looking for you than to pad along in the silence of uncertainty. He didn't need much light to find where he was going – the few long matches he struck and held up to create a pool of light about his own width were enough – he just needed to go down, and keep going down. In many ways his destination made it easier – coughing and blundering through the smoke, the warders were doing their best to establish a perimeter, armed with batons and truncheons, to hinder would-be escapees. The thing they were not trained to prevent was people trying to break in.

*

Outside the prison, the guards were surprised by a number of things. First was the absence of any kind of prison riot. Smoke billowed into the courtyard from the windows, rolling into the fog – but no cell doors were unlocked and, though the prisoners shouted and screamed and coughed and banged their bowls on the metal doors to create a clamour of scrapes and wallops that drowned out all human voices, no one who wasn't a prison guard emerged from the darkness coughing black phlegm.

Second was the absence of fire. The smoke was dirty and stank of charcoal and burnt toast, but the guards running through the corridors with their buckets and sticks could find no glimmer of light to suggest an open flame as they tripped over each other's feet and tumbled down stairways and into walls, feeling and fumbling their way through the darkness by guesswork alone.

The last thing that took some warders by surprise was the least probable of all. Milling in the dark, looking for another shadow to give commands or establish order, trying to strike lights to their lanterns and shouting out, 'Who's there? What's there? Hello?' some noticed sharp sounds, like a singer's intake of breath before the final song and, turning from the group, looked into a pair of bright green eyes.

'Hello,' said Lin Zi. 'Will you dance?'

Below ground level, Lyle's fingers groping through the dark found the door he was looking for. It wasn't a particularly exciting door, and when the lock clicked under pressure, it led to a not very interesting flight of stairs dropping further down into darkness – pure darkness, not a trace of smoke except that which drifted in with Lyle: the utter darkness of a windowless space made of very thick brick. Lyle kicked the staircase thoughtfully – it hummed with iron. He ran his hand across the wall – it was cold and metallic. Smiling, he closed the door behind him, and reached into his bundle of goods for a couple of the long glass tubes Tess had brought him. He tipped a liquid from one on to a small stock of powder at the bottom of the other, shook gently and held it well away from his face. With a *phuzz-hiss* the mixture started to glow, giving off a thin white steam and an angry noise as the little parts of the powder bubbled up and down like pebbles in a storm. By this dim light, Lyle picked his way down the metal staircase, on to the metal floor below, past the silent metal furnaces with their pipes and coal-black open doors, and across a room at the far side of which a metal door sat with the foreboding look of a door not intended to be opened by those who Did Not Know. Underneath it, however, Lyle could see a faint orange light. He walked over, took a deep breath, and hammered on the door.

A shadow passed across the orange glow. A voice said, 'What in the name of the Lord is going on up there?'

'Bloody fire, isn't it?' snapped Lyle, matching the accent of the speaker, one that he associated with somewhere near the waterfront. 'And here's me sent to save your hide.'

'Only the gov'nor can open this door! Who is that, anyway?'

'He gave me the damn key,' snapped Lyle, fumbling in his pocket for the lock picks. 'You want to burn?'

'Can't leave! I need to speak to the gov'nor!'

'You want to die, mate?'

'Is that Steerwell?'

'No, it bloody isn't,' snapped Lyle. 'Now I'm leaving, and you can do what you want, all right?'

'Wait, wait, wait!'

There was a clacking from the other side of the door, and the voice went on, 'I heard the bell but, you know, they said never to open it up unless . . .' The door swung open. The guard on the other side looked into Lyle's face and said, 'Hey! You're not from around –'

Lyle, grimacing apologetically, hit the man as hard as he could. This didn't have quite the desired effect – the man staggered back, clutching at his nose and screaming, 'That bloody hurt!' Lyle stepped forward, grabbed the man by the back of the neck and rammed a tube of too-thick-looking clear liquid under his nose. The man struggled for a moment, coughed, rolled his eyes, then he went limp in Lyle's arms. Lyle lowered him carefully to the ground, stepped by him, hesitated, then stepped back. He pulled out the guard's notepad and stub of pencil, found a clean page and wrote in large letters,

You have been rendered unconscious by the use of chloroform. Please seek medical attention at your local infirmary. Do not ingest alcohol for at least a week, preferably two (or smoke generally), take some days off work, and do not be alarmed by any contact sores – they will pass in time if you do not pick at them. Apologies for the inconvenience.

Feeling a little happier, Lyle left the note face-up on the man's chest and hastened down the corridor. When he reached the solid iron door at the end, the magnet tried to meld itself to it. Lyle slid back two bolts and set to work at the lock.

Tonight, it is Lin Zi's turn to dance. There is no other word for it, no other way to describe it: Lin Zi beats out every step to an invisible rhythm, taps across the courtyard to an unheard melody, spins to a distant trill in the music, rolls to a drumbeat in the mind. The legs she kicks out from under their owners, the shoulders she taps in passing, the noses she tweaks, the hair she tugs, the jackets she tears, they are nothing but steps along the way, downbeats at the beginning of every bar. When the men shout and try to catch her, when they reach out into the fog, she has already spun on the tips of her toes, laughing, and is away. The dance is only a simple thing, easy as a child's skipping game, but ordinary pleasures have such delight for Lin. She leads the warders of Pentonville Prison around in circles and across the yard and through the fog and hardly notices them, lost entirely in the song that tonight only she can hear. And as she dances, she lights up the night, in every way imaginable.

Later, when asked, she'll shrug and say it was simply the logical outcome of magnesium and black powder meeting the vapour in the air.

Down in the depths below Pentonville Prison, Lyle clicked back the last spring in the lock, and carefully pushed the door open. He picked up the guard's discarded lamp by the door and held it up, looking into the shadows of the small iron room beyond. Iron walls, iron floor, iron ceiling, with a single iron bowl in the corner. Next to it was a shape that was either a man huddled, or a smaller sleeping animal; it was hard to tell, the creature was curled in so tight on itself. Lyle cleared his throat and felt like an idiot.

'This is going to sound unlikely,' he began, 'but are you Tseiqin?'

The black shape in the corner didn't move. Lyle raised the lamp to let more light fall on it, but it had its head turned away and didn't react.

'All right: iron prison, iron walls, armed guards, buried away, there's definitely something wrong; sorry, it was a stupid question. Let me put it another way. Are you prepared to speak to me?'

The bundle raised its head. Lyle saw bright green eyes and a face the colour of swept Scandinavian snow. The face said, 'Your bones to dust, Horatio Lyle.'

Lyle stared at it in horror, let the voice sink down on to his senses, let memories sit up and start rattling the cage, let the realization sink through every part of him until there was no getting round the inescapable, unavoidable truth of the matter. He put the lamp down carefully on the floor, for fear of dropping it, and said, 'Oh bugger.'

In the darkness, Lord Moncorvo started to smile.

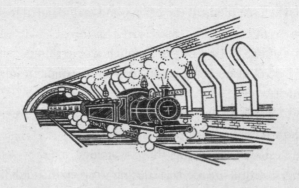

CHAPTER 10

Enemies

'I've been cleverly manipulated by evil people, haven't I?' said Lyle.

Lord Moncorvo made no reply, but watched Lyle beadily from his huddle in the corner. 'And I really thought this enterprise would be a good thing. Open-mindedness, sympathy, understanding and all that.'

'Is something going wrong in your life, Mister Lyle?' Lord Moncorvo's voice hadn't changed. It still had the sound of polished black leather, if black leather could speak. But his face — that was different. There was no longer the charisma and command Lyle had remembered, but something shrivelled, pointed and pale, the way Moncorvo's companion, Lady Lacebark, had looked when she died, all the beauty and magic faded from her features.

'I'm waiting to find out how much worse things can get,' replied Lyle. 'I'm assuming a trap, a plan, something of unspeakable cruelty, yes?'

'If so, I wait with the same anticipation as you do, Mister Lyle, to see how it might transpire.'

Lyle hesitated, watching those watching eyes. A sense of growing, dreadful unease was starting to creep through his initial horrified reaction. Cautiously, every word an age, he said, 'You . . . weren't expecting me.'

'No. Should I be?'

'Old Man White says hello.'

Moncorvo's eyes flashed, in a moment of . . . something . . . although his face remained empty and cold. 'Old Man White?'

'Yes, he says hello.'

'How do you know him?' Anger in his voice? Hard to tell, the hate drowned out everything else.

'He's worried.'

'He should be.'

'Why?'

Moncorvo shifted, smiling a tight, bitter smile. 'I am good at not answering questions, Mister Lyle. Why do you think he should be worried?'

'I take it you don't like Old Man White?'

'As I said . . .'

'You're very good at not answering questions. My God, but you must be one of the few people in this world whom even the saints would hate, Moncorvo.'

'But Horatio Lyle is beyond hate?'

'Don't test me,' Lyle muttered.

'It is no great vice to confess to hate — in fact, it probably helps cleanse the soul. I will be punished for hating you, but in admitting that I wish to see you burn to dust and ash, perhaps I'm a little bit closer to enlightenment.'

'Oh, let's not play the recrimination game, Moncorvo. When it comes to first principles you were the man standing there with the very sharp knife, and besides, I'm working within something of a time limit here.'

'Why are you here, Mister Lyle?' Lyle didn't answer.

Moncorvo started unfolding his long thin body from its corner. His fierce green eyes glittered. 'You hate me,' he mused, 'you are afraid of me . . . yes, I think so. Afraid — you believe so greatly in your own, arrogant, petty, ignorant self-righteousness, you do what you think is "right" without regard for the bigger consequence — but you would not be here without a reason.' He stood up — he seemed to droop in on himself, standing, as if over time the bones had bent or become rubbery, unable to support his weight. 'Why are you here, Horatio Lyle?'

'I thought I knew.'

'I don't think it's revenge.'

Lyle looked up sharply from his study of the faint lantern, anger settling across his face. 'I'd have bloody good motive, which is an important thing in my line of work.'

'You're too weak for revenge, Mister Lyle. You don't have the stomach for it. Do you even have a gun with you now?'

'No, but I've got all my own brain,' he spat. 'How do you know Old Man White?'

'Which answer would upset you more? Friend or enemy?'

'Oh, for God's sake.' Lyle stood up sharply, crossed the small space between them and dragged Moncorvo up by the lapels, pushing him against the wall. The man was light, astonishingly skinny under his loose black clothes; Lyle, who wasn't a particularly strong man, lifted him easily. He glared into his emerald-green eyes, a few inches away. 'Let's just clarify this. I have gone to great trouble and personal risk to get down here. I've been chased, half-drowned, kidnapped, arrested, tried without due process, locked up, burnt enough carbon compounds to give me a dodgy cough for the rest of my days and generally had an unsettling philosophical change of perspective thrust upon me by the various believers of this life, by all the secret people doing their secret things for secret petty stupid causes and I'm sick of it.

'So, here's the way it goes: you can tell me the things I want to know, or you can not tell me, and I can leave ignorant and go on holiday just as Tess always wanted. Alternatively, I can leave knowing things that might actually help you stupid bastard people with your stupid bastard plans to survive beyond the next few days. Frankly, I'm nearing the point where I don't care; because, you know, the whole right and wrong thing is excellent up to a point, and that point is *now*. So . . .' He smiled a tight, unsympathetic smile. 'How do you know Old Man White?'

Moncorvo grinned. 'Was that meant to be intimidating, Mister Lyle?'

'Right!' Lyle let go of him, turned, scooped up the lantern and marched for the door.

He got two paces beyond it when the tired voice said, 'Mister Lyle.'

Lyle turned, eyebrows raised. 'Yes?'

Moncorvo opened his mouth to speak, then hesitated, smiling a self-reproving little smile. 'Remarkable. You've been standing in that doorway for less than a minute and already I find myself curious as to all things in your life, wracked with a fascination that I can't seem to shift, despite myself. So . . . how, precisely, are you going to help my people?'

Lyle edged back into the doorway, put the lantern down and folded his arms. 'If I said "the Machine", with a definite article in front of it and a strong emphasis for dramatic effect, what would you reply?'

Moncorvo was silent a long while. Then he said, 'You are helping to build it?'

'I bet you think I would.'

'It would either have been you or . . .'

'Berwick?'

Now it was Moncorvo's turn to raise his eyebrows. 'How much exactly do you know? Or perhaps it should be – how much has Old Man White told you?'

'Oh no. I've played that game too, these last few days, and I'm sick of it. You tell me about the Machine and it's just possible that some good comes of it, nothing more.'

'All right.'

'And don't try . . . Really?'

'Get me out of here, and I'll tell you everything I know. Which is . . .' he smiled again, revealing sharp white teeth, '. . . quite a lot.'

For a second Lyle froze on the spot, trying to absorb the words he'd heard. Then he laughed, a short humourless chuckle, emanating from a face that could have intoned a funeral chant. 'No, sorry, not a hope,' he explained.

'Why not?'

'Shall we go back to first principles with that question?'

'Is the Machine being charged?'

Lyle hesitated, caught off guard by the other man's question. Moncorvo drew himself up, and edged an uncertain pace forward. 'Has Berwick completed the discharge mechanism? Did he get the explosives to work?'

'How much do you know *exactly*?' asked Lyle. 'And no hedging melodramatically around the scientific details, please; I like things with numbers, letters and equal signs.'

'In this . . . place . . . this prison of iron and magnets,' hissed Moncorvo, 'I can feel nothing, taste nothing, all senses are flat to me, it is . . . a death. One small black increment at a time, a wasting away, a constant, dull, driving pain. That's your doing, Mister Lyle.'

'Tell me what you know!'

'Get me out of here first.'

'No! No, I'm sorry – somewhat – a little – perhaps – but no! You're such an enthusiast for the continued survival of the Tseiqin, you know so much, tell me! Let me help you – help them!'

'You are our enemy!'

'Yes, and you're mine, and it's all deeply confusing and frankly I don't know what I'm doing here. But this . . . this Machine, this device of Havelock and Berwick, if you know what it is, how it works, how it functions, tell me and I can stop it. Probably. With a bit of luck.'

'You? How? Why?'

'You know well enough how good I am at stopping things I don't like,' snapped Lyle with an edge of cruelty. 'You and I have already tested this hypothesis to the utmost. As for why . . .' He hesitated.

'I would have thought you were the kind to build this device, Mister Lyle, not destroy it.'

'It's indiscriminate.' Lyle was surprised to hear himself, but he was beginning to feel that way about a lot of things.

'That's it?' Incredulity spiked the flat cold of Moncorvo's voice.

Lyle glared. 'The Machine is indiscriminate,' he repeated. 'That's what Old Man White says. I find it hard to believe, but if it is true . . . so many dead in a moment . . . Not one chance, not a moment to explain, no . . . no justice. I've met some bastards in my time, Lord Moncorvo, from murderers up to the moral turpitude of cattle rustling, and you cap the list. But until I know, until I *know* that every one of your kind is as cruel as you, I have no . . . there is no mercy in it. There is nothing in the Machine to make it different from what you would have done to us. It is without feeling, judgement, empathy. You'd build one in an instant, I think, my lord, if it worked your way.'

'Of course. And I respect the man who does so.'

'You respect Augustus Havelock?'

'As a man who does what he believes needs to be done.'

'And you expect me to listen to all this?'

'I notice you haven't walked away.'

'No, that's something I really should learn,' muttered Lyle.

'So,' said Moncorvo easily, 'what do we do now, I wonder?'

Lyle stepped back from Moncorvo. 'Look, I'm not here just to cause riots or to break out dangerous prisoners. I was here to get the information I need; and above all other things, more than almost anything else ever, I am *not* here to get *you*, of all people, back out *there*. I get in under a fake name and am never recognized, never seen, just another face in the crowd, you understand? I can't go around breaking people out of prison willy-nilly, it's not the law!'

'And is the law so important to you?'

'The law is bloody well all we've got!'

'But you are thinking how to get me out.' It wasn't a question, it wasn't even smug – just a flat statement of fact, waiting on a plan and an answer.

Lyle scowled. 'You tell me just one thing – one thing only and maybe I'll help you, all right?'

'All right.'

'Where is Berwick?'

'I don't know. Don't you?'

'Oh well, goodbye then.'

'If I needed to, though, I'm sure I could find him.'

'Really? How?'

'If I told you that, it would hardly give you reason to get me out, would it?'

Lyle groaned, ran his hands through his hair and turned a few times on the spot in uneasy tight circles. 'All right,' he muttered. 'Let me think, let me think . . . you evil Tseiqin, need to save all Tseiqin, can't let Machine detonate, you hate me, I hate you, probably back-stabbing along the way, but you *can't let it work*. You know something, I help you, you stop it . . . what have I missed? I let you go, you try and stop the Machine. Can you? Can you really stop it? In here you could survive if it really does work by electromagnetism, iron walls, Faraday cage, but could you? Finding Berwick, he can finish it . . . would you hurt Berwick?' He looked up sharply, turning the words into a question. 'Would you hurt Berwick?' he repeated, louder.

'That is one of those areas where you and I may have to compromise.'

'If I let you out and you're lying, you'll die from the Machine anyway.'

'So what harm is there?'

'Don't even ask me what harm there is,' said Lyle. 'You of course realize that I have no concrete plan on getting you out.'

'How did you get in?'

'Oh, got myself arrested, incarcerated, used a high-velocity device to attach a rope to a wall, had Tess scale it, drop in some lock picks and a lot of smoke bombs, had a distraction outside, fireworks, smoke, bangs, a lady who swears she's good at causing havoc and who may not lie, you know . . . the full works.'

'Is there still a lot of smoke?'

'There should be. Plenty of fog, too.'

'So the risks are somewhat less?'

'I imagine so. And it's possible . . . I have a few ideas.'

However, what these ideas were, no one had a chance to discover. In the darkness above the iron room with its iron walls and iron doors, the warden of Pentonville crawled from one patch of darkness towards another, holding a gun in his shaking hand. 'Keep away!' he shouted.

Nothing answered in the darkness. 'I know about you! I know about your fears, your magics, they told me everything! Keep away!'

A swirl in the fog – he fired, the flash temporarily blinding him, so sudden and bright and white in the night. When the darkness returned it was even thicker, pooling around him. 'You can't get to him,' he called out, louder. 'There are iron walls and iron doors and iron stairs and iron floors, your kind are old! Dead! You will die, that's what they said, you are going to die and . . .'

A faint sound, a footfall somewhere in the smoke, and the warder's voice disintegrated into a whimper. 'Keep away,' he muttered, turning on the spot, raising and lowering the gun like a see-saw as if uncertain whether his attacker would be dwarf or giant. 'Keep back.'

A movement right by his shoulder: something cool, but not as ice cold as the gun in his hand, brushed by his neck, making him jump. A voice said, 'Now, not too fast, sir, not too fast.' The blade against his throat was bronze; the edge wasn't hard or cold enough to be iron. A white-gloved hand patted him on the shoulder; the wind-chime voice seemed oblivious of the gun still held in his hand.

'But . . . you're a woman,' he whispered.

'If I weren't hardened already by the shocking failures of your gender, I would be indignant,' sighed the voice in his ear. 'As it is, I am, so I'm not.'

'You did all this?'

'Not at all. Flash bombs and smoke bombs and shots in the night and doors unlocked and pathways cleared – I could not do all this. As you said, the floors are iron, the stairs are iron, the walls are iron. You make my skin crawl, and it's not just the smell of your breath smothered in the smog.

'I simply like to dance, sir. You see, I know that my kind are faster, stronger and smarter than yours. I am alone, but I see in the dark: I see you all running like frightened animals, some overcome with the smoke, coughing and cowering in the dark. It is easy in this chaos of bangs and booms to separate you out one at a time, and leave you sleeping in the night. We live in an understanding with the world around us, comprehend the currents of this world, in a way you people can never begin to conceive. On the other hand, my people never invented the waltz, or the polka, or the mazurka or the stripping of the willow or even the morris dance, although perhaps we should be grateful for that. It is for the sake of the waltz, sir, that I let you live. Run away, little human, and tell your masters that the Tseiqin have come for one of their own.'

He ran, and didn't think twice about it, as he stumbled on into the dark.

The bells were striking half past three when the lights stopped exploding in the courtyard of Pentonville Prison, bright white *fizz-bangs* that seemed to conduct through the fog like electricity through water. At least, that's what Tess thought they struck. She recognized the half past strike, and the bells, flat and distant, but it was hard to remember what hour it was. Despite herself, she was beginning to yawn. The darkness had settled to a complacent, busy silence, full of distant trains, the stamping of the bored horses and, from inside the prison, the occasional exclamations of a guard.

'Bigwig?' muttered Tess. Her head was drooping lightly on his shoulder.

'Yes, Miss Teresa?' Thomas's cheeks were glowing scarlet at the proximity of a lady's – at least, in theory – head anywhere within a half-foot of his own suit.

'Got summat to eat, bigwig?'

'What with the High Velocity, Low Torsion Wind . . .'

'The big thing with the gears an' all.'

'. . . Device, and the ladder and the smoke bombs and the spare packets of potassium chloride you made me pack and . . .'

'You never know when you might need pota . . . potass . . . that stuff! It's a vital component of all things what go bang!'

'. . . I fear I neglected to bring breakfast.'

Tess looked up sharply. 'Were that . . . *sarcasm*, bigwig?'

In the light of the single lantern on the carriage, Thomas's face was nothing more than an innocent grey shape. 'Miss?'

'You ain't never learnt sarcasm, bigwig. It ain't what you're all about.'

'What exactly am I all about, Miss Teresa?'

'You,' she poked an accusing finger into his chest, 'are all about doin' what is needed to be done when asked, right? We ain't needin' cheek from you.' She looked worriedly into the smoke and fog. 'After all, what'd be left for me to do then?'

Before Thomas could think of an appropriate reply, there was a sound from near the open prison gates. It went like this:

'Oh my god oh my god it's alive he's alive help me immediately aaaahhhh!', and was accompanied by running feet.

Tess said, 'That sounds like Mister Lyle.'

'Are you sure?'

''Course. He ain't never good at spinnin' the yarn, like.'

Thomas called out, 'Mister Lyle?'

In the darkness, the running stopped. A more normal voice said, 'Thomas?'

'We're here, Mister Lyle!'

'I can't see a bloody thing.'

'Where are you?'

'Somewhere in the courtyard, I think. Shouldn't there be guards everywhere?'

'Miss Lin had a word with them.'

'What, all of them?'

'I think so.'

'How?'

'She can see in the dark, can't she?'

And right next to Lyle's ear, a voice whispered, 'I'm here, Mister Lyle.'

Lyle jumped. 'Bloody hell, don't do that!'

A warm female hand settled on his shoulder. 'It's all right. The guards are . . . indisposed.'

'How indisposed, exactly?'

'I promise you, only one or two had anything even slightly broken, and those are unimportant limbs only.'

'My God, did you attack an entire prison's worth of guards?'

'No, no, not at all! I lured half of them into one of their own cell wings and locked the door on them. Then there were the ones who ran away to seek help and I think are now somewhat lost in the fog, and the rest were . . .' In Lin's voice, the sound of a shrug. 'Night-shift duty only, I imagine. Doesn't pay well enough for them to stay.'

'But . . . I had a brilliant plan! An excellent, superb, utterly infallible escape plan, a work of true genius! I was going to save the day dramatically for the greater good!'

'And I had flash bombs,' replied Lin. 'And may I say, an exceptionally invigorating time. Did you find what you were looking for?'

'*Well*, it depends on how you look at it,' muttered Lyle. 'Did you *really* . . .'

'Mister Lyle,' said Lin, 'I am a Tseiqin. I have spent my life learning how to fight, how to maim, how to injure, how to induce every conceivable kind of distress with the minimal possible effect, in fact, on . . .'

'I'm beginning to regret that I asked.'

'And today,' – Lyle sensed her grin in the dark – 'I am learning about the miraculous properties of magnesium and air.'

'Oxygen.'

'I beg your pardon?'

'Not just air – oxygen.'

She replied, 'I can see why you are a popular man around town, Mister Lyle. *Did you find out what we needed to know?*'

'Not in so many words.'

And from the prison gates, a voice said, 'Interesting. I had thought we needed a plan of escape. It would appear the path is already clear.' Moncorvo stepped forward, into the night, and drew a long, deep breath of dirty fog and swirling smoke, as though it was the taste of the sea.

Lyle sighed. 'It's going to be a terrible day,' he announced. 'Miss Lin?'

'I'm here.' Her gentle hand, on Lyle's shoulder. He smiled

grimly and said, 'Thank you.' In a second he had grabbed the hand, and turned on the spot, dragging Lin's head back and down. He drew a magnet from his pocket and rammed it tight against the small of her back. Her face distorted in pain.

'Tell me,' he hissed in her ear, 'tell me why *that* man is free,' indicating Moncorvo. 'Tell me why you sent me in there to get him out, tell me why you lied, tell me why you didn't tell me, tell me what you really *want*!'

Lin, dancing Lin, struggled; but the magnet burnt even through the clothes on her back. Its influence took the grace, the strength out of her body, and seemed to make her thin and limp. 'He's the only one with answers!' she gasped. 'Believe me, we like him no more than you do!'

'Flattery,' sighed Moncorvo.

'You let me go in there for *him*,' spat Lyle. 'You *used* me to free him, you used me and I trusted you.'

'I suppose I should interrupt this,' said Moncorvo, flashing a smile. 'This is hardly the time for recrimination, Lyle. I suspect even this lady's excellent handiwork will not keep us safe for long. Many people will not take my escaping lightly. Should we not find a means of transport, perhaps?'

Lyle hesitated. 'You . . . and he . . .' he began, glowering at Lin.

'I'm not on his side!' she snapped. Lyle's grip relaxed and she pulled away from him, eyes glowing with anger. '*Yes!* We did use you to get him out, because we couldn't go down to that iron prison with iron walls and hope to win. But Moncorvo is as much our enemy as he is yours. I'm sorry we weren't honest with you, but this — all of it! — is a necessary evil.'

'Don't tell that to Mister Lyle,' murmured Moncorvo. 'He sees everything in black and white.'

Lyle stood, looking as if someone had merely assembled his limbs in a Lyle-shaped bundle and forgotten to animate them. He suddenly looked very small and tired. 'Miss,' he murmured, 'I do not, and never will, trust you. *Never*. I hope we understand each other.'

'Absolutely, Mister Lyle,' she replied calmly.

'Right. *You* watch *him*,' a finger jabbed from Lin to Moncorvo, 'and somewhere a long way from here, we'll sort out this whole bloody mess.'

CHAPTER 11

Institute

'Thomas! Tess!'

Lyle had the tone that Tess associated with bathtime – an unstoppable command that made all cringe before it. He strode out of the darkness towards the waiting carriage, and stared straight at Thomas.

'Thomas, I need you to take Tess home immediately.'

'Is something wrong, Mister Lyle?'

'Yes, very; now please do as I ask.'

'What's happened? Did you find the Tseiqin under the prison?'

'Yes, and things are very wrong.'

'You gettin' us . . .' Tess's words disintegrated into a yawn, then re-emerged at the other end '. . . out of the way so as we're not causin' trouble?'

'I think it's a lot past your bedtime, Teresa, and I'm afraid I don't have time to argue this .'

'What's the matter? There ain't . . .' Tess saw something move in the shadows, and heard that *voice*, that voice she was never going to forget, even though she couldn't see the face, that voice like black leather if it could speak, that voice like the flow of oil across a still surface in the moonlight, that voice that said . . .

'I see you keep your pets, Mister Lyle.'

Tess looked at Thomas, and saw how pale he'd gone. Lyle grabbed Thomas by the shoulders and gently shook him. 'Thomas, now is not the time.'

'My God,' whispered Thomas, 'she *did* bewitch you, didn't she? It's all gone wrong!'

'This is *me*, I swear,' hissed Lyle. 'This is me from top to toe, I know what . . . well, no, I'm working out what I'm doing as I'm going along. Please, Thomas, I can't deal with all this now. Get Tess back to your father's house, *please*. I'll send someone as soon as possible.'

Thomas didn't seem to see, his eyes burning into the darkness. '*Him*,' he hissed. 'He did it, he's . . .'

Moncorvo drifted into the light of the carriage, directed a humourless smile at Thomas and said, 'Master Elwick, I am pleasantly surprised to see you endure.'

Thomas gabbled, 'Mister Lyle, you've got to make this stop! He's evil, he's the enemy, he's everything that's wrong with *them*. Please, you've got to go back, we can't let him out! Not *him*!'

'I know, lad,' muttered Lyle. 'I'm sorry.'

'Sorry? He will burn everything! Please, you've got to . . . you can't . . . he said that . . .'

'This is what has to be done.' Lyle's voice had that firm edge to it again. 'Thomas, please understand, this is what is *necessary*.'

'Must we wait here much longer?' asked Moncorvo. 'I do believe the police will come *eventually*.'

Thomas sagged, and looked wearily at Tess. 'Are you ready to go home, Miss Teresa?'

'Very!' squeaked Tess, her wide eyes not having moved from Moncorvo's smiling face. 'Very, very now, please!'

'Then let's go,' he murmured, turning away. 'There's nothing more to be done here.'

Lyle watched them drive off into the night.

Dawn across London in early spring. The still, dead time when the morning shift of factory hands is still sparse enough to comprise just the odd face here and there where later there will be bustle, and when that face, being anomalous, is more sinister for its passage down the empty street. The sun, when it rises, hardly warms, hardly illuminates, merely dispels the dimness to a paler form, without ever bothering to cast colour into it. It sends thin shadows from chimney stacks across dull slate roofs, catches thick smoke and lets it blend into the heavy clouds. It tickles the edge of the silvery fog, weighed down by smoke above and now nudged by dew below, trying to rise in the morning light. At this hour, the sounds that are usually never heard, become bigger – the murmur of pigeons perching in the gutters, the slamming of a distant door, the whistle of a train, the bell of a ship coming up the estuary and the *sloshsloshslosh* of its paddles, the dripping of the broken water pump down on the square, the coughing of the sleepy cab horse in its mews, the rattling of beer barrels being rolled down the street.

In the suburb of Hammersmith, the butler in his nightrobe opens the door to young Master Thomas, and gapes with astonishment. 'Sir! What are you doing up at this –'

'Not now,' says Thomas. 'There's a young lady asleep in the carriage. Please see that she is put to bed. Preferably without disturbing her.'

Horatio Lyle stared across the Thames as the sun began to rise, and tried not to yawn.

'All right,' he said grimly. 'Tell me how much worse today can get.'

'You could sleep, Mister Lyle,' suggested Lin.

'I'm not letting *him* out of my sight.' Lyle glaring at Moncorvo. 'No thank you very kindly.'

'We'll not let him do any harm,' insisted Lin.

'I'm not being used and discarded like a snotty handkerchief! I'd like answers or . . .'

'Or what, Mister Lyle?' demanded Moncorvo. A smile twisted at the corner of his mouth. 'How exactly will you threaten us now?'

Lyle leant back against the cold stone of the Embankment wall. 'Well . . .' he said carefully, 'it seems that what you lot are dealing with is a machine designed to kill by magnetism. So . . . whatever this device is, however it works, it's going to be using either a lot of magnetic material, or a lot of electricity, or a lot

186

of both, neither of which you people are exactly equipped to deal with.

'*Sooo* . . . it further seems to me – and I want you to know that I'm very tired and this is all good stuff considering how little sleep I've had – it further appears that no amount of knowledge about the Machine is going to help you, unless you have some-one else willing to help you. Someone with a good understanding of electricity and magnetism and other unusual forces. And no allergy to iron and all its doings. What do you think?'

Lin beamed. 'Mister Lyle,' she declared, 'have I mentioned that I've always respected your work?'

Lyle gave an empty smile. 'Miss Lin,' he said, 'I never knew you cared. Go on, my lord, say something useful, that will make this farce worth my while.'

'Oh, Mister Lyle,' sighed Moncorvo, 'how have you made so much of such a little, scuttling life?'

'Come on,' snapped Lyle, 'out with it.'

Moncorvo glowered at Lyle, then glanced more nervously at Lin. 'I know you know Augustus Havelock. He is a gentleman of . . . influence. The essence of "having friends in high places" – friends, patrons, employers, supporters, call them what you will. There are those who believe that my kind are a dying species, that we are somehow . . . *less* than these monkeys who currently lord it over the earth.'

'See how I don't hit you?' murmured Lyle. 'I'm becoming wiser each day I live.'

'It came to my attention,' stated Moncorvo with a show of patience, 'that certain parties within Her Majesty's Government

who were . . . hostile . . . to my people, were attempting to construct a device capable of causing my kind great harm. I
investigated further, and found that the mandate for this construction had been given to Augustus Havelock.'

'Given? By who?'

'"Whom",' corrected Lin with a smile.

'What?'

'"Whom." Good grammar is important' – she intoned the
words like a chant – 'as it allows easy blending with the most
hostile of environments for successful completion of your aims.'

'My God,' muttered Lyle, 'that's told me. What was the question?'

'By whom?'

'Oh yes, right. Who exactly gave this "mandate" to
Havelock?'

'Among others, Lord Lincoln.'

'Lord Lincoln is involved in this? A royal aide?'

'Of course. He is one of many who believe that my kind
are . . .' Moncorvo twiddled his fingers in the air, as if trying to
pluck the correct sentiment out of nothing, '. . . abominations,
I suppose, will serve. Surely you must have deduced this in your
many dealings with his lordship?'

'Certainly Lord Lincoln would appear to be chiselled from an
iceberg. I could see how he might be less than sympathetic. So
there's government involvement?'

'Of course. Indeed, it was largely through the support of
some of Her Majesty's Government that, as I learnt, Havelock
was enabled to construct some sort of machine underneath the
city.'

'Underneath? Where?'

'I don't know.'

'Wonderful. Let's limit the story, then, and get to what you *do* know.'

'My attention was somewhat occupied during this period, you understand . . .'

'Yes, yes, I know, with a scheme for domination and demi-godhood, I was there,' muttered Lyle, waving his hand dismissively. 'What exactly do you know?'

'Havelock employed Berwick to design the Machine. That was almost five months ago, shortly around the time of my . . . arrest. I became aware of Berwick's involvement: I had men dispatched to follow him, and I knew that Havelock had turned to him because there was something missing, a component in the Machine that they couldn't get right but that he hoped Berwick would be able to supply. I also knew that Berwick was eagerly working to achieve this aim. I had his friends, his movements, everything about his life monitored, in the hope that it would lead me to the location of the Machine itself – but unfortunately, it did not. He was not, it seemed, working on the Machine site directly, but at a laboratory underneath Baker Street Station which was guarded night and day by . . .'

'Yes, yes. Where's Berwick now?'

'You don't know?'

'No,' said Lin quietly. 'He vanished a few days ago.'

'But Havelock's looking for him,' added Lyle. 'And Old Man White has said the Machine is almost ready to do . . . whatever it does.'

'I see.'

'A bad answer, my lord,' said Lyle. 'It means you're thinking something you don't want me to know, because you are buying time to consider and contrive something evil; sorry to be morally crude about it. But the only reason you're out of prison is to help us find Berwick before Havelock does, so please stop now.'

'Berwick is the key to the Machine; yes,' murmured Moncorvo, although not apparently to anyone else. 'The Machine works by somehow . . . exploding magnetism. Does that sound plausible to you, Lyle?'

'Exploding magnetism? No, not really. Most of the time magnetism is just a field, an area of influence . . . you can strengthen it, although, like gravity, it is theoretically infinite if infinitesimal over a distance, but "exploding"? Exploding implies *poof!* There and gone in an instant. I suppose a single burst of current could produce that effect, but only through massive, *massive*, unthinkable amounts of energy. As for changing the field, making it a weapon – that would require something spectacular, a . . . I don't know . . . a small volcano or artillery barrage or thunderstorm or a bomb . . .' He trailed off.

'Lyle?' Moncorvo's eyes were bright.

'What exactly,' Lyle's voice was distant, his gaze fixed on the vague eastern horizon, 'was Berwick's contribution to this project?'

'I don't know. But I understood it to be significant.'

'"Significant",' repeated Lyle, who liked to believe in scientific precision. 'What exactly does "significant" mean when it's not hiding in the dictionary between "signature" and "silence"? I mean, *huge* amounts of energy, you'd have to . . . build up a charge, we're talking . . . miles and miles of . . . but then if it's underground, have to be in a Faraday cage to keep it in and then . . .'

'What are you thinking, Lyle?' asked Moncorvo quietly.

'You said you could find Berwick. How?'

Moncorvo hesitated, but only for a second. 'When we were watching him, we built up a coherent view of all his comings and goings, who he deals with, who he doesn't – and in the process we learnt an intriguing thing.'

'Mmm?' Lyle's voice was hardly there; his eyes still roamed some other world.

'Have you heard of a man called Stephen Thackrah?'

'No.'

'He co-authored a number of Berwick's papers, particularly those relating to explosives.'

'Don't be absurd. Berwick never worked with anyone.'

'He did with Thackrah. That gentleman's expertise is, interestingly, in explosives.'

'I've never seen his name anywhere.'

'That's because Mr Thackrah is the son of a dead Yorkshire convict, and a Jew.'

Lyle sucked in a long, unhappy breath. '*Oh*. I see.'

Lin looked bemused. 'I don't.'

'You're new in this place, aren't you?' said Moncorvo, not kindly.

'It can be . . .' Lyle looked awkward, '*difficult* being Jewish in some areas. Not least if your father wasn't renowned for good behaviour.'

'Why?'

'Well . . . because . . .' Lyle hesitated, looked surprised. 'You know, I'm not entirely sure. I think it has something to do with theology.' He spoke the words in the awed tone of someone aware that here were mysteries beyond his comprehension, and best left that way. 'But I still don't *entirely* see how this helps us.'

'Thackrah works at the Royal Institute, ostensibly as an assistant librarian, although in practical terms he is more likely to be found experimenting, on Berwick's authority. He is a trusted confidant, a friend and ally of Berwick, and, moreover, he has links in parts of the city where a man might wish to take shelter, should he not want to be found.'

'You think Berwick would go to him for help?'

'I do.'

'And you think Havelock . . . what . . . wouldn't notice something like that?'

'I do.'

'*Why*, exactly?'

'Because, Mister Lyle,' replied Moncorvo, 'you know as well as I do that Augustus Havelock does not have the imagination for details.'

Lyle opened his mouth to say 'Yes, but that doesn't matter in the least. Just because he doesn't notice anything that isn't immediately relevant to him, it doesn't mean he's stupid, just . . .' and stopped himself. He thought about it. '. . . just ignorant.' He shrugged. 'All right. Why not? It's something, it's more than anything else, why not! Let's find this Thackrah!'

'I knew we could rely on you, Mister Lyle,' Moncorvo said, in a voice that sent a shudder down Lyle's spine.

Tess, Thomas and Tate sat in Lord Elwick's dining room, around lunchtime, eating breakfast.

'Bigwig?' said Teresa.

'Yes, Miss Teresa?'

'You think Mister Lyle is bewitched?'

'I don't know, miss. He seemed to be behaving normally – for Mister Lyle – last night. But then, why did he break *him*,' the hate was obvious in Thomas's voice, 'out? I just don't know.'

'Bigwig?'

'Yes, Miss Teresa?'

'What are you going to do if he is bewitched?'

'Me?'

'You're oldest, you gotta do something,' she said smugly. ''Cos of how I'm the lady an' all.'

'I'm honestly not sure what I could do if . . .'

'Only it seems as how,' went on Tess coyly, 'if Mister Lyle is bewitched or confused or dead or missin' his brain or anythin' like that, then I ain't goin' to have nowhere to go, so I might as well stick 'round here, if that's all right with you, bigwig.' Thomas turned white. Tess grinned an indescribably evil grin. 'So . . . whatcha goin' to do about it, bigwig?'

Before Thomas had a chance to respond, the answer came through the door for him, and the answer was angry. Or as angry as anyone chiselled from an iceberg could be.

The Royal Institute was situated in a part of London that was, in every sense, 'royal'. Kensington Palace sat just across Hyde Park from Buckingham Palace, which in turn looked down the Mall, used for royal processions, to St James's Palace, by the park of the same name, where the common people queued to catch a glimpse of the reclusive, widowed queen. Nearby on Piccadilly the great of several nations visited the Royal Academy, and the area's elegant shops sold goods that only the most indulged of princes could afford, and every watchmaker was by royal appointment.

Among all this, at the boundary zone where the arched arcades and flush carriages began to be displaced by the tighter passages of southern Soho, and the bobbies dared not venture in groups of less than four, was the pillared front of the Royal Institute. Horatio Lyle always felt out of place in the Institute. Although technically he was a member, his ideas were sometimes too radical for many wealthy members who saw science as a hobby rather than a means of advancing mankind, and whose enthusiasm, at least to Lyle, didn't always make up for an absence of experimental method. A glance at the lecture notices for the week produced in Lyle a mixture of awe and contempt; his eyes lit up to see '*Darwin – the debate rages!*' while his face fell in response to '*Newton and Hooke – the particle model is the* only *model!*' and '*Miasma and the ether – a radical reassessment of the airborne inter-spatial medium*'.

'Amateurs,' he muttered, marching up the steps.

'You have better theories, I suppose?' Moncorvo demanded.

'I just don't like the idea of everything being explainable by a big intangible wobbly "ether" that I can not examine! It's as bad as saying that there's . . .' Lyle cut himself off, but it was too late.

'Magic?' suggested Moncorvo, raising one eyebrow, a trick Lyle had never quite managed, even in front of the mirror.

'Pretty much.'

Lin said, 'You know, things could be worse!' She ignored the glares that descended on her like fiery meteors. 'Think what an opportunity this presents us for reconciliation and understanding! A chance for two bitter, angry, life-long, pig-headed enemies to work together for a common cause!' She beamed. 'Isn't that nice?'

'*Nice?*' hissed Lyle.

'Well,' she went on, 'it's far better that you work together out of your common desire for reconciliation and understanding than that I bang your heads together until you cry.'

They considered this. 'You are a traitor to your kind and will die in your own pitiful loneliness,' replied Moncorvo.

'You're a bit odd, miss,' admitted Lyle.

'See! The two of you practically agreed there!'

And, in fairness, the scowls that greeted her were almost identical.

Lyle pushed back the doors to the Royal Institute, stepped into the hall, and said, 'If we're going to find Thackr—'

A voice to one side of him boomed, 'Young man, could you please help me with this?'

Lyle turned, with the words, 'Sorry, sir, in a bit of a rush –' on his lips – and deflated mid-mumble.

The man who'd spoken was shortish, sported huge grey side-whiskers, and had a wrinkled old face that looked out from under an enormous pair of eyebrows.

Lyle stood and gaped while Lin peered over his shoulder. Moncorvo drummed his fingers.

The old man, sensing something amiss, said, 'If you would be so kind, sir; my man appears to have abandoned me . . .' and indicated a large box at his feet, wrapped in brown paper.

A nod, and a tiny squeak that might have been a word was evidently the only answer Lyle could give. He edged forward and struggled to lift the unwieldy box. The man smiled thinly and said, 'Please be careful, there's some very fragile equipment in there . . .'

'Lyle,' snapped Moncorvo, 'we hardly have the time.'

Lyle shot Moncorvo a glare. Lin peered at the box and said, quite reasonably, 'What exactly is it?'

'Ah!' exclaimed the old man with a widening smile. 'A young lady with an interest in science! Are you aware of the wave-particle debate?'

To Lyle's surprise, Lin said, 'Yes.'

'Excellent, excellent. And I don't suppose by chance you are familiar with the current work in the field of electromagnetism on the debate as to whether the flow of electricity, the current down a wire, is in the form of particle movement or waves?'

'Of course.'

'Well!' The old man looked as though he could have danced on the spot. 'This device – careful, dear boy, careful –' gesturing urgently at Lyle – 'is part of an attempt to determine the very nature of electricity, whether it is merely a charge on mass, or a free-flowing wave, part of a field, to attempt to determine, if you will, the very stuff of . . . of stuff. To understand the properties of mass through an analysis of current, voltage, drift, charge, and so forth, and thus break more ground in the great particle-wave debate that for so long we have been unable to reconcile and . . . do be careful! It's very, very fragile! If you'd put it here . . . very gently . . . thank you, dear boy, you are a saviour.'

'Can we get on?' demanded Moncorvo.

Lyle ignored him, and went on staring. The old man shuffled nervously in the face of Lyle's gape. 'Can I help you with something, young man?'

'You're . . .' whispered Lyle. 'I mean, you're . . . you're . . .' The old man waited patiently for Lyle to find the words.

'You're . . . the most . . . the work is just . . . everything about . . . there wouldn't *be* modern science without . . .' squeaked Lyle, flapping his hands uselessly in front of him. 'I mean, you're . . . you're . . . you're *him*!'

'Yes . . . I suppose I am. And who are you?'

'Lyle, we don't have the time!'

'I'm . . . I'm your most . . . I mean, I admire . . . the work you do is just . . . I mean . . . I really think that you're the most . . . everything is just . . .' Lyle gave up. 'You're just . . . very good, sir.'

The old man beamed. 'Why, thank you. It's always nice to hear that sort of compliment, particularly at my age.'

'Well, it's . . .' He shrugged uselessly. 'You must hear it all the time, sir, but I just think it ought to be said.'

Lin put a polite hand on Lyle's shoulder and steered him away, with a murmured, 'I thought that was very nice of you.' Glancing back, she nodded at the old man and said, 'A pleasure meeting you, Mr Faraday.'

'You too, miss.'

Lin led Lyle gently away.

Lord Lincoln. There was no really satisfactory way to describe Lord Lincoln, Thomas concluded, since the man spent so much of his time perfecting the art of nothingness. His face revealed nothing, his clothes said nothing about his character, his eyes reflected no emotion, his bag bore no badge, his shoes had no stains on them, his face was scrubbed to a perfect glowing cleanliness, his voice didn't tremor more than a semitone around a single, flat, nothing note.

Thomas knew that, theoretically, the absence of distinguishing features should tell a good detective as much about a subject as two scars and a hare lip. But today, he wasn't feeling at his objective best. Lord Lincoln didn't so much sit in the chair at the end of Lord Elwick's dining table, as fold himself into it like a paper doll, each limb crinkling up to form a new shape defined entirely by right angles, back as straight as a brick wall, hands folded neatly on the end of the table.

Lord Lincoln smiled. It was the smile the alligators use when watching their prey nibbling at the water's edge.

'I am glad to have found you both in good health,' he intoned. Tess sidled closer to Thomas; Tate cowered in a corner. 'Mister Lyle does not appear to be at home. I had hoped to find him here.'

'We ain't seen him!' exclaimed Tess.

'Indeed? When did you last see him, then?'

Thomas and Tess exchanged a look. She said quickly, 'A few days ago. He were busy.'

'Busy? Doing what?'

'Didn't rightly say, did he?'

'Perhaps we can help you, my lord,' offered Thomas.

'Perhaps you can,' murmured Lord Lincoln, his eyes moving from one face to another. 'Last night there was an . . . *incident* . . .' the word forced itself between his teeth, '. . . at a local prison. Significant damage was caused, by systematic use of specialist equipment – fireworks, and smoke bombs that blinded the guards, as well as acts of assault by at least a dozen heavily armed individuals.'

Thomas and Tess swapped a look, and Lord Lincoln's smile narrowed. 'I don't imagine you have any knowledge of such an event.'

Thomas shook his head. Tess said, 'I ain't knowin' nothin', guvnor my lord.'

'I really don't see how we could help,' added Thomas. 'Terribly sorry, sir.'

'Naturally, the idea that either of you, or Mister Lyle, could be involved in such an activity is . . . implausible. And yet – I hear rumours that Mister Lyle has not been himself these last few days. Acting irrationally, perhaps against the better interest of the public, hm?' Only Lord Lincoln could make an inexpressive 'hm' sound so menacing, a tiny invitation to step into damnation, a polite request that you confess now before the knives come out, an inarticulate warning of nasty things to come.

Tess mumbled, 'Ain't knowin' nothin', sorry.'

Lord Lincoln sighed and sat back in his chair. For a moment he drummed his fingers, then declared in a harsher voice than before, 'I know of few individuals who could produce the equipment used last night – certainly *They* never would.'

'They?' echoed Thomas.

'I think we need no explanation as to who *They* are,' snapped Lincoln, a little too quickly. 'And Horatio Lyle is . . .' He hesitated. As if trying to pluck a thought from nowhere, he gestured, a black iron ring the only ornament on his hand. 'Let me rephrase. Horatio Lyle is a law-abiding citizen. The idea that he would participate in an attempt to free this . . . gentleman . . . from a prison is laughable. And yet . . . did he ever mention a man by the name of Berwick?'

The question came so suddenly that Tess almost answered. She bit her tongue to keep silent.

'Berwick?' mumbled Thomas, the tips of his ears beginning to burn.

Tess, more composed, leapt in. 'Yes, he mentioned Berwick. Science type bloke, right, bigwig what his pa knew. I heard him mention Berwick.'

'Recently?'

'Nah, few months back,' said Tess easily. Now she was getting into the swing of it; she was more relaxed, leaning out past Thomas and almost, but not quite, daring to meet Lord Lincoln's eyes. Tess had learnt at an early age the secret of lying – to know just enough to be convincing, have just enough truth in her words to be persuasive and believable, mixed in so thoroughly with the lies, that only the best-informed of detectives could begin to disentangle the two. 'Was he the bloke what was in the prison?' Under different circumstances, she could have been wearing a halo, her face was so angelic.

'Where is Mister Lyle?' asked Lord Lincoln with an impatient look.

'Dunno.'

'I'm sorry, my lord, but we are currently unaware of his whereabouts; although if we could help we would be only too happy –'

'Let me be infinitely clear.' Lord Lincoln's words bit through. 'Your Mister Lyle may be involved in something very rash. He may be entangled in events better avoided; in matters that are far over his head.'

'What's changed?' asked Tess with a laugh.

'The nature of his enemy,' replied Lord Lincoln. 'I cannot but consider how much Lyle may have informed you children of the situation's true nature. I know you were with Lyle at Baker Street Station the day before yesterday, young woman – and I also know that even if he abandons the children who are his care, Mister Lyle rarely travels anywhere without his dog.'

Three pairs of eyes wandered to Tate, who was unconcernedly scratching his ear. Aware that attention was on him, he looked up, saw Lord Lincoln's glare fixed on him and growled, revealing surprisingly pointed teeth and a lolling pink tongue.

The children sat in obstinate silence. Lord Lincoln spread his hands upon the table, as if measuring out its width. 'You both know what the Tseiqin are, and that they would have killed you, and Lyle, before now. Since I think you both are involved in what Lyle is doing, I will say no more, but this. The Tseiqin are *all*, all of them without exception, aiming at the destruction of this city, of its people, and of your friends. Are you sure that in protecting Mister Lyle you are doing the right thing?'

When they didn't answer, he added, 'Should you wish to confide in me any thoughts about where he might be or what he plans to do next, oblige me by doing so.' Lord Lincoln rose, and

Thomas instinctively got to his feet as well, but was waved away. 'I will see myself out. It is in Lyle's best interest that we speak soon. And, perhaps, in yours too. Consider what I've said. I'm sure you will.'

CHAPTER 12

Benwick

The place was full of sugar. It crunched underfoot, it was sprayed across the wall, it had been caramelized into the ceiling, it was a sharp, teeth-tingling spice on the air. Swirls of brown sugar, and crunchy bags of white, had spilt out across the floor together to create the effect of marble-patterned snowdrifts, solidified here or there into amber and black burnmarks. Little growths of stalagmite-like sugar hung from crusted tables and workbenches. In an area of dim light at the far end of the room, a slouched shape in grey and faded green scurried around a lantern, muttering.

Lyle, Lin and Moncorvo approached cautiously. Lin cleared her throat, and the figure jumped, its arms and legs flying outwards so that it seemed to grow in every direction as the slouch was displaced by a volume of flapping limbs. 'What – who?' it demanded.

'The same to you too,' replied Lyle. 'Why all the sugar?'

The man looked ill at ease. 'Uh, just something that someone was working on.'

'Thackrah,' said Moncorvo briskly, 'where's Berwick?'

The man, Thackrah, cringed and tried to speak.

'Ignore him,' Lyle quickly said, indicating Moncorvo. 'Are you Stephen Thackrah?'

'Maybe?' hazarded the man.

'In God's name!' Moncorvo strode forward and grabbed the man by the arm. Looking him intently in the eye, he muttered, 'Tell me where Berwick is.' His voice, to Lyle's ear, was flat and unpersuasive, not at all the melody he associated with Tseiqin speech.

Thackrah wrenched himself free of Moncorvo and backed away. 'Oi! Lay off!' he retorted with a distinctly East End abruptness. 'Who the hell are you, anyway?'

'Forgive him,' said Lyle, stepping forward and pushing Moncorvo aside. Whether from surprise or anger, Moncorvo's face was white, and in the dim lamplight Lyle saw for the first time how heavy and deep the shadows ran under the Tseiqin's eyes, and how far his cheeks had sunk over the bone. 'He's just a tactless dolt. My name is Horatio Lyle.'

'Lyle? Like Harry Lyle?'

'His son.'

The other man's face lightened, if only a little. 'I *am* Thackrah,' he confirmed, holding out a cautious hand. 'I've heard good things about you, Mister Lyle.'

'Thank you.' Lyle shook his hand, noticing the length of the fingers, and how prominent the veins were. 'I'm so sorry about my . . . companion's rudeness. We mean no harm in saying we are looking for Berwick.'

'Why ask me?'

'Because you know Berwick,' said Lin. 'You help him.' Lyle noted Moncorvo's distant look. His face had become the white mask of a tragic clown.

'Me? No no no no no, I'm just an assistant librarian, I wouldn't . . .' began Thackrah.

'Why all the sugar?'

'What?'

'The sugar.' Lyle's face was a picture of polite enquiry. 'Fuel, maybe? Attempting to build some sort of bomb, explosives, Mr Thackrah? I'm thinking that perhaps Berwick asked you to do a little nosing into explosives?'

Thackrah shifted unhappily from foot to foot. 'Er . . .'

'Maybe very high-velocity explosives, perhaps designed to do something very specific – an exact function. Did Berwick mention anything like that?'

'I'm just the librarian . . .' Thackrah tried again.

'And I bet you have a lot of time for sitting around reading?'

Thackrah looked away, defeated. 'He didn't say what to do if people came *asking*! He just wanted a place to think, that's all he said; to think and work on the regulator in peace and quiet.'

'What's the regulator?'

'It's the . . . thing for regulating . . . the thing.' Gesturing vaguely with four fingers, two thumbs and a lot of elbow, Thackrah tried vainly to explain exactly what thing regulated what, using, it seemed, nothing but flapping. Huffing with futility, he said, 'Look, I just help him out with research and things, that's all he asked!'

'Mr Thackrah, I've had a very long day,' said Lyle. 'Please, *please* tell me that he came to you a few days ago with this regulator thing and asked you to find him a place to stay and it's somewhere south of Scotland and you said yes and you're willing to divulge the address.'

'But . . . but he said that . . .'

'Mister Lyle.' Lin's voice came through sharply, suddenly alarmed. She stepped forward, staring fixedly at Thackrah. 'Has someone been here already?'

Thackrah hesitated, and Lyle's heart sank. 'Tallish gentleman, thin brown hair, smartly dressed, slightly aquiline nose?'

'I wouldn't say aquiline as such . . .'

'So much for Havelock not knowing,' muttered Lyle, but Moncorvo didn't seem to hear. 'Mr Thackrah, please, if you believe in anything at all right now, believe that Berwick is in danger.'

'How can you be sure?'

'By the pricking of my thumbs. Did you tell Havelock where to look?'

Thackrah shook his head. 'I told him I didn't know.'

'Did he believe you?'

Thackrah looked wretched and said nothing.

Lyle sighed. 'He'll work it out. He always does in the end.'

Thackrah mumbled, 'If you are Horatio Lyle, then Berwick said you were to be trusted – but Mister Lyle, I don't trust your friends.'

'Neither do I,' said Lyle, 'But please, I promise I will do everything within my power to keep Berwick safe. Where is he?'

Tess and Thomas sat in silence. Each studied the floor as if it was the most important thing in their life.

Thomas cleared his throat. The grandfather clock in the corridor went *Tock*. *Tock*. *Tock*. *Tock*. Somewhere downstairs, someone dropped a plate and went, 'Bugger!' in a loud, unashamed voice.

Tess glanced up, accidentally caught Thomas's eye, and looked away again. Outside in the stables, a horse stamped its iron foot against the cobbles, and made a deep *whruph* through its nostrils.

Tess said, 'I dunno much . . .'

Thomas said, 'If Mister Lyle is wrong about this . . .'

Tess said, 'That Lord Lincoln is an *evil* bigwig, bigwig. He's the sorta bigwig what gives your kind a bad name.'

Thomas said, 'But he knows things, and he's always been on our side . . .'

Tess said, 'Yeah, but what side were that if it ain't Mister Lyle's?'

Thomas stared at the floor. Tess went on, 'I ain't sayin' Mister Lyle is right all the time, 'cos he ain't. But I ain't trustin' the bigwig, and I ain't trustin' that Havelock fella to do what's good an' all.'

Thomas thought about it. Then he looked up, a slow smile spreading across his face. 'You're right, Miss Teresa. If we aren't on Mister Lyle's side, then we aren't on anyone's. What do you think we should do?'

Tess folded her arms. 'Nothin'.'

'Nothin'? I mean . . . nothing?'

'Nothin'. The bigwig will be expectin' us to go an' do somethin'. I just bet he's watchin' this house, hopin' as how we'll go an' get involved. So, we does nothin'.'

'That's not very helpful.'

'Yeah.' Tess grinned a wide, nasty grin, 'But have you got summat smarter?'

To Thomas's surprise, he found himself starting to think about it.

Berwick. What exactly does that word make Lyle feel? Berwick: a name that over the last few days has lost any association with face or personality. It has become an idea – the idea that Berwick has the answers, that Berwick can solve the mystery, that Berwick *knew*.

It is difficult to remember how this had started, how he's got involved. Event on event had piled up, so the distant recollection that he'd been concerned at first for a friend, has been smothered behind the concern for so many other things. It is hard to think past the immediate moment, to assemble thoughts and pick out priorities, list each order of concern.

So here is Horatio Lyle in a cab, squashed between his deadly enemy and a lady with green eyes who likes to dance. They're being driven towards Smithfield, past the meat market, through the remnants of the ancient city wall, past all those mean houses and flea-ridden little music halls where, he remembers with a start, the whole thing began just a couple of nights before.

So here is Horatio Lyle, climbing out of the cab in a smelly little street where brown-stained washing drips brown water onto the sludge-encrusted cobbles and the doors hang loose on rusty hinges and the reddish bricks are coated with black stains and green slime where water runs down from a broken pipe, and where the water from the pump at the end of the street comes out a greyish colour and smells of dead eels.And here is Lyle, knocking on one door and suddenly feeling so, so tired, not really sure if he can put up with this for much longer, just wanting to sleep and forget the whole thing, and saying to the lady who answers, 'My name's Lyle. I'm here to see Mr Andrew Berwick, please.'

The lady squints past him at Moncorvo and Lin and says, 'Who's the foreign lassie? I ain't havin' no women in the house!'

And Lin, to Lyle's surprise, says, 'I'll wait outside,' and Lyle knows there's something wrong there, something not entirely to do with the image of Lin he's built up these last few days, but by now he's so tired, so close, he doesn't really care.

So here is Lyle, climbing a flight of stairs that shriek like a Greek funeral under his footsteps; here is Lyle, knocking on a gloomy little door; here is Lyle, staring into the one eye and one revolver barrel that peer cautiously round the crack in the door; so here is Lyle, saying, 'You make trouble.'

And here is Andrew Berwick, a short, ginger little man who speaks with a thick Scots accent and has more freckles than he has hairs on his head, stepping back as he pulls the door open and blurting, 'Horatio? What in the name of all that is holy are you doing here?'

And suddenly, there was no more time left to think.

'Well may you ask,' muttered Lyle, ducking under the low doorway into a room smelling of damp and unwashed clothes and which also carried the sharp whiff of metal. 'I'm going to make a deductive leap and suggest the gun is a reaction to quite how deep into the effluent you've managed to waddle.'

'What do you know about it?'

'Enough to find you, which is what Havelock too will shortly do, if he's got any brains – and, which, regrettably, beneath that lack of imagination, he has.'

Moncorvo entered the room. Berwick leapt back, gun raised, and squealed, 'What the hell is *that* doing here?'

Moncorvo didn't answer. Eyebrows drawn together, he gazed at Berwick as if discovering a bomb ticking down to ignition. Lyle murmured, 'You would not believe.'

'Yes? After what I've seen these last days, lad, you wouldn't credit any of what *I* now believe.'

'You know, statements like that are always a challenge. All right: this is Lord Moncorvo, in my opinion one of the most evil creatures to walk the earth, a gentleman who attempted to trans-form his species of tree-loving, mind-altering people into rampaging semi-gods, whom I encountered during this process and had the good fortune of sending to prison as a consequence. This same gentleman was also at the time, unknown to me, spying for his kind on the works of highest government, obtained infor-mation regarding the construction of a device which attempts to use magnetism for the destruction of his aforementioned morally questionable race, although as it may turn out, not universally morally questionable, though that too is questionable in itself. To obtain this information I recently broke Moncorvo out having been informed that *you*,' Lyle found himself suddenly angry, tired and weary and aching and *angry*, 'that *you* were working for *bloody* Augustus *bloody* Havelock in constructing this device and had recently gone underground for reasons unknown and though it pains me to admit it, this same gentleman is at least partially responsible for my being here right now and my getting just a little bit loud! Do you still think that you can outdo me for bizarre and improbable circumstance?'

Berwick thought about it. 'Nah. I reckon that about caps it.'

Lyle realized he had been shouting. He sagged. 'I'm sorry.'

'Why did you run, Berwick?' Moncorvo's voice sounded like uncut stone.

The other man eyed him suspiciously and murmured, 'Horatio, there's some things you didn't mention about your life.'

'You too,' conceded Lyle. 'I'm not sure which of us is more surprised. But good God, why did you agree to build the damn thing?'

He shrugged. 'It just had the scientific appeal of a good – no, a *brilliant* idea.'

'That's a terrible answer.'

'It appealed to my vanity, nonetheless.'

'*Why?*'

'Horatio.' Berwick's eyes glowed. 'The thing is beautiful. The science of it, the maths, the structure, the building of it, the perfect working function, the perfect form, the perfect effect – the Machine is beautiful.'

'You and I need to talk,' said Lyle.

And here is the Machine. Every part glows, honed, carved, polished to lock precisely into place with the next part. It is a giant clockwork maze, a thousand intricate little pins hooking into a million intricate little cogs which spin a billion chains and each one works, a perfect function. Even broken down on paper into lines, into pure mathematical formulae, the thing is perfect, every number clicking into place like beads on a rosary, *snap* equal zero *snap* equal one; nothing out of place, not a minus sign ignored, not a fraction inverted, but the whole as pure in conception as it is in construction. Even the colliers, who have no grasp of the science that has gone into the pistons that reach up thirty yards overhead, even the porters and the men who pull the handles to release the billows of steam when the pressure climbs too high, even the nimble-fingered women whose job it is to crawl underneath the main hub of the furnaces when the chains get tangled, can sense that it is a work of scientific genius, a work of mechanical art – the Machine is beautiful.

More to the point, as the last whirring hub falls silent and a few sparks drip from overheated wires, the Machine is ready.

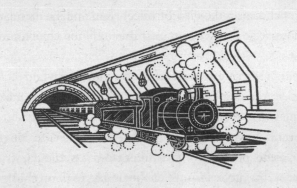

CHAPTER 13

Murder

'What is it?' asked Lyle, turning the thing over in his hands. It was approximately a foot in length, tube-like, but with a strange bulge at either end that looked as though it fitted into something else. Inside, the thing was made of little gold wires that gleamed in the candlelight from the table at the end of the narrow bed in the small room. Impatiently Berwick waved the papers on which the thing had rested. 'A regulator, a regulator!' he exclaimed, and waited for the light of comprehension in Lyle's face.

Lyle looked confused. As did Moncorvo. Berwick sighed. 'It's what they need to finish it: this is the final piece of the Machine.'

'Well, yes . . .' Lyle peered at the diagrams on the table, leafing through them. 'Yes, fair enough, but what *is* it?'

'It synchronizes the flow of the current and the detonation of the explosive so that they occur at precisely the same time, in the same space.'

'*Right*.' Lyle carefully put the long tube down and picked up the papers, turning them this way and that. 'And this makes the Machine work . . . how?'

'Horatio, I expected more of you,' said Berwick. He pushed the gun aside, pointing out the interest of a particular drawing. 'Observe – the precise nature of the timing requires construction of machinery so fine – not to mention an entirely separate circuit through which the control current can run, as a mere fraction of the energy being deployed, so that . . .'

'This is a bomb,' murmured Lyle, whose attention had already been seized by another paper. 'A very, very *big* bomb.'

'Take all the explosives of the Crimean War and compress them together and you wouldn't have as much power as I do inside that chamber.' Berwick's face had lit up. 'It took years to make this.'

'Years? But you've been working on this for . . . what? Five months?'

'Yes, but it's been years since they started trying to make the Machine work. I've simply provided the key, the know-how, the knowledge of how to control the explosion so that the current passing around the detonation chamber flows at the exact moment of the blast, forcing the magnetic field to collapse and . . .'

'You make the magnetic field collapse into the explosion and then push it back out again.'

'Exactly! But bigger, much bigger; the original field is just the field around a current – and what a current! But by exploding it, we can force a wave of magnetism that can travel many miles before dissipating into the background field of the earth's own magnetic field.'

Moncorvo, if he understood what was being said, showed no reaction. Lyle's face, however, showed incredulity. 'But that kind of power! No, and that kind of detonation, I mean . . . the thing must be *huge*! It must be . . . well . . . it must be . . . *no*, and there's no way you could get that kind of energy, it'd take . . . oh . . . it'd require . . . *so much*, I mean just . . .'

'Billions,' agreed Berwick in a low, excited whisper. 'Billions of coulombs, we store them in capacitors, thousands of them, it takes days to charge, each one bigger than a man, and the explosive is actually four and a half hundred explosives compressed together for the detonation. It's . . .' He shook his head and let out a long breath, 'beautiful.'

'It's a disaster in waiting.'

Berwick shrugged. 'Maybe that too.'

'And this regulator thing?'

Berwick picked it up again, and grinned. 'Ah, well, yes, that's where it was all going wrong for them, you see? That's why Havelock needed me.'

'Why? I'm guessing by the name "regulator" it's involved in somehow . . . regulating . . . the whole process?'

'Quite, quite! You see, we can generate a current big enough, we can store it while trying to extract the necessary charge, we can even construct and contain a big enough explosion, although I must admit even I was taken aback a little by the scale of the construction. But in order to collapse the magnetic field, we needed to ensure that the passage of charge through the coil around the detonation chamber is exactly synchronized with the explosion itself. That's what this does.'

'This thing?' Lyle waved doubtfully at the slim tube.

'Yes!' Berwick looked quite offended. 'I mean, obviously, it fits into the larger structure, has its place, but essentially . . . yes.'

'Havelock asked you to make it.'

'Yes.'

'Five months ago?'

'Yes.'

'And you did?'

'It was an adventure, Horatio, a challenge. How could I resist?'

Lyle hesitated, then shrugged – in one sense, he could understand Berwick's response. 'Willpower?' he hazarded. He saw Berwick's face and sighed. 'Nevermind. When suggesting this idea to you, did he ever mention the Machine's ultimate purpose?'

'No . . . not really. He said it was an experimental device for Her Majesty's Government. I did think about the possible consequences, if that's what you mean. Strangely enough, the idea that it was going to be used in a war waged against people with an intolerance for high magnetic fields and ferrous material generally, didn't leap to mind.'

'Surely not.'

'You may be used to this world, my boy,' said Berwick primly, 'but believe me when I say that even as a child I regarded fairy-tales as simply another way to get me to eat cabbage.'

'Scientists are a species unto themselves, aren't they?' asked

Moncorvo. Lyle didn't feel he expected an answer. He glared at Moncorvo, and turned back to Berwick. 'I'm assuming you found out about the whole Tseiqin business?'

'Oh yes. Very much so.'

'*How?*' Lyle's voice was pained with the effort of restraint.

'It all happened very fast. I was on Baker Street Station – there was a lab underneath Baker Street, you see. Havelock said it was better to keep the work secret . . .'

'I've been there, flooded that.'

'Oh, really?' Berwick didn't seem too bothered. 'Well, I was on Baker Street Station, when, without any warning, this group of men ran at me. Just like that. *Poof!* I didn't know what to do; I panicked, obviously. One second, perfectly fine; the next second, running people. I can't really explain what happened – but they attacked me, and some other men came at them. Afterwards Havelock said they'd been set to look after me, but I hadn't even realized until then that I merited a guard. There was shooting, shouting, all that – I hid under a bench.'

Moncorvo gave a derisory snort. Lyle frowned. 'What then?'

Berwick hesitated, then said, in a precise, quiet voice, 'I saw them die. All of them, all the men who'd run at me. I saw their faces on the floor next to mine, I saw them bleed. Their blood was white, Horatio – but I suppose you know about that. It didn't react to the air, it didn't turn red, it was just . . . white. And their skin was almost white, their eyes green, and . . . dead. I've never seen dead eyes before. They didn't change in the light, they didn't crinkle, they didn't widen; they just stared, right at me, but not at me, through me, like . . . anyway, mustn't give inanimate objects character, it's a foolish habit. Havelock said I was in danger, that I couldn't go home, that I couldn't leave work, now that completion was so near.

'I said, "In danger from whom?" He told me that there was an enemy, that my Machine . . . that the Machine was a weapon. He said it was a crusade, a holy war, a war of survival, and that I was the key. We were so close.'

'Go on,' murmured Lyle, when Berwick didn't seem about to move.

Berwick's eyes became focused on something beyond the room. 'I am not a soldier. Havelock said that they weren't human; and their blood . . . is not human, Horatio. But their eyes, when they were dead, were . . . sad . . . so sad. They . . . say those men were there to hurt me. I didn't have time to see. They were probably right. I saw them die, they stared at me. Am I going to kill the rest of them? Havelock doesn't even know how many there are in the city – he guesses hundreds . . .' Another *hmph* from Moncorvo, but Berwick didn't seem to notice. '. . . but what if there are more? All those unexplained bodies in the street, struck down by an invisible wave of magnetism, never knowing what the Machine was built for, what it was about. Dead bodies with dead eyes. Would you finish the Machine, Lyle?'

Lyle didn't answer. Berwick smiled faintly. 'You are part of this, I suppose.'

'No,' said Lyle coldly. 'I'm not.'

'Then why are you here?'

Lyle thought about it, then shrugged. 'People just keep on breaking the bloody law.'

'Is that it?'

'It's the best explanation I've got. Somebody shoots someone, somebody else decides to shoot back — how many bodies do you need before it stops being murder and becomes war? That's about the extent of my reasoning: sorry, I haven't really thought about it much.'

Berwick let out a sharp breath. 'Ah. So you *are* here to stop the Machine.'

'Pretty much.' Lyle was surprised to find himself sounding so certain.

Berwick waved the regulator in Moncorvo's direction. 'Do you . . . trust these people?'

'No!'

'But you still want it stopped.'

'It's not science, it's a crime,' said Lyle impatiently. 'You know that.'

Berwick was thoughtful. Eventually he smiled. 'Fair enough, lad. But you see, I have this problem.'

'Does the problem wear a top hat and have a voice like . . . oh, I don't know, the sound silk would make if you polished an iceberg with it?'

'You've met him.'

'Oh yes—' After a while Lyle added, 'You know, not to be crude, but that means you're right up to your neck in manure.'

'How, exactly?' Berwick looked confused.

'Well, I could inform you that I can protect you from the wrath of Augustus Havelock and hide you and he need never find you despite your having betrayed him and his Machine by absconding with the final part and necessary information to complete it, *but* . . .'

'It'd be a lie?'

'You probably *can* evade him,' said Lyle. 'But I suggest that to do so you move away a lot further than back home to Aberdeen. And you'd never again be able to see or speak to any of your friends or family.'

'Why's that?'

Lyle met Berwick's eyes and said, perfectly reasonably, 'Because he'd kill them all if he thought you could know of it.'

'I see.' Berwick suddenly looked a lot smaller.

'On the other hand,' Lyle forced a grim smile, 'he won't just kill them out of pique; it's all about you being aware, about you knowing that poor Aunty Maud was mown down in the street because of you, and nice Uncle Godfrey was drowned as punishment for your sins! There has to be that contact, that awareness.'

'You're not painting a pretty picture, Horatio.'

'I'm painting an honest one.'

'Where's the Machine?' Moncorvo's question came so suddenly, it caught both Berwick and Lyle off guard.

'What?'

'Where is it? It's a very simple question.'

When Berwick didn't answer, Moncorvo said briskly, 'Lyle's ramblings imply that it would have to be big – exceptionally big – to generate the power you require. But there is nowhere in the city I can think of which could conveniently house such a structure. So – where is it?'

'It's a good question,' admitted Lyle. 'I'd like to know too.'

'Underground,' replied Berwick quietly.

'Where underground, exactly?'

'It hardly matters – your kind wouldn't be able to get within half a mile of it.'

'I could,' said Lyle.

A shadow passed over Berwick's face, an instant of pain. 'Would you destroy it, Lyle? All of it, not just the key? It would be . . . hard, when you see it.'

'It's monstrous,' snarled Moncorvo.

'It is misguided,' agreed Lyle. 'But where is it?'

'When Bazalgette built the sewers a few years back,' Berwick's voice was distant, still faint with doubt, 'he was approached by the government and asked, in the course of his works, to extend an extra tunnel underneath the city itself into a space of the government's design, a complex capable of housing more of the pumps that he was attempting to build to control the flow of water through the system. He agreed – the money was excellent for the project, even if the secrecy was alarming. At high tide, it is hard to get there: too much of what he built crossed through the old sewers which flow into the river. But at low tide, it is possible to go down into the sewers and follow the signs.'

'What signs?'

'Markings on the wall. You wouldn't notice them if you didn't know they're there. Two cogs, one inside the other; they look almost like the face of a clock, if you look right, counting down.'

'I've seen that mark before,' said Lyle quietly.

'So have I,' murmured Moncorvo. 'Is this thing . . .' a gesture at the regulator, 'the only one of its kind?'

'Yes.'

'And these papers . . . ?'

'Are the only things which will tell you how to build it? Yes, there are no copies.'

'And without it the Machine can't be completed?'

'That's correct.'

'And you are the only one who knows how to finish the design.'

Berwick's eyes strayed uncertainly to Lyle. 'I suppose I am . . .'

And too late, Lyle realized. He saw Moncorvo, standing next to the table at the end of the bed, standing next to Berwick's forgotten revolver, and thought, *stupid, stupid, stupid, stupid!* and pushed Berwick to one side and made a lunge for the gun. So did Moncorvo, and Lyle knew that if he'd been standing just a bit closer, he wouldn't have needed to call himself a fool.

Lin Zi, when informed that women were not welcome in the house, had done a number of things. The first had been to let out a profound sigh at the absurd rules of society and their cruel and inexplicable restraint and denial of natural biological incentives, emotions and needs, not to mention the lax attitude of some women within the country towards their God-given rights as social equals to men and failure to capitalize on their obvious advantages in life. The next thing she did was to walk to either end of the narrow, squalid street, smiling politely at all strangers she passed by and causing most to run on in uncertainty and fear, just to make sure that the street was *clean*. Clean of anyone else who might have an interest in the little house with its little occupants. The final thing she did was to find a drainpipe that wasn't made of such thin metal or so rusted away by neglect and the secretions of fungus, and climb it hand-over-hand on to the rooftops above the street. She took a deep breath of slightly cleaner, above-street-level air, tried a cautious step and nearly fell over as the tile under her foot clattered away to the ground below. Sighing, she tried another, picking her way on hands and feet across the rooftops until she judged herself to be directly above the room inside which she could hear Lyle, Moncorvo and Berwick talking in low, worried voices. She stretched back on the sloping, slippery tiles, and listened, quite contentedly, to everything that passed.

When the gunshot came, it was so close and so loud and so immediate, that Lin nearly fell off the roof again, which would never have done, as much for dignity as anything else. And to her surprise, she found that the sound made her angry, which hadn't been part of the plan at all.

A gunshot in the gloom.

Lyle was surprised at how big the sound was in the small space. Certainly, the tight walls should amplify noise, make it shatter through the eardrums and churn the stomach, make it as much of a physical punch as a sense or signal to the brain. But he found it hard to believe that the thin walls, which after all were incapable of keeping out water, cold or wind, were capable of keeping in such a sound. Against something so sudden, violent, unnecessary, all the plans in Lyle's head suddenly seemed futile and childish.

He felt physical pain, but was surprised not to find himself shot, or indeed hurt in any particular, and cursed his own imagination for running away with itself, so certain of death that it had already provided all the sensation without bothering to check for the proof itself. He knew he had missed the gun, he knew that Moncorvo had caught it and pushed him back in a single sweep, that the push had been weak but enough, because he was off balance and moving too fast, knew that he'd looked into the muzzle and seen the flash, knew that there had been no sound of bullet striking wall, no reassuring flat *thud*, but something entirely softer breaking in its passage.

So Horatio Lyle, not so dead after all, having seen Moncorvo fire, watched Berwick die. And Berwick looked at the blood seeping into the fabric of his shirt, and said, very quietly, 'Oh. But . . . I thought . . . aren't we . . . ?'

Lyle caught him almost before he hit the floor, with every limb flailing. He screamed at Moncorvo, 'He's on your side! *Murderer*, he's on your side!'

He looked back at Berwick, but the man's eyes were already wide and lifeless, staring at an invisible point on the ceiling, too much of the white showing around the pupils. His mouth was hanging open as if it was about to drool. Moncorvo put the gun down carefully on the table next to him – where the iron had touched his skin, it burnt, and his arm shook, but Lyle had no doubt he could fire again if he needed to. Moncorvo said, 'The regulator, please,' and his voice was hoarse.

Lyle looked at the regulator in Berwick's fingers, looked at Berwick and carefully laid him down on the floor. 'Murderer,' he hissed. 'He trusted *me*, you didn't have to . . . he was on your side.'

'A weak man who would have run and been caught,' replied Moncorvo coldly. 'Havelock would have found him, and Havelock would have destroyed us. This way, the Machine will never be complete. A man who did not comprehend necessity.'

Lyle tried to speak, and found that nothing in particular came to his lips. He felt he should be screaming some sort of abuse or prayer, either in anger or sorrow, he wasn't sure which; but that too didn't seem a good enough response, just somehow too easy and obvious to be real. He knelt next to Berwick and felt the blood pool around his knees and slip around his fingers and didn't bother to think.

Lyle said again, 'He trusted me.'

'And you never trusted me,' replied Moncorvo. 'And there you were wise.'

'He wanted to help! Why the hell didn't you see that?'

'He didn't want to help, Lyle; he simply didn't want the responsibility of doing what had to be done.'

'Murderer.' It seemed the only thing Lyle could say. '*Murderer.*'

'You are wrong, if you think this is *not* war, Lyle. You hypocrite – you hide behind your high morals and lofty judgements, and say that everything is within the law. Is life within the gift of the law? Is the future of a whole people? Can you legislate, Lyle, for two sides who *must* seek to destroy each other, if either is to survive? You coward! You run from what *must* be done, and cower in the blissful ignorance and righteous veil of what *should* be done. I have saved my people! Give me the regulator!'

Lyle plucked the regulator from Berwick's fingers, and held it out. Moncorvo snatched it away and, in the same sharp movement, threw it hard against the wall. His throw wasn't strong, but neither was the device; it smashed into dozens of bronze shards and fragments of wire. Lyle watched it bounce down the wall, and felt nothing. Moncorvo said, 'The papers, please.'

Lyle rolled up the papers, and handed them over. Moncorvo touched their ends to the candle flame. Both watched for a long minute, while the fire caught and burnt its way down to the end of the roll. When it reached Moncorvo's fingertips, he dropped the last ashes on the floor, and stamped on them to put out their worm-like glimmering edges.

In a distant monotone, Lyle said, 'If I should happen, for whatever reason, to survive the next few minutes, I will find you and see you utterly destroyed.'

'Mister Lyle,' replied Moncorvo, 'your death is as much a pleasure to achieve as a needful thing to be done.' He reached out for the gun, fingers curling round the butt.

Lin said brightly, 'My lord, I want you to consider carefully the effect a bolt of bronze will have on the back of your neck and spinal chord, should my finger happen to slip accidentally while holding this trigger.'

Lyle saw Lin standing in the doorway with a small crossbow. He found to his surprise that at that moment he didn't care what happened. Lin's eyes were fixed on Moncorvo's hand as blood started to seep between the cracking skin where his fingers touched the iron. She said, 'I should point out that such an impact would cause extensive damage, perhaps severing the spine, almost certainly puncturing your windpipe, and maybe even catching the jugular on its way out – I think at this range it would go all the way through, and probably dent the wall. This would be unfortunate: the cleaning up will be a horrendous task. But I suspect it will be the women who are required to perform it, typical of the patriarchal society within which we live, alas. But however you regard the messiness or even social ramifications of your demise, you may take comfort in the fact that it will be very, very fast.'

'Miss Lin,' muttered Moncorvo, 'you and I are of the same blood. You know that Berwick had to die, for us to be safe; Old Man White knew. If you had not known this, you would not have let me alone long enough to do the deed that you were unable to complete.'

Lin's smile stayed perfect. Wearily, Lyle heard her say, 'My lord, the Machine is monstrous, and so are you. These things are not so far apart, in my estimation.'

There was distant shouting in the street, and a clattering too, the artificial *clicker-clacker* of the bobby's rattle. Lyle wondered who else had heard the gunshot, and whether they also had forgotten to feel in the few seconds after its sound, the mind overwhelmed instead by all those little chemical signals saying, *Survive and run or stay and die.* A small part of his mind clicked into place, which said simply, *This is a bad place to die.* He looked up and saw Moncorvo's eyes fixed on his own, saw Moncorvo's blood running down the end of the gun, white and slippery, and knew he was right.

Perhaps Moncorvo saw this in Lyle's eyes, because his fingers, impossibly, tightened around the gun. He said through clenched teeth, 'Miss Lin, I have spent an eternity these last few months sleeping on iron floors and surrounded by iron walls, and it has burnt the magic out of me. I am no longer beautiful to the eyes of humans, I am no longer powerful, I am no longer what I was. Lyle did this, and for his death I am happy to die.'

He brought the gun swinging upwards in one simple movement, and Lin pulled the trigger.

This is what Old Man White had said to Lin, while Lyle lay sleeping on his couch.

'This time is a time for humans. For humanity. Our time is long past. We must accept this, and embrace their future, their skills, their souls, their abilities, revel in what they find beautiful, since that which we loved is long since destroyed. The faerie and the Tseiqin will not survive in this world, regardless of what we do – and one day perhaps humanity will be in the same position as us, but today is their day.

'However, this Machine – this creation of mindless destruction, merciless judgement – is wrong. And if its construction is to be the herald of the new age of humanity, I would rather that it burnt, and those burnt who made it, and those who conceived of it burnt, so that this new world may not be shaped in its terrible image.'

Lin had thought about this, and asked the fatal question. 'And Lyle?'

Old Man White had shrugged. 'He may have the knowledge to build the Machine – maybe he lacks the will, but that is a thing which others can provide. I would have humanity survive and grow and prosper, but not so this knowledge. Do we understand each other?'

She had nodded slowly, her eyes elsewhere. 'Indeed, sir. I believe we do.'

The body, that a moment before had been Lord Moncorvo, lay on the floor by Lyle's feet, his white blood mingling with Berwick's red, together staining a girlish pink. Lyle shuddered and looked away. For the first time he was starting to feel sick, something that in years of detective work had never really happened, after the first corpse.

There was shouting in the street below. Lin reloaded her little crossbow with a neat *snicker-snack* and said in a businesslike way, 'If you wish to remain at liberty, Mister Lyle, I suggest you run.'

Lyle looked up with the eyes of a dead man. 'What exactly were your orders, Miss Lin?'

'Mister Lyle, we do not have time for this.'

'*Tell me.*'

She hesitated, then stared him in the eye. 'To protect everyone: the whole, the mass; utilitarianism and all that – the ideals of Bentham – the good of the many – and so on and so forth. To stop the Machine.'

'To let Berwick die?'

'And to let you die if you knew how to make it work.' There was no apology in her voice. 'The knowledge of the thing must die. Now may I advocate your leaving here?'

'Lin, I can make it work,' he replied with a sad smile. 'Now that I know what "it" is.'

She nodded. 'I know. And I choose to let you live, Horatio Lyle.'

He sighed. 'Not that I'm ungrateful, but one day you may regret that, miss. Promise me you'll look after the children? And tell Tess . . .' He hesitated, then smiled a little wider. 'Tell her to have a proper bath after.'

She hesitated, then nodded. 'I give you my word, Mister Lyle. For whatever that means.'

'Thank you.'

He staggered upright, like a drunken man, *so tired*, pulled the door open a crack and peered out, closed it again and leant on it. 'Miss,' he said wearily, 'I think you might consider leaving by the window.'

Footsteps on the stairs; shouting. Lin hesitated. 'But . . .'

'No killing of policemen, please. Whatever the consequences, no more killing.'

She nodded and moved swiftly towards the window. Behind Lyle, there came a hammering on the door. 'Open up! Police!'

'Lyle, you have knowledge, I can't just *let* them come in here and . . .'

'Miss Lin, I'm a copper, and this is a crime. I'm not running away this time!'

Lin hesitated, then tried again, pleading. 'Havelock will come and he will . . .'

'What would you have me do, miss? Be a fugitive for the rest of my life? Berwick was right. These things are not so easy; I do not have your talents.'

By the window she paused. The hammering became louder, and the door shuddered as if something heavy had smashed into it. She smiled, and bowed her head. 'I wish you well, Mister Lyle.'

'You too, Miss Lin.'

And she was gone.

Lyle rubbed his eyes and wondered if they'd let him sleep, just a little. He stepped back and opened the door, no matter what the consequences.

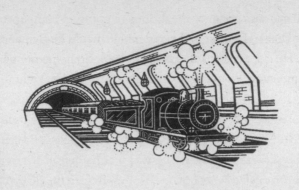

CHAPTER 14

Beneath

At midnight there was a quiet knock on Thomas's door.

He said, 'Mmmnnn!'

From outside, Tess's voice hissed in a dramatic whisper, 'Get your lazy bottom 'ere, bigwig! There's detecterin' an' all that sorta happenin' tonight.'

It was perhaps a little past midnight when Lyle, seated in the Smithfield Police Station, folded his hands on the table, leant forward, and looked the youthful and somewhat confused detective straight in the eye. He said, 'Lad, take it from a copper, trade secret, one to another. You've heard my story now three times, and the more you shout at me and the more you insist that I've pulled any damn trigger the more I'm going to clam up and the less the beak is going to be impressed when he demands evidence. So, if I were you, I'd switch tactics. You've been the tough copper very well, your guv would be proud – but right now I'd go for winning sympathy, and give your very tired suspect a clean blanket, a cup of tea brewed from leaves only used three or four times, no more, and a pot of boiled peas, and send him to bed with a reassurance that you'll consider all the evidence before you rush to conclusions, right?' Before the detective had a chance to reply, he added, 'Oh, and while I'm on the subject, I'd be very careful who you tell that one of the corpses currently in your basement is bleeding white blood.'

The detective hesitated. 'Isn't there . . . a scientific explanation for that?' he hazarded.

Lyle sat back and gave the young man a look that needed no translation.

The detective shifted in his chair and, for the fourth and last time, mumbled the desperate fall-back words, 'Let's go over it one more time, shall we?'

Lyle sighed, and began again. 'My name is Special Constable Horatio Lyle, and for the last few days I have been investigating the disappearance of a man called Berwick . . .'

It wasn't the whole truth he told that night. But, he reasoned, the whole truth could get a man killed.

Thomas found Tess and Lin Zi sitting by the fire in the second drawing room. Tate was curled up at Tess's feet; Tess wore a nightgown ten years too big for her. Lin was looking, even to Thomas's eye, a little flustered.

Still sleepy, Thomas mumbled, 'What's the matter?'

Tess said, 'All hell breakin' loose on the manure cart *again*, bigwig. Where do we get summat to eat right now?'

'You're hungry?' he hazarded.

'Just thinkin' of how we might need food for our adventure an' all what we're goin' to have to have 'cos of how no one else seems up to it.'

'It's a little more complicated . . .' began Lin.

Tess turned to glare at her. 'Miss, ain't I never gone an' told you what a *Good* brush with death and adventure involves?'

Lin raised one enquiring eyebrow. Tess opened her mouth to speak. But to her surprise, and his too, Thomas got there first. 'It involves *preparation*, it involves *consideration*, it involves never rushing into things on an empty stomach, never permitting the gentlemen assigned to follow you to achieve their aims; it involves packing provisions and preparing food for the journey; it involves large quantities of ammonium nitrate and surprising amounts of magnesium and phosphorus; it involves a practical grasp of the nature of oxidization and an awareness that at all times, regardless of any strain being put upon the venture, all actions must be carried out with decency and decorum, correct?'

Tess gaped at Thomas, who responded uncertainly, 'Is that right, Miss Teresa?'

'Well . . . it's good as how you're learnin', I suppose.'

Thomas beamed. 'So what's the adventure this time?' He was beginning to feel more awake.

Lyle slept. Or rather, Lyle dozed; it was hard to tell which images in his mind were dreams, and which were a relentless reliving of events over the last few hours, a retreat through the mud of memory in search of the moment when things might have gone differently: *here* or perhaps *here* — a word, a warning, a thought, a different turning, a step taken in a different place. Sleep was too grand a word for the dark daze in which Horatio Lyle drifted, curled up on a hard bench in a cold cell beneath the police station. It is hard to say how long he lay in this state. The darkness gave no indication of time, and after such a long while moving and searching, a moment of sleep — a second in which the mind and body could begin to unclench from all the running and the arguing and the fighting and the fearing and the guilt — would have been worth an hour under normal circumstances.

He trusted me.

Murderer.

I choose to let you live, Horatio Lyle.

Dreams and memories mixed together, not caring which one carried the title from this particular race. But even asleep, a part of Lyle didn't close its eyes, and a thought loitered at the back of his mind, listening, despite the absence of consciousness, for the footsteps in the corridor, for the key in the lock, for the shadow in the door, for the voice to speak, for the enemy to work it out, as he always did, as he inevitably would.

Lyle slept, and Lyle waited.

Thomas was straining to sound like his father.

'So . . . to clarify. Lord Moncorvo is . . . and Berwick is . . . and Mister Lyle has been arrested on suspicion of all . . . *that* . . . by the police and is being held until more evidence becomes available, or until no evidence comes at all. But the police serve the government and Havelock has infiltrated the government and he might go looking for Lyle and even if he doesn't, the Machine is still down there and your kind can't go close to it because it's magnetic. So you're here to *protect*,' the word was a snowball rolling across a sheet of ice, 'me and Miss Teresa until such time as Mister Lyle is released. At which point you're expecting us to help you destroy the Machine.'

Lin studied the ceiling, and seemed to like what she saw. 'That's more or less it, funny little human thing,' she agreed. 'Except, of course, there is one minor problem that may assail us well before this moment of triumph.'

'We're gonna have a moment of triumph?' asked Tess uncertainly.

'Of course you are! You and the little Thomas person are going to save Mister Lyle, going to prevent the Machine; going, in short, to overcome your unfortunate evolutionary shortcomings and prove that despite how small you are, despite your complete lack of grammatical control, despite even a shocking propensity for pickpocketing . . .'

'Is prop . . . propen . . . is that anything like "proper"?' asked Tess.

'Despite all of this,' Lin went on, unflustered, 'you are Mother Nature's improbable final answer, and you are going to do your duty!'

There was silence while this sank in, before Thomas finally said, 'Didn't you mention some sort of minor problem, miss?'

'Well, *yes*.'

'May I ask whether you mean the word "minor" in the same

way as we mean "small", said Thomas primly, 'or if your ki . . . if you have another way of understanding it?'

'*Well*,' said Lin, 'the problem is that Augustus Havelock has contacts throughout Her Majesty's Government.'

'Yesss . . .' offered Tess. 'An' this is bad 'cos . . . ?'

'Augustus Havelock will probably soon be aware, if he is not already, that Mister Lyle is under arrest on suspicion of Berwick's death.'

'An' . . . I'm guessin' as how you're buildin' towards summat what's gonna make me cry an' all, so any time you say . . .'

'Havelock will also be likely to realize that now Berwick is . . .' Lin waved her hand as a tactful substitute for the word, the weighty, despairing word, '. . . and Moncorvo is . . .' the same gesture, slightly less emphatic, '. . . there's only one person left in the whole British Empire who is capable of completing the Machine.'

She waited for the realization to hit. Tess looked at Thomas; Thomas looked at Tess. Tate looked at the bowl of chestnuts by the fire and wondered if they were edible.

Thomas said, 'I'm sorry, miss, who would that be?'

Lin rolled her eyes. 'And this is the future of mankind.'

Tess nudged Thomas in the ribs.

'Ow!' said Thomas.

'Don't be a baby, bigwig,' muttered Tess. 'I think as how she might be lookin' at us for a reason.' She turned to Lin. 'It's that metaphor stuff again, ain't it? The euphe . . . euphemi . . . that thing where you says one thing but you really mean another an' you kinda think as how the person what you're talkin' to is goin' to work it out 'cos they know what you're talkin' about even though you ain't gone an' said it an' all.'

'That makes even less sense, Miss Teresa. Not that you don't make sense, I don't mean to imply that – I'm sure the fault is entirely mine and wouldn't want to cause offence at all, but . . . could you please explain?'

Tess looked exasperated. To Lin she said, 'You're talkin' about Mister Lyle, ain't you? You thinkin' as how Mister Havelock's gonna want Mister Lyle to finish the Machine.'

Lin beamed. 'And yet inside your respective skulls there's so little cranial space for brain!'

Tess looked at Thomas and shrugged. 'If summat's goin' bad,' she confided, 'I always know to blame it on Mister Lyle really.'

Thomas frowned. 'Mister Lyle is in trouble?'

'Of course he's in trouble,' Lin exclaimed, 'you strange little ape-descended creature, you!'

'What . . . will this Havelock person do?'

Lin looked uncertain. 'I'm hoping that Mister Lyle, acting *nicely*, won't betray my people to an ignominious and cruel demise.'

'What'd the big words mean, bigwig?' hissed Tess.

'Erm . . . something like unfair and nasty. Why shouldn't he, miss?' Thomas's voice was very polite, but there was something hard behind his eyes. 'Why shouldn't he help Havelock finish the Machine? After all, from what you're saying, Moncorvo' – a scowl – '*killed* – he went and *killed* – Berwick, Mister Lyle's friend. Why shouldn't Lyle finish the Machine?'

Lin stared at him in surprise, then said in a calm voice, 'If I were to die right now in front of you, young Master Thomas – if I were to fall down without a sound and die – would you not call for help? Would you stand back and watch and do nothing and have my body buried in an unmarked grave and give it no other thought, simply because of *what* I am? You are so young, and yet you have already seen such evil, and much of it, I confess, from my kind. I am older than I seem, older than I pretend, and I have seen evil performed by all the peoples of all the empires of this world – the Chinese murdering the Tibetans, the Hindus murdering the Sikhs, the Turks and the Russians fighting for a scrap of land the size of Wales, the English and the French slaughtering each other for a field of opium. Should all the Frenchmen die for fighting you? Should all the Russians be condemned for one Tsar's interest in the Black Sea? Maybe you think they should. But I like to think, Master Thomas, that you have enough of that insight Mister Lyle values so preciously to see that I am not your enemy, and that if the Machine were to be completed, if I *were* to die right now in front of you, you would be as shocked and appalled as if a friend were dead.'

Silence. Tess looked uneasy. Lin added, 'Oh – and Havelock will probably kill Lyle anyway, once he's done.'

No one moved. She smiled grimly. 'The future of a friend may be in your hands, little humans.'

A footstep in the corridor.

A key turning in the lock.

A shadow in the door.

Sleeping, waking, dreaming, remembering, doesn't particularly matter any more.

A voice.

'Good evening, Horatio. You do seem to be in a conundrum.'

*

Lin spells her plan out in full detail.

This is Thomas's reply:

'What? I mean . . . no! I'm sorry, that wasn't very . . . uh . . . but it's . . . I mean, surely if there's . . . uh . . . but isn't that . . . Miss, I'm sure you mean well – well, I think you might . . . sometimes . . . mean well, but this is just . . . it's not as if . . . uh . . . it's just not very hygienic.'

And this is Tess's reply to Lin's plan:

'*Well*, if it's underground where you'll be wantin' to go, I know this very nice lad what owes me a favour. You've got somethin' big an' hidden underground, he'll know where to find it.'

Tess beams at Thomas, and though Thomas knows, in his heart of hearts, that what's proposed is absurd, laughable and stupid, he also knows that it's probably the right thing to do.

Then Lin adds, 'Oh, and I think we should really hurry.'

'Why?'

'Because Mr Havelock will obviously attempt to catch you two in order to manipulate Mister Lyle.'

Thomas looks surprised. 'Why would finding us make any difference to Mister Lyle?'

Lin gives a look and says nothing.

'This is a bit of a pickle.'

'I beg your pardon?'

'A bit of a pickle.' Lyle smiled. 'A conundrum.'

Augustus Havelock struck a match to the lamp in Lyle's cell, and sat down next to him. Choosing his words with care, he said, 'I saw Berwick's body.'

Lyle didn't reply.

'And Moncorvo's, broken out of prison yesterday by an unknown stranger, who left a note on a chloroformed guard, and acquired his pick locks and smoke bombs having used a device that could practically shoot through walls.'

Still Lyle said nothing.

'I also saw the broken remains of the regulator, and the ashes of the drawings for its replacement; and I saw Thackrah, and my servants saw you.' Havelock lounged back against the wall and said in an almost kindly voice, 'So, Horatio Lyle, you are my enemy at last.'

'I suppose I am,' said Lyle. 'I think it was always going to happen.'

'I am glad.'

'You are?'

'I understand, Lyle, that underneath the naivety and the foolishness and the childish games, there are few others who I would respect more as an enemy.'

'I'm thrilled. I can't rebuild it, you know.'

'I think you can. I think, Horatio Lyle, that you've seen the plans, you've seen the regulator, you understand the science. You and Berwick were, after all, friends; he taught you while he worked with your father. I think you can build the Machine, and I think you will.'

'Because,' sighed Lyle, 'if I don't, you'll threaten the children, won't you?'

'Quite.'

'You're going to tell me that you will hurt them and anyone and everyone else I've ever known or loved, and I'll be left alone, in the dark and so on.'

'A crude summation. But I think that, in your own way, you understand what I am prepared to do.'

'Except,' Lyle said easily, 'there's only one problem.'

Havelock raised his eyebrows and waited.

'The thing is, if you so much as touch one of the children, I mean actually hurt them, actually cause them harm, rather than merely threaten and posture, you know and I know that I'd never help you ever in a thousand years and would, in fact, seek to destroy you. It all comes down to a test of wills – you can't risk causing harm to those I care for, because, if you do, you will lose me for ever. And I can't risk letting you harm them because I'll never forgive myself if you do. The question therefore becomes one of who, in this regard, has the stronger will?'

Havelock thought, then nodded with a concerned look of agreement. Then he stood up, and very calmly hit Lyle across the face as hard as he could. Lyle fell, turning away instinctively and shielding his head with his hands. Havelock waited a few seconds, until he was sure Lyle was listening, then leant down and said quietly, 'The police will hand you over to me, because in the end I am more powerful than they. The Machine will destroy the Tseiqin because in the end I am more resolute than they. The children will try to help you, and fail because I am more prepared; your friends will wonder where you are, and forget because I am more persuasive than they; and you will rebuild the regulator and you will make the Machine work because, I promise you, the one thing you lack and that I possess without limit, is *will*. I trust we understand each other, Horatio Lyle?'

Lyle pulled himself up, one cautious limb at a time, and shuddered, and said nothing.

And here is London, in the darkness of the night.

No fog, tonight; for once, the rain has banished it. For a brief, brief moment before it is obscured by smoke rising from the factories that rumble away throughout the night, the air smells fresh. And here is Teresa Hatch, running to catch a hansom cab, remembering old friends and the way into the sewers. She is thinking of machines that churn beneath the city, and Mister Lyle and what he knows and whether he was wise after all, and wondering if maybe this adventure itself was so smart, and whether it'll end in breakfast after all.

And here are colliers still carrying coals down from a canal, even though it is night: more coals than burnt even in winter, and not just into the city, but down, into the sewers, into the tunnels and the darkness and the stench below the city where so many new tunnels have been dug: the pedestrian tunnel at Rotherhithe, where ladies of the night ply their trade, and the tunnel at King's Cross where the new-fangled Underground line wheezes towards Euston Square. In the old sewers that lead out to the river, the tide turns and slushes thick goo out by Woolwich. And somewhere, underneath it all, the Machine waits and burns.

And here is Old Man White, staring out across the city, suddenly not sure, not knowing: no one has come to report, no one has brought news, not even Lin, who is usually so punctual. He does not know what will happen, nor where, and that is not the way things have worked in the past.

And here is Thomas Edward Elwick, carrying bags laden

with chemicals and tubes and wires and tools and strange bent things that he's sure Lyle would know how to use and which Teresa pretends she knows how to use but which probably are only useful for those rare and special occasions when you want to dissect the gut of a sheep or carry out some other improbable scientific activity, and which tonight serve only to weigh him down – but tonight, it's best to play safe. He realizes he's never done anything like this before – at least, he's never done anything like this alone. But as Tess rightly says, 'It's all right, bigwig, I'll see that you ain't too beat up an' all.' Maybe not so alone then.

And here is Horatio Lyle, wishing he was somewhere else.

It occurs to Lyle that if he had gone safely away on holiday, odds are the Machine would have been completed some time or another, with Berwick or without. It would have been used, and the Tseiqin would have died, and he would never have known nor cared, and would probably never have wondered where the people had gone who a few days ago he regarded as his unmitigated enemies. He wonders at what point everything changed, and whether it can ever be changed back. Probably not, he decides. Life is never that convenient.

At first they ride in a carriage; he can't tell where. They blindfold him, and he is amazed, angry, disappointed that the police gave up so easily, even though he knew it would happen. He hears a bobby say, 'He's all yours, sir,' and recognizes awe in the young copper's voice as he talks to Havelock. He hears the exchange of money.

They go down. In some areas of the city there are places in the middle of the street where it is possible to descend, via grates across the road, or other access points, to the widest tunnels. He smells the river, then he smells the throat-shrinking, gut-churning stench of the sewers, and feels it as heat on his face, as if the filth under his feet through which he slips and slides, a hand under each elbow to guide his way, is somehow in the air too, coating his hair and skin, sinking down inside.

They walk. At some points the water is up to his knees, at others he feels the tunnels slope upwards, with dry paving underneath; sometimes he hears the distant pouring of water down a wall; a few times he bangs his head on the ceiling and has to walk bent over double. He knows they're getting close when he smells smoke and the heat rises and rises past the point where you previously thought it would be unbearable, to the level where it seems to eat all moisture out of the skin, make the hair crackle and the flesh tighten so that when he twitches his fingertips, he can feel the stretching and distending of every cell of skin on his hand. As they get near, he hears the thumping of machinery, the huge *whumph whumph whumph* of pistons moving up and down, the *clatterclatterclatterclatter* of tiny gears meeting and parting, the *click clack click clack click clack* of pins falling into place, the *chumphachumphachumphachumpha* of steam venting, the featureless roar of furnaces like the breath of a whale-sized snake exhaling, and the fires crackling, and more still. He feels the hairs on the back of his hands rising, on the back of his neck, the bite of static in the air, hears the faint *pop* as someone who has iron nails in their boots lets off a spark while he walks along a gantry, the loud sizzle as someone who has nothing at all to earth him in his boots lets off a spark from the end of his fingers as he accidentally touches an iron rail and swears.

Finally they take off the blindfold. Horatio Lyle sees the Machine; and what Berwick failed to mention, what wasn't explained on the diagrams, was that, for ease of conductivity, all the wires, the miles of wires that wrap around the core of packed explosive contained within an iron shell, the thousands of wires that run together towards the thousands of giant, man-sized capacitors that stand upright like a mummy's tomb in rows and rows across the gloomy cavern floor, overshadowing the tiny shapes of moving people, hundreds of them turned to insects under the scale of the thing; what no one bothered to explain, was that the wires that lit up the cavern containing the Machine with reflected firelight, and made it glow, were made of solid gold.

Havelock said proudly, 'This is the Machine.'

Lyle wished he could answer, utter something especially witty or glib, and found he couldn't speak. Havelock smiled. 'The capacitors are something you are familiar with, I think – their place in the system is based on your design. It functions well.'

Lyle let out the breath he hadn't realized he'd been holding and pulled free of the two men who had guided him through the sewers. He moved to the edge of an iron platform above the stairs to the sewers, and looked down at the moving buzz of activity a long way below. 'This must cost . . .'

'The annual produce of India,' replied Havelock primly. 'I doubt you can conceive of the wealth or scale. It took an empire to make it viable.'

Lyle looked up at him. To Havelock's surprise, Lyle was smiling. 'Augustus, although you and I personally despise each other and I wish nothing but a prolonged and agonizing downfall for your good self preferably involving kneecaps, I must confess to being very, very impressed.'

'Horatio, I am pleased you begin to understand,' replied Havelock.

'Of course, the odds are absurdly small that something this big is going to work, that there won't be a squashed mouse somewhere in the gearings that causes the whole thing to blow up.'

'On the contrary. When you have built something as big as this, it is very easy to see where the problems may lie.'

Lyle stared back out across the Machine. At length he said, 'Is it charged?'

'Oh yes. We just need to complete the discharge mechanism. Which is, I believe, where you will help.'

Lyle looked up at the ceiling. He decided there was no way to determine whether the looming blackness overhead was actual cavern-top or simply a thicker layer of darkness somewhere this side of it. Behind him, Havelock said, 'We could *not* waste time with persuading you, Lyle. It would have been surprising, if pleasing, had we been able simply to proceed to the main event.'

'I can't repair it, you know. I only saw the plans for a second.'

'But you are Horatio Lyle, a friend of Berwick and the son of Harry Lyle, a man who spent his tenth birthday party trying to analyse the bicarbonate that went into the cake, *and* a knowledgeable scientist in your own right!' replied Havelock. 'I think a glance is more than enough, at something so dear to your heart. After all, it was so nearly you, rather than Berwick, who was recruited for this project.'

'I can't make it work!'

'You mean you *won't* make it work. That, Mister Lyle, is something I am more than capable of rectifying.'

'There is *nothing* you can do, Augustus. You can't find *them* and *I* can't fix it!'

'Horatio,' chided Havelock, 'I am a man of greater means than you can even understand.'

At roughly this time, in the house of the senior Thomas Henry Elwick, Peer of the Realm, a window on the fifth floor very quietly went *click*. It was slid carefully upwards, a hand groped inside, and a voice beneath the hand muttered, 'Get a move on, will you?'

'You want my boot up your nose?' was the delicate reply from the owner of the probing hand. There was a scrambling in the dark, and after a moment a man slipped through the open window on to the floor of the room. He was followed by another, then a third, each wriggling through the window like fish through a cranny in the rocks, all bending backs and flopping limbs.

One said, 'Which first?'

'The girl,' replied another. 'She's more likely to scream.'

'Mr Havelock said as how they weren't to be damaged,' pointed out the third. 'He needs them, he said.'

'He said as how they weren't to be damaged *much*. Come on.'

The three slunk towards the door, opened it a crack, peered out. The corridor was empty except for a single, snoring footman, a bottle open by his side, head lolling against the wall, curled up on a stool too small for a man half his size. Ignoring him, they picked their way quietly down the corridor to the next door. It was locked. One pulled out a pair of lock picks from his coat pocket and set to quietly, as if he hadn't a care in the world. Another smelt the breath of the sleeping footman and wrinkled his nose in disgust. 'Rum,' he hissed.

'So much for Lord Elwick's staff,' muttered another.

The lock clicked. They pushed the door back. The room beyond was shuttered and dark, its only illumination the faint lamplight that seeped in from the corridor. In the bed a figure lay, its back to the door, curled up and almost invisible under the blankets. The first intruder crept towards it, and reached out to put a hand over its mouth before it could scream.

The figure rolled over, opened its eyes, and smiled.

One yelped, 'Bloody hell! It's got a bloody beard!'

'You must be the gentlemen sent to find my son,' said the figure in the bed, sitting up swiftly and pulling out a hunting rifle from under the sheets. Outside, the drunken-seeming footman had suddenly acquired from inside his jacket a small but effective-looking pistol; at the end of the corridor, more shadows crossed in front of the light.

Lord Elwick smiled grimly. 'I'm sorry – you missed him. But *I* have so been looking forward to talking with you.'

His name was Scuttle, he was twelve years old, so he claimed, and he was born to rule. More precisely, he ruled the north side of the riverbanks at low tide that ran between Blackfriars Bridge and the Tower of London. No mudlark, snipe or spoon hunter could enter his domain without first begging an audience from Young Master Scuttle. His throne was an old bathtub with a hole in it, that, turned upside-down, allowed him to sit cross-legged, like the old prattler up on Cheapside said the Rajahs did in India. He wore a velvet burgundy jacket the thickness of a spider's web, and a crooked top hat supported only by his protruding ears. He kept order over his assembled courtiers, who had an average age of about nine, with a hook of the kind used by dyers to hang clothes to dry above the vats.

It was ten thirty in the morning when Tess, Thomas, Tate and Lin found him. Tate had been snuffling his way through the carcasses of boats rotting on the low-tide mark and his coat had quickly turned muddy brown from the slime thrown up by his paws and low-slung belly. Thomas was struggling to move under the weight of bags and equipment thrown across his shoulders – with which load neither of the ladies had offered to help, he noticed, with a pang of resentment that immediately made him guilty at the immaturity of his own feelings. He had, after all, volunteered to carry the bags, as befitted the man of the party. Lin and Tess had accepted his offer with, he couldn't help but feel, a slightly too cheerful expression on both their faces.

The presence of Lin brought a swift reaction from the crowd of children gathered with their goods for barter around the bathtub where Scuttle regally sat. Anyone over five foot tall was suspect in the eyes of the mudlarks, who cringed back from Lin with a look to Scuttle for guidance. Thomas, meanwhile, was trying in vain to shake some of the mud off his trouser legs. The mire from the banks of the Thames, all thin green slime on thick grey-brown sludge, had somehow crawled as high as his knees, even though he was sure he had walked with utmost care and discretion from the steps at Blackfriars Bridge.

Scuttle said, 'Oi, you here for the barter?'

Thomas tried not to gape. Lin beamed, and said, 'Aren't you a quaint little specimen?'

Tess marched up to the bathtub, ignoring the ooze of the mud and the rag-tag children who scampered out of her way. 'Right, you, you owe me big, an' now's the time when it gets paid chop chop, all right?'

Scuttle said, 'You can't go an' talk to me like that! Ain't you got no dec . . . deco . . . dec . . .'

'Decorum?' suggested Thomas politely.

Scuttle's eyes narrowed. 'An' who the hell is this?'

'Bigwig, this is Scuttle. Scuttle, this is bigwig,' said Tess brightly. 'Bigwig's really called Thomas, I just call him bigwig 'cos of how he is. Scuttle's really called Josiah, but he don't like as people know that, 'cos it sounds all stupid.'

'An' what about the lady what ain't normal-looking?'

'Oh, you must mean me,' exclaimed Lin. 'I'm a knife-wielding fiend from ancient lore, a demon in the night, a dream in the moonlight and, may I say, I also make splendid chow mein. How do you do?'

'Tess!' wailed Scuttle. 'You gone an' met all funny sorts!'

'Never you mind that,' she exclaimed. 'We need to go in the sewers, an' *you*' – an accusing finger stabbed at Scuttle's chest – 'are gonna take us there.'

Seated on his bathtub, Scuttle flinched. 'But Tess . . .' he wheedled.

'Don't you go an' try an' get out of it. I done you plenty of good in the past. I lifted stuff what has kept you in bread an' nice clothes when you was still scratching for teaspoons in the old tunnels, so watch it.'

'Why you want to go there anyway? It ain't nice down there, Tess, an' besides' – he leant towards her conspiratorially – 'some of the snipes been goin' missin', ain't they? Down in the new tunnels, it ain't safe like it used to be.'

'You mean, it ain't safe like it used to be when the only thing what you had to worry about was bein' attacked by rats or flooded by the tide or getting lost or havin' poo drop on your head?' asked Tess sweetly.

Thomas had turned green.

'All right, all right, I see what you're on about,' muttered Scuttle. 'But that don't explain why you wanna go down there!'

'I wanna go down there,' replied Tess in a voice of infinite patience, ''cos there's this evil bigwig bloke what *don't* want me to go down there. I wanna go down there 'cos there's this Machine what's gonna kill these people an' though I ain't too sure of what these people are about, my guvnor says they're all right really an' as how it ain't right to go judgin' many all at once, an' maybe he's got a point there 'cos if you just say, "They're all bad" then you'll hurt everyone even if they ain't all bad, an' that's summat I don't rightly like the sound of. I wanna go down there 'cos this nice miss says my guvnor's down there, an' 'cos he needs savin', an' I wanna go down there 'cos I just find them sewers so *nice*, see? Now you gonna help or do I 'ave to sock you one?'

'Miss Teresa!' squeaked Thomas indignantly.

'Stand back, bigwig,' barked Tess. 'This is lady's work.'

Scuttle wilted under the force of Tess's glower. 'Oooh . . .' he complained. 'You gonna get me in'na so much shitty poo, Tess.'

She grinned. 'You just about hit the nail on the head there.'

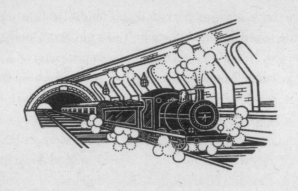

CHAPTER 15

Tides

Later, Lyle wanted to kick himself for not having worked it out before. Later, however, wasn't early enough. Later, he remembered it all in flat, unsympathetic statements, cold grey images, nothing really left for feeling, although he could remember the sensation in his throat from all the shouting, and how tall Havelock looked. Mostly he remembered the moment when he had realized – with a sudden blooming of understanding after the sneaking build-up of information which warned him – *he could . . . he might . . . he can go so far . . .*

He had wondered why, Havelock had just left him in a darkened cell with confused strangers and their voices. They didn't know him; he didn't know them. After maybe an hour in the dark, the door had been opened. Not just Lyle, but all of them, the cell's many occupants, had been prodded out at gunpoint into the dull orange glow from the furnaces, and lined up. Several of the faces had surprised him: some were older than their owner's voice, some younger, in a mishmash of characteristics that, as far as he could tell, had almost nothing in common, except that they were all clearly in disgrace with Havelock. And they were afraid.

When they were all lined up, Havelock walked down the line, a bobbing face on a black shadow in the dull light of the furnace, seemingly oblivious to the heat rushing out from every inch of the bellied metal giants. He got to the end, where Lyle stood next to an oldish man with the beginnings of a rough beard, took a revolver from one of the men guarding them, checked that it was loaded, raised it and, without a word, shot the man next to Lyle.

Lyle would remember the strange seconds of silence that followed, and every time he did so, the silence seemed to have been longer as people saw but failed to understand exactly what had happened. He would remember blood on his face from the shot, the other man's blood, and that where a human being had stood, now there was just a prostrate creature on the floor, wheezing for breath, clinging to a hole in his chest and sobbing and choking and dying all at once, his face the colour of tomatoes, his fingers pale as snow. Only when a woman fainted, three places down the row, did the rest begin to stir and shout and scream, and only then did Lyle kneel next to the man and tear at his clothes to see the wound, and press down as hard as he could while the blood flowed between his fingers like water squeezed from a sponge.

Havelock leant over Lyle to peer at the dying man with an

expression of mild curiosity, and said calmly, 'Well, he might survive for a while.'

And the little piece of Lyle that was a detective before it was a scientist, that was a copper and, more to the point, an angry one who had seen too many bodies, who knew that no matter what it did, the world would not yet change – that piece of him cracked. He threw himself at Havelock with all the strength he had and actually managed to get his slippery, bloody fingers on the man's throat before he was pulled back and pushed to the ground, kicking and biting at anything that got in his way.

Havelock watched dispassionately while Lyle struggled, and then remarked, 'Oh, look. I do believe he's dead.'

Lyle sagged on to the floor and put his head in his bloody hands, then tucked it in towards his knees like a child afraid of spiders. Havelock prodded the man's body with a toe, and murmured, 'I wonder what he was called?' And turned to the next one in the line, and raised the gun.

'Please, stop.' It was barely a whisper, a sigh from somewhere inside the bundle that was Lyle. 'Please.'

Havelock raised his eyebrows. 'I trust you understand this game, Horatio Lyle. I really do hope it is something you may comprehend.'

'Please.' Lyle looked up at Havelock and whispered, 'Please.'

Havelock hesitated, then lowered the gun. He squatted down so that his face was level with Lyle's. 'This, Horatio,' he explained gently, 'is why you are weak. I don't need the children to control you; I don't even need your friends. I can take anyone off the street, and kill them before your eyes, and you will know that they are dying not for their own insignificant merits, but because of *you*.

'This makes you easy – very easy – to control, in a game hardly worth my time or their blood to play. So, we will be simple, indeed childish, about these things. You *will* rebuild the regulator, and I will *not* go down the line killing every single person in it before your eyes. And if the regulator does not then work, I will go into the streets and kill, and make sure the bodies are laid at your door. Do you understand me?'

Lyle nodded.

'Excellent! There, now, that wasn't so hard, was it, Horatio? In the end, it will be much, much easier for you to build me a regulator that will kill hundreds of unseen, unknown Tseiqin at a stroke, than for you to watch a single person die and to *know* it's your responsibility. I suppose that makes you a hypocrite; but frankly I'm more inclined to think it makes you a coward. To work, then! So much to do, such a busy time.'

And he turned and strode away.

All roads lead to London. This is a firm conviction held by most Londoners, who know that in every hamlet and village in the country there will sooner or later be a sign or a milestone indicating that in this general direction is the metropolis, and you should count yourself damn lucky to be going there, whereas in London itself, not a clue is given as to how you can escape its boundaries because, after all, why would you want to?

In a similar way, there was a general sense that all things in London eventually led to the river. Although many inhabitants of the city lived in the shade of the hills beyond its northern bounds, even along the modest slopes of Pentonville Road or down near Charing Cross an unspoken feeling prevailed that the trend in London was *downwards*, bending towards the water. Of the railway stations that supplied London, only a small number did *not* cling to the banks of the Thames, and those few, such as King's Cross and Paddington, were nested close to a canal anyway, as honorary riverside ports.

This trend of the city towards the river had both helped and hindered the designers of the new sewer system, opened with much aplomb when the first pumping station belched into life just beyond the city's south-easternmost extremities. Gravity had been the mechanism that also, with a lesser degree of success, powered the old sewer system. This had broached the riverside with a number of tunnels that slipped discreetly out into the water to the east of the Houses of Parliament – and whose contents had in recent memory caused such stinks throughout the whole river that parliament had been forced to close, for fear of deadly miasmas carried by the smell of sewage. Then, and only then, had the funds for a new system been provided – but the old tunnels remained.

One of these tunnels came out half a mile downriver of the Tower of London. It had a small opening barely large enough for a child, let alone the fully grown Lin – and for the rats that snuffled, oblivious to humankind's presence nearby. Until, that is, Tate barked at them and charged with teeth bared. It was here that Scuttle stopped, sniffed the air and announced, 'Righty-righto. This'll do.'

Even then they had to wait for the tide, which had been rushing in and lapping the sides of the tunnel when they arrived.

This took time. And time was something Thomas felt they couldn't afford.

This is why:

Horatio Lyle sits at a workbench in the light of a single dull candle underneath the black cavernous roof, and chews the end of a pencil.

He lays out paper in front of him, considers its blankness, half-closes his eyes, and remembers the images that Berwick had shown him, the shape of the thing, the details of its design, every dot and line. And he knows that this, here before him, would be a futile exercise were it not that, now he understands *what* the Machine is, now he realizes the scale of it, he knows it can work, and he knows how to finish it. He knows too that somewhere inside, there is a tiny, tiny part of him that thinks it is amazing, an achievement, a scientific miracle, and *wants it to work*. The thing is so very simple, the work of a few hours if you knew how to do it. His pa would have called it 'elegant', and so it would have been, if you forgot its purpose or the men with cruel faces leaning over his shoulder to watch him work.

He puts pencil to paper, and starts to draw.

The tide never changes so slowly as when you are sitting there to watch it. Usually the Thames was nothing more to Tess than a big, wet *thing*, that meant you had to go up- or downriver to find a bridge, if a ferryman wasn't about; an occasionally inconvenient sloshy bit – not that she, Teresa Hatch, would ever be caught going *south* of the river, where expanding suburbs stretched towards such mysterious places as Vauxhall and the

Elephant and Castle coaching inn. On that side of the water the brothels and music halls were practically one and the same, though more recently hidden behind the giant yellow-brick wharves built up by the shipping companies to receive their wares.

They waited until the sun was just a mucky brown splodge somewhere out towards Richmond, shimmering dirty off the changing tide. As they waited, Thomas twiddled his thumbs and tried to think about maths and geology and science and other essentially healthy things, and not at all about betrayal and death and sewage; *especially* not about sewage. He hadn't thought to find an older pair of trousers for the adventure, there'd been so much to do . . .

Tess thought about when she was growing up, and going underground into the sewers had been another way of life to consider, another means of surviving. She'd known other street children who, in their time, had decided to hunt down there for the things that people forgot and left behind – although Tess had never quite understood how some of the things that could be found in the sewers had ended up down there. Sometimes the other children would come back with no more than a few brass buttons or a shoe so rotten and muddy it would crumble in their hands; sometimes they'd come back with a spoon or a lost far-thing eaten away by the slime; sometimes they wouldn't come back at all, and their friends would wait all day on London Bridge for the tide to turn, to see if the body would be carried by or just washed straight out to sea. The most prized posses-sions of the sewer hunter were a watch, and a knowledge of the tides gathered from the pilot master or the man who ran the naval clock down at Greenwich that signalled local time to the passing ships. Compared to what happened if you got lost in the sewers, Tess had decided a life of crime wasn't so bad.

And Lin thought about . . . nothing. Nothing at all. Perhaps, deep down, she didn't dare.

'What we're lookin' for,' explained Tess in her special patronizing voice reserved for stupid people, friends, acquaintances and the general populace, 'is this big place what has a Machine what we reckon's gotta be really big an' all, right, an' it's in the sewers an' it were built by this bloke what built the new tunnels a few years back, an' we reckon as how it's got these big pumping things inside of it, an' lotsa people gotta be workin' round there so you must've seen *summat*, an' we wanna go there. Oh, an' it's run by these bigwigs what are all big on machines – but like *Machines* with a big "M" 'cos of how it's all nasty an' clever an' stuff – an' it's real important that we get there all healthy an' all, right?'

Scuttle scratched his chin, which wasn't due to sport a beard for proper sagely effect for at least another six years, and murmured, 'Well . . . I might just know this thing what'll interest you.'

Horatio Lyle puts the pencil down, looks up from his piece of paper and says, 'I need some things.'

Havelock shrugs. 'We can do anything.'

CHAPTER 16

Machine

Scuttle scuttled. This, Thomas realized, was precisely the motion that characterized him; there was no other way to describe the boy's movement through the tunnels. As they worked their way into the darkness, lighted only by a lamp that gleamed reflectively off rats' eyes and dripping slime, the short, jerking movement of Scuttle as he lunged from tunnel mouth to tunnel mouth was exactly as his name suggested – a crab-like motion; alternatively, with that nervous quality of a pigeon constantly turning its head to spot the vulture. Thomas watched Scuttle for all he was worth and tried to think about the physical properties of a crab's movement, about what each joint did and whether it was a more efficient way of moving than, say, swinging a leg from the knee or riding a penny farthing. He tried to think about the science of scuttling, until his eyes ached; anything, *anything* to get his thoughts away from the smell, and the heat whose suffocating punch to the chest had knocked through him like a door slamming in the face, and from the strange liquid that swilled above his ankles and had seeped through his shoes to make his socks sticky and his feet wrinkle like pink apricots. Next to him, Tate paddled through the stuff, bounding ahead as best he could to bark at the rats that lurked in every corner. They rippled away from Tate's teeth in a black tide, their feet making a splishing sound like raindrops in a puddle as they retreated from the light of Scuttle's lantern, and Tate's growl.

When Scuttle eventually stopped, he did so beside, as far as Thomas could tell, a dripping wall no more nor less foul than any other encrusted, rough brick surface in the endless maze of darkness. Scuttle raised the lantern to the wall and, while Thomas nearly gagged, brushed away a coating of thick brown muck to reveal a small marking.

It had been scratched crudely into the brickwork – two cogs, one inside the other, like the face of an odd-looking mechanical clock. Thomas drew a sharp breath, and instantly regretted doing so as it burnt its way down into his lungs. Tess squinted at the marking and said, 'What's this about?'

'Dunno,' said Scuttle, 'but they've been croppin' up all over since the new tunnels got opened an' some of the old 'uns what dares says as how they're markin' out territory, see?'

'What's *territory* about?' demanded Tess suspiciously. 'Who's pretendin' to be the bigwig?'

'Dunno. *But* . . .' Scuttle grinned. 'I do know as how there's places down here what weren't *never* put on the map.'

Havelock hadn't lied. They had *everything* Lyle could possibly have needed, and more, laid out in a workroom of a size and scale that 'til now he could only dream of, a miracle of technology, efficiency and proper scientific practice.

Yet oddly enough, it was the *more* than what he just needed, that interested him most. He bit his lip, and found himself thinking, inexplicably, about voltages.

They found more of the marks, cut into the brickwork with a penknife and mixed with the notes of other sewer hunters going *l l l r l 2l 3r l* . . . as they indicated their passage through the tunnels. At some points the tunnel became so low they had to bend down and crawl, with their heads bumping against the roof; with every bump Thomas imagined living, slimy things creeping into his hair. In other places the tunnels were so wide and dry they felt like a passage in a castle, cold and sterile, rather than a sewer. Sometimes they caught glimpses of daylight, seen through grates high above; sometimes they had to pass under veritable waterfalls of leakage, ducking through sheets of water that poured through the brickwork. Every time they reached another corner, Scuttle checked his watch and murmured, 'We don't want to get caught by the tide none,' and tried not to look afraid.

'We keep goin' 'til *I* gets bored!' replied Tess firmly. 'An' if you're lucky an' all, we'll 'ave found my guvnor by then and *he* can do the worryin' for us.'

It was underneath a shaft of light from somewhere a long,

long way overhead, that Tate started barking. He splashed forward, sniffing the walls and the air, and leapt up and down, sending flecks of brown muck spattering out from his ears and coat, and barked yet more.

'What's up with little Tatey-watey?' Tess crooned at him. 'Is little Tatey-watey bored, is he, is *heee* . . . ?'

If it's possible for a dog to look condescending, Tate managed it, nose wrinkling up in irritation and huge eyebrows sinking over his brown eyes. He scampered down a tunnel and waited impatiently for the ignorant humans to follow him.

Lin peered after him and murmured, 'I do believe the dog-creature wants your attention.'

'He's a dog,' replied Tess. ''Course he wants attention. But you can't give him none, else you'll spoil him, an' you can't spoil him, can you? No you can't, little Tatey-watey, no you *caann't* . . .'

'Miss Teresa?' said Thomas uncertainly.

'Whatcha want, bigwig?'

'Well, Miss Teresa, maybe Tate has a scent.'

'A wha'?'

'A scent.'

'A wha'?'

'A scent, Miss Teresa?'

'Bigwig, I ain't gonna repeat myself again none.'

'Erm . . . perhaps he can *smell* something that we can't.'

'What, down 'ere?'

'Maybe. Apparently a dog's sense of smell can be a thousand times more sensitive than a human's — I mean, as if we could see and the colour red was actually a thousand colours, and . . .'

'Tatey-watey sees colours?' hazarded Tess.

'No, I mean . . .'

'He might smell Lyle,' said Lin quietly. 'I think that's what the little gentleman is trying to say.'

'Well, yes. Yes, it is.'

'I can't smell nothin'.'

'Well, apart from . . .'

'Yes, apart from the squelchy stuff, bigwig!'

Tate, who clearly felt that initiative was being lost, barked again. Tess frowned at the shadowy shape he made in the gloom, then turned to Scuttle. 'Oi, you, what's down that-a-way?'

'Nothing,' said Scuttle simply. 'Just more tunnels an' a brick wall.'

Tate kept barking. Lin stepped carefully into the tunnel, reached into a pocket and pulled out a very small bronze knife. Tess stepped back instinctively. 'It's hotter down here,' murmured Lin. 'And I feel . . . strange. More than just a brick wall.'

Tess scowled and turned to Thomas. 'Have you noticed how it's always you an' me what have to go an' save Mister Lyle from all the silly things what he's gone an' got caught up in, bigwig?'

'Well, I suppose on occasion . . .'

'An' do you know he only gives me five shillin's a week pocket money?'

'You have pocket money?'

'Yes. What do you get?'

'Well . . .' he hesitated. Somehow he didn't think Tess expected to hear, 'I don't get anything, I just tell the butler to go and buy it for me, but when I'm eighteen I'll get an allowance and part of Wiltshire.'

But Tess had already moved on. 'An' *now* we gotta go an' save him *again* an' this is you an' me followin', with all due respect, miss, this lady what has evil green eyes an' ain't like normal people, an' a lad what refused to give up his special blanket 'til he was nine . . .'

'Oi! You said you weren't tellin'!' squeaked Scuttle.

'. . . an' a doggy-woggy with big ears!' Tate growled. 'So what I'm sayin', bigwig, is as how you an' me gotta be real clever an' all to make up for this, or maybe how it's me what's got to be clever, an' save the day against overwhelmin' type odds!'

'Oh. Yes.' Thomas thought about it, straightened up proudly, banged his head, hunched again but repeated nonetheless, 'Yes! That sounds about right!'

Tess grinned. 'Just checkin'. Let's do the adventurin' bit, then.'

They marched off, into the darkness.

The tunnel was long, featureless and hot. As they walked, it got hotter and darker, and the walls became narrower; and still the temperature kept climbing – until, without warning, Lin stopped dead and murmured, 'I can't go further.'

Tess and Thomas turned. Even Tate stopped his insistent snuffling to stare at her. Scuttle raised the lamp, and in the dull glow Lin had turned white. She was swaying slightly, leaning against a wall, seemingly oblivious of the slime. 'Oh God,' she whispered. 'Can't you feel it?'

'It's a bit hot?' suggested Tess.

'Miss, are you all right?' ventured Thomas. He'd always secretly hoped a lady would swoon in his presence, so that he could leap valiantly to her rescue. Now, however, deep in a sewer, with a woman who filled him with apprehension, his dream was suffering from malign circumstance.

Lin gave them a look of disbelief, then forced a smile. 'The future leaders of mankind,' she sighed. 'How do you get by?'

'I think she's bein' mean about us,' muttered Tess in Thomas's ear.

'You're very, very close to it,' murmured Lin. 'It's . . . a sickness . . . a coldness, an acidity, right ahead. That way, keep going,' she said, pointing with her chin down the tunnel. 'The closer we get, the more it hurts.'

'What? What what what what what?' demanded Tess, bouncing on the spot.

'The Machine,' Lin replied. 'Berwick didn't say, Lyle didn't say, but I can feel it. It gives off a magnetic field, it's like . . . walking across broken glass, and the feeling's been growing all the way down this tunnel. I can't go any closer. If I do, I'll die.'

Tess looked at Thomas, who looked helplessly at Lin. He said, 'Will you be all right, miss?'

'Just make it stop,' she hissed. 'That's all, just make it stop.' Then a thought struck her and she added, 'And get Lyle out alive. And please don't tell him I said that.'

'But it seems like a *nice* thing –' began Tess.

Thomas nudged her and said, 'Right, yes, of course, Miss Lin, naturally.'

'But . . .' Tess tried again.

'We'll just be off.'

'We will?' piped Scuttle.

'Yes,' said Thomas, sticking out his chest defiantly. 'We will.'

For a moment, just a moment, Tess looked at him in awe. She murmured, 'You ain't takin' charge, are you, bigwig?'

'Uh . . .' Thomas wavered.

'Seein' as how you're oldest an' all,' she added.

'Well . . .'

She patted him on the shoulder. 'I think it's sweet as how you're tryin'.' Then to Lin, 'Goodbye, miss! Don't go an' do anythin' evil while we're gone, right, 'cos that'll be *bad* an' I'll sulk an' you wouldn't want to see that.'

'Oh, she's 'orrid when she sulks,' said Scuttle. His tone made Thomas feel, just for a second, alarmed and protective, and he wondered why.

'Come on!' boomed out Thomas in the voice he hoped generals used when marshalling their troops. The three of them, and Tate, went on down the tunnel, leaving Lin alone in the darkness.

Havelock stood behind Lyle's chair. He was watching everything Lyle did. So did others. Men and even a few women, from the dimness away from the candle on the table, all observed Lyle, as he worked at slipping wires into frames or twisting circuits together. They took in every movement, every breath. Each time one of them didn't follow his reasoning *exactly*, they'd call a halt, to study what he'd done, interrogating him about every twist and turn, until finally the voice of dissent would say, 'Ah, I think I see what he's trying to achieve.' There was to be no error.

There was, however, a suspicion growing at the back of Lyle's mind, that these very, very clever brains – these exceptionally well-educated scientists watching his every movement, studying his every thought as he twisted infinitesimally small circuits into being at the heart of the Machine – might just be the kind of people to miss the Obvious Thing.

The tunnel stopped. It ended at a brick wall down which water dribbled in black rivulets defined by almost five years of seepage. Tate sat on his haunches and glared at it. Tess folded her arms and said, 'I ain't impressed by this, bigwig.'

'I'm sorry, Miss Teresa,' Thomas heard himself say.

'Well, don't just say that, *do* summat!' snapped Tess.

'What do you want me to do, miss?'

Tess stared at him as though he were an idiot. 'You're carryin' most of Mister Lyle's kitchen, bigwig.'

Thomas noticed again the weight of the bags across his shoulders.

'Blow it up or summat! There's gotta be summat in there what'll go "Bang"!'

'Aren't we supposed to avoid things that go "Bang"?' asked Thomas in a pained voice.

'I won't tell if you don't,' she replied briskly.

'Are you both always like this?' asked Scuttle.

Thomas was thinking. 'Maybe . . .' he felt stupid as he said it, 'there's a secret door?'

Tess stared at him in despair. 'You takin' the pi . . . I mean, you havin' a laugh, bigwig?'

'I'm just saying, if perhaps we searched . . .'

'You just think people go round buildin' secret doors everywhere, do you? There's always this book you push that makes the shelf come out, or a bit of string you pull or a brick you kick or summat?' 'Cos I'm tellin' you, as someone what knows about gettin' into places where you don't belong . . .'

Thomas kicked a brick hopefully. 'Ow!' He hopped up and down, clinging to his foot.

Tess grinned. '*Hah*. Told you.'

Overhead, something went *thunk*. Somewhere near by, something else started whirring. Tess's face fell. 'I ain't never gonna be able to talk proper sense to you again, am I?'

Thomas's face had broken into a huge grin. He gazed expectantly at the brick wall. Nothing happened. At his feet, something went *shurlp*. He looked down. So did Tess. Seeing them do so, Tate also looked down – then started barking furiously as, beneath his feet, a small section of floor started to move, creaking back while slime oozed over its edge into the darkness below.

The thing opened up into a dark shaft. The lamplight gave no clue as to whether there was a floor below. But there were the rungs of a ladder, and they looked clean and fresh. Tess said, 'I just get this feelin' as how we're gonna 'ave to go down there.'

Scuttle looked green. 'Er . . .' he began.

'Yes?' asked Thomas politely.

'You wanna go *down* there?' Scuttle squealed.

'Yes,' said Thomas, in the same tone of uncomprehending goodwill. 'Do you think we shouldn't?'

The only answer was a little noise of distress.

Tess scowled. '*Men*,' she hissed. Snatching the lantern from Scuttle, she started to climb.

Lyle put down the last piece and studied the thing in front of him. It wasn't as neat or as finished as Berwick's piece of work, but it would do. Hammered together from scraps, it would serve the purpose for which it was made.

Havelock leant over Lyle's shoulder. 'Very good. Yes, I think I see what you've done.'

'You claim to be a scientist, Augustus,' Lyle coldly replied. 'But I doubt you have any idea of what I've done.'

Havelock's eyebrows twitched; his mouth tightened. He reached out and wrenched Lyle's face round so he could see into his eyes. 'Are you going to double-cross me, Horatio Lyle?' he hissed. 'Would you dare?'

His fingers dug into Lyle's skin, dragging red marks across his cheek and jaw. Lyle tried to shake himself free, but the grip tightened. 'Would you let so many die to save your enemies?'

'It works!' said Lyle quickly. 'I swear – I swear it works, I swear.'

And as he swore, just one wire under his fingers, one tiny piece a bit too long, that he bent back on itself to shorten to the correct length, ready to snap – bent back and *round*, a hook under his fingers . . .

'Please stop,' he whispered. 'Please . . .'

Tying positive to negative, and all eyes were on Havelock, and Havelock's eyes were on Lyle's, and it didn't seem to occur to him that fingers can work by touch alone. 'Please . . .' Or that you can have *more* than what you need to build a thing.

Havelock let go. Lyle lapsed forward, clasping the new, strange, lumpy regulator, not nearly as neat or shiny as Berwick's device, but just as well informed. Havelock took it carefully from Lyle's hands and turned it over, examining it with narrowed eyes, then scrutinizing Lyle, and Lyle decided that

Havelock read faces better than he did machines, and that under different circumstances that might almost be an irony.

Havelock smiled. It was his first genuine smile that Lyle had seen, full of satisfaction and triumph, almost childish in its glee. 'I choose to let you live, Horatio Lyle,' he said. 'At least, for now.' He straightened up and said briskly, 'Let's finish this, shall we?'

Lyle followed Havelock without a word, without being told to and without being told not to. He followed him from the workroom beneath the furnaces, across bridges spanning rivers of cable, down flights of stairs, and along passages that smelt of burnt metal and coal, through caverns piled with nothing but soot and wood, metal and wire, across gantries where the workers with black-stained faces watched the Machine waiting below, through billows of venting steam and past walls of fat pipes that hummed and hissed like a breeze gusting through a rusted organ. At the hall of capacitors, thousands of them that grew around him like trees in a forest, Lyle thought he saw a shadow move, and dismissed it. Then, at the start of the metal casing that stretched five hundred yards ahead and contained, somewhere inside, more explosives than the mind could comfortably conceive – even a mind as well adjusted to explosions as Lyle's – he thought he heard a footstep somewhere overhead, a familiar pattering. For a moment, he nearly smiled. At the circuit-breakers, giant switches spun on a handle that took five men to move and snapped like a crocodile's jaws when the connectors were swung into place, he felt almost ready for what he knew was about to come.

He watched with no sign of emotion as Havelock disappeared into a small shed built within the cavern. Through this there passed a giant's thickness of arm, composed entirely of cabling, each individual cable fatter than Lyle's wrist, and hundreds of them to boot, carrying the regulator. He waited without particularly caring that he couldn't see while men wired in the regulator, and briefly met the eyes of the scientists as they struggled to make his cruder device fit the area that had been designed for Berwick's. That took nearly half an hour. He waited patiently, sniffed the air and smelt . . . brass, gold, bronze, iron, coal, smoke, dust, static, sweat, sewage, stagnant water, soot, salt, sugar and perhaps, somewhere close by, the tiniest, tiniest hint of ammonia, where there shouldn't have been anything of the sort.

Havelock emerged, without the regulator in his hand. Everyone stood well back.

Lyle said, 'Is there a lever marked "Bang"?'

Havelock didn't grace him with a reply. He waved up at a man on a gantry. The man on the gantry waved at someone down on the floor. Someone down on the floor waved at someone else in the red-black haze of darkness. Somewhere, very far off, a piston went *umph. Umph. Umph. Umph umph umph umphumphumphumph . . .* A whistle blew. Lyle looked up and heard the sound of venting gas, the familiar *eeeesssshhheeekkk!* as it poured from a hundred different, overly stressed pipes. Little cogs started to click; somewhere a turbine went *duummmduuummmmmduuummmmmm . . .*

Teams of men started pushing the circuit-breakers shut, huge twists of metal clacking into place. If it was possible for the temperature to rise, it did, and so did the light as fires were stoked and sparks began to flash, little white-blue flickers in the darkness and a rising redness that crept surreptitiously towards the top of the cavern underneath the city. In the streets above, pigeons scattered; underneath Lyle's feet, the ground hummed, a resonance that passed right up through his stomach and rattled around his teeth and head. Metal shook and strained.

Havelock looked at his Machine, and laughed.

Lyle said, 'I'd stand a little further back, if I were you.'

Havelock's eyes flickered to Lyle, and now, for the first time in what felt like far, far too long, Lyle smiled.

Later, Tess would say that it wasn't that exciting. Watching capacitors charge and discharge was like watching cliff-face erosion — exciting if you could see what was happening just at a moment of crisis — but otherwise an unfulfilling experience. A charge that was stored in a forest of clay and metal discharged, as invisible as the current that had fuelled it in the first place. It did so from a thousand capacitors all at the same time and was, needless to say, invisible to Tess's eyes, except for the odd hotness in one or two cables where the quality was lower than the required standard, and where resistance raised the temperature to a dull, ruddy glow.

The discharge of the capacitors themselves was, therefore, unspectacular.

The arrival of the charge at the point where the current divided — part to the coil that ran round and round the central metal core that filled the main hall which housed the Machine, part to the detonator that set off the shaped charge inside its bowls — approximately 0.00001 seconds later was, Tess grudgingly admitted, more interesting. It was interesting for the way in which a large part of the shed that housed the regulator exploded outwards in a jabbing shard of blue-white lightning; it was interesting for the way in which the ground boiled with racing electricity that dug itself into the earth; it was interesting for the way in which every single cable that ran from capacitor to the regulator suddenly exploded dancing sparks; it was interesting for the way clay boiled around the capacitors, the way wooden platforms too close to the cables caught fire, the way the furnaces screamed, the way the pistons churned, the way the lightning flashed across rotting pools of dripping sewer water and turned every droplet to a flying electrical snowdrop; it was very interesting for the way the single thin wire that carried a tiny, tiny, *tiny* part of charge from the regulator to the detonator that should, if all things had gone well, blown the explosive to collapse the magnetic field just *so*, only to blast it out again in a tidal wave of raw magnetism – it was interesting to see how that hung so loose and forlorn, just beside the detonator. Cutting the wire had been Thomas's idea, although judging by the fireworks, Tess was beginning to think it might not have been such a good plan after all.

CHAPTER 17

Circuitry

And the regulator exploded.

Horatio Lyle, when he had decided that short-circuiting a device that was designed to carry millions of volts at any given second would be an interesting thing to do, had ironically been more concerned with the effect of said millions of volts trying to earth themselves anywhere within a fifty-yard radius, and what this might do for the soles of his shoes than any more material consequences of his action. Now, the thought seemed a silly one – there was far more to be concerned about than elementary electrical physics, strange though the idea could be.

He did what he always did when something exploded violently, which was to throw himself to the floor with his knees tucked in and hands over his head and wait for the worst to stop. The ground beneath his fingers and his knees tingled, it burnt and bit with energy as the electricity in the Machine, suddenly very, very confused about where it was going, went down into the ground, boiling it too close to the shattered remnants of the regulator and there was so *much* of it, artificial lightning, a man-made monster, a crude imitation of nature, of something *he'd seen before*: Havelock had spent a fortune on building something that could have come naturally from the sky. And now Lyle was *angry*, so angry, at every second of the last few days spent being lied to, chased, manipulated, used, a pawn in other people's battles. For them it was a war, for them there was no limit and they would kill to make something as futile as this, to make artificial lightning and leave behind the bodies and murder and plot and scheme and steal and threaten and kidnap and bribe and blackmail and think nothing of it because they had a *cause* and somehow that made everything all right, and they had threatened the *children*.

Another blast shook Lyle where he lay. The force of it sent bubbles into his ears and made his nose ache, the prickly heat in the earth stinging his fingers. He started to crawl away on his belly, wriggling like a snake from the dancing lightning, eyes half-closed against the sudden explosive glare of sparks and fire erupting underground, all across the length of the Machine – no wonder his Pa had disliked short circuits; what a mess, what a waste . . .

Another blast and there was something around Lyle's ankle, restraining him. He looked back to see broken metal and torn walls and falling shards of fire and torn wire ripping through brick and stone, and to see Havelock's face pressed to the earth but looking at him and Havelock's bloody hand clinging to his ankle, anchoring him. He kicked, and when that didn't shake Havelock, he rolled over and kicked again with his other foot, hitting Havelock across the top of his head and the grip went slack. Lyle tried to crawl up to his feet, reached out to grab a pipe, part of a bank of pipes that ran across one wall, and burnt his hand, staggering as the faster, smarter part of his brain instinctively let go before he even had time to register the pain. He pushed himself to his feet and turned, looked up, saw the broken wire leading to the detonator at the start of the hundred-yards-long metal case of explosive. He grinned, and saw a shadow move and felt he now knew absolutely what had to be done. He ran towards the detonator, looking for a path up to the broken wire, saw a ladder of black rungs on a black wall hiding in the darkness, looking thoroughly uninviting, and raced towards it, pulling himself up with a strength he was surprised to find he had, and not a little pleased, grateful that his body knew when it was an emergency. He peered over the gantry and looked straight into a pair of laceless leather boots that looked far too big for the ankles that housed them. He looked up from the leather boots, past a pair of pinstriped trousers held up with string and a red velvet jacket and into a small, spotty, frightened face that went, 'Uuhhh!'

'Who the hell are you?' demanded Lyle.

The child said, 'Are you Tess's guv'nor?'

'I guess so, previous question still stands, and what are the soles of your shoes made of?'

'Wha'?'

'I'm just thinking that if you're going to stand in the middle of an electrical disaster, you might want to do it somewhere where the current won't be inclined to earth itself *through* you.'

'Wha'?' squeaked the child.

'Never mind,' sighed Lyle, heaving himself up and carefully manoeuvring the boy to one side. 'Let's just trust to luck, despite the futility of the idea.'

Somewhere in the distance, something irritably chemical met a spark, and did the irritable chemical thing, sending a rolling wave of yellow fire and acrid smoke spilling out across the Machine. The child mumbled, 'Tess said as to how she should say hello an' that she's gonna rescue you.'

'She did?'

'Yep.'

'Why isn't she *here*, then?' asked Lyle, patting down his pockets and finding them embarrassingly empty. 'What *are* the soles of your shoes made of, by the way?'

'Oh, she's tryin' to sabotage the Machine type thing,' said the child.

'But I've already done that!' wailed Lyle.

'We noticed that, Mister Lyle! An' I went to all this trouble!' said an indignant voice from somewhere below. Lyle peered down to see two familiar faces and a large nose peering back up at him. 'Oi, you!' said Tess, stamping an indignant foot. 'Me an' bigwig, though it were all my work, see, well me an' bigwig had a really, really great *plan* for how we was gonna save you *an'* save Miss Lin *an'* destroy the Machine an' then how you'd give us more pocket money an' . . . hello Scuttle . . .'

'Uuuhhh,' mumbled Scuttle, who was by this point trying to eat one of his own fists and doing surprisingly well in the effort.

'Well, if you'd been here thirty seconds *earlier*,' said Lyle, 'I wouldn't have gone and short-circuited the damn Machine as was my intention all along anyway, thank you kindly.'

'What, *all* along?' demanded Tess. Somewhere, something overhead rumbled and creaked, masonry bounced off the iron carcass of the explosive core, the useless, dead coil of wire around it sparking and bending indignantly under the pressure. 'Even with the bits where it were goin' horrid an' you needed rescuin'?'

'I'm glad you're all right, Mister Lyle, sir,' added Thomas.

'Well, yes, another time, maybe,' said Lyle, flapping indignantly. 'You . . . what's your name?'

'Scuttle,' mumbled Scuttle.

'Josiah,' said Tess gleefully.

'Little spotty person,' said Lyle firmly, 'you'll be wanting to stand *well* back. Thomas, did Tess make you carry the bag of goodies?'

Tess and Thomas were by now clambering up the ladder on to the gantry, which swayed as smoke started rising from somewhere in the distances. Lyle thought, And all that coal . . .

'Here, Mister Lyle.'

Thomas slung the bags off his shoulder. Lyle opened it and gave a gleeful laugh at the sight of the tubes, bottles, glass contraptions and metal twists inside. 'Oh, you two are very, very good,' he said happily.

'Is that like pocket-money-increase good?' asked Tess, her face a picture of innocence.

A scream from somewhere in the direction of the furnaces, a roar of gouting flame. 'We'll negotiate later, shall we?' sang out Lyle, pulling a small dynamo from the bag, all wire, coil and magnet. 'Let's see how this goes.'

He picked up the trailing end of metal that ran into the end of the explosive core and happily attached it to one end of the dynamo's trailing wires. Tess yelped, 'But I just went an' cut that!'

'I know, and I'm very impressed,' said Lyle. 'But now that there's no risk of a current travelling through the coil *simultaneous* with the detonation, it's all right to detonate, as there is no magnetic field to collapse.'

Three blank faces and Tate's nose stared back at him. Lyle sighed. 'This is the lever marked "Bang", Teresa.'

'Aaahhh,' said Tess sagely.

'Oh,' said Thomas helpfully.

'Wha'?' said Scuttle vaguely.

'Never mind, another time,' said Lyle. He turned the handle of the dynamo. It took a few seconds, but it came. The spark jumped from the dynamo to the wire, and sank into it. Nothing happened.

'Wha' happens now, wha' happens now?' shrieked Tess.

Lyle peered at the giant iron cage, and tried to remember that somewhere inside there were more explosives than the Crimean War had used. Inside the cage, something on the edge of hearing went *click*. Something else started to spin; he felt warm air brush his face.

'Erm . . . I think we run.'

'Really?' asked Thomas.

Tess gave him a sidewise look. 'Ain't you never learnin', we is *always* runnin', bigwig!'

And she turned, and she ran, Tate bounding along beside her. Thomas hefted a bag, Lyle hefted another, and followed. Scuttle was rooted to the spot. Lyle hesitated. 'Look, lad . . .' he began, and then thought better of it. 'For goodness' sake,' he muttered, and grabbing the boy by an arm half-carried and half-dragged him along the gantry, after the shape of the retreating Tess.

Behind him, the explosive core – the last part of the Machine, the part of chemicals and acids and very carefully shaped and timed devices that would have made Stephen Thackrah sob to behold it and was, in its own, horrible, terrifying way, a work of beauty – rumbled and roared.

The explosion was meant to be contained, caged in iron, designed to affect forces that were invisible to the naked eye. But perhaps the lightning storm, perhaps the shock of chemical blasts everywhere, perhaps the design was of itself flawed – Lyle never quite found out. For the first part, the initial series of blasts within the cage, the iron frame held, contained every blow though the shock made the metal bulge in ugly grey spots that ruptured and warped around the heart of the core, while pipes screamed and hissed as they blasted out hot air and steam and chemical smoke and purple-brown flames from the heart of the core, one detonation at a time.

Where the iron cage failed looked no different from any other part of the system, but Lyle heard it go, and he felt it go, and when he risked looking back, he saw it, a flash of yellow and red somewhere in the endless dark of the tunnels behind, like staring straight at the evening sun after a day spent hiding in the shadows. He felt the burning of it as everything, *everything* went wrong, as the floor shook and the ceilings shook and the walls shook and mortar dust and sewage and water and sparks and wire and metal and dirt and wood and coal and dust and heat poured down like an avalanche, scratching and burning and punching and stabbing. He screamed out, 'Everyone down!' and they didn't argue; even Tate didn't argue, but threw himself wisely under Tess as she flung herself at the floor, perfectly prepared to be squashed in the name of being shielded.

The shock hit from behind, knocked them flat and pressed them to the ground and shook and shook and shook and tore and broke, shattered the glass of the lantern, tore the pipes from the walls and played a one-note melody behind the eardrums, a roaring that became the memory of a roaring as loud as the real thing that became a buzzing that became a whine in the skull.

The lights went out in the underground cave of the Machine.

It was water that made Lyle open his eyes eventually – a long eventually. It dripped down from the ceiling and pooled around his fingertips, and smelt of the river, and that not a pleasant smell. It was the only sound, a relentless *drip drip drip drip* that, as he listened to it, seemed to get even more insistent. He sat up and felt mortar dust on his eyelids and tongue. He fumbled for the bag at his side and in the utter darkness felt his way to a pack of matches, striking one off the wall in a fat yellow phosphorus flame.

'Any limbs broken?' he asked in a little hoarse voice.

In the darkness of the tunnel, shapes moved. Tess picked herself up and felt her head, where her hair had turned the colour of the pale dust that floated through the air, and the colour of the match that illuminated it. Tate crawled out from under her and sneezed, shaking dust out of his coat, only for it to be almost immediately resettled. Scuttle said in a little voice, 'Tess? I don't think I like this sorta thing wha' you do nowadays.'

Thomas crawled on to his hands and knees, coughing dust from his nose and mouth furiously. The match in Lyle's hand guttered and went out. He struck another and fumbled in his bag until he found a small metal tube and a pair of pliers. He dropped the match into the tube which immediately went *whumph* and spouted dull red flame from its top. He cautiously wrapped the pliers round the tube and used them to hold it away from his skin as it hissed and smoked. Without a word he handed the pliers to Thomas, and a large handful of matches and a fistful of frosty glass spheres to Tess. In the darkness, there was no sound but the *drip drip drip drip*, each drop pock-marking the dust.

Tess quietly struck a match, and held it to the bottom of one of the glass spheres, which burst into bright white light. Lyle said in his best dignified voice, trying to ignore the coating of dust that covered him head to foot and probably didn't aid his attempt at authority, 'Now . . . does anyone here know a way out?'

'We just followed Tate,' admitted Tess. 'Sorry.'

'If you followed Tate in here, I'm sure we can follow him out again,' replied Lyle calmly.

Scuttle, however, had already lost interest, and was watching the water dripping down, with a growing expression of horror that even Thomas found himself suddenly rapt with. Lyle swallowed and said very quietly, 'What's the problem, lad?'

'Water,' whispered Scuttle.

'In the loosest sense, I suppose so,' said Lyle. 'Is this bad?'

Tess had started to turn green; Thomas didn't dare meet anyone's eye.

'Tide,' whispered Scuttle. 'Tide's rising.'

Lyle took a moment to appreciate this, then let out a long breath. '*Right*,' he murmured. 'I think it's time we moved, with some haste.'

'Run like buggery?' hazarded Tess.

'Language! But yes. I think that might be about it.'

CHAPTER 18

Rising

They run through the darkness.

It takes a silence and the dull flicker of firelight to realize how far they are beneath the city, how lost from all common sight. It takes an awareness that these shadows really could be endless, that the walls are heaving and the water dribbling in through the cracks, that the dust is the new underground fog, that every other shape might be living or might be dead and there is no time to find out, no way to know, for the full horror to settle in. No one speaks — no one dares. They run, Tate bounding on ahead, and they follow blindly in the flickering dark.

And here is the Machine.

Metal bent like a corkscrew, the dripping of chemically dead liquids, as inert now as glass, running down the side of a shattered frame. Edges as sharp as diamond, lines as twisted as a madman's mind, torn metal shaped like a spider's web broken in a gale, boiled earth, running water carrying fluorescent traces of oil that shimmer dull purple whenever they catch dying firelight, the glow of embers and the rolling hiss of steam, broken walls and torn masonry, and everywhere the dead glow of tarnished gold burnt black, the jagged shape of a lightning strike etched into clay, melted wires stuck like frozen water in silvery shapes to the walls, icicles of copper and puddles of tin and here or there a running foot looking for a way out in the darkness, stumbling from ember to ember trying to find a light, a sound, an exit, a way up, while all the time the water goes *drip drip drip drip dripdripdripdripDRIPDRIPDRIPDRIP* through the roof and sloshes into the dust and traces little clean rivulets of shininess down the walls of black dirt and soot as, with a final coughing rumble from somewhere inside its miles of gears and cogs and cables and ideas, the Machine dies. At least, this Machine dies.

And here is the Machine, picking itself up, patting itself down, feeling inside its coat pocket and finding a revolver, with only one shot fired. After all, while the idea survives, can the Machine ever really die?

They came to the hall of capacitors, the tree-like clay coffins now dark shadows stretching out in neat rows as far as the eye could see, which in the dark wasn't very far at all. They went in single file between the columns of silent, identical black shapes, glancing at every turn down each row in search of more shadows.

There were things still alive down in the dark, and as they walked the light cast the shadows of the capacitors long across the halls and the voices began.

'Who's there?'

'Help me!'

'Please, is anyone . . .'

'I can't see . . .'

'Can't get out!'

'. . . help . . .'

'Is there anyone who can . . . ?'

As they walked, they grew slower and slower and slower until Lyle finally stopped, head on one side, listening to the voices. Finally he said, 'We can't . . .' and found that he couldn't finish the sentence. He tried again. 'No one should . . .' He stopped. He looked at his feet, then looked up and gave it one last shot. 'This isn't a war.'

As he spoke, shapes moved in the darkness, drifting towards the light. 'Thomas, Tess – you, Scuttle, whatever your name is – shout. Give them instructions. If they follow us, the light, the sound of voices, we can help them get out.'

Shadows, people, men, women, drifting forward, some of them covered with thick black streaks where the blood and dust had mixed to paste on their skins. Tess bounced up and down, waving her makeshift torch and calling, 'Oi! Everyone, this way, *coo-eee*! We're goin' towards a way out, come on! *Coo-eee!*'

Thomas held up his torch and shouted seeming just a little embarrassed, 'Everyone over here! Do try and come here, we'll help you if we can!'

Lyle shouted, 'If you can hear me, try and follow our voices and light, we're going for an exit. You need to leave here before the tide rises, do you understand me?'

Scuttle shouted, 'Erm . . . hello! I dunno what's goin' on, but we gotta be out of here soon, right?'

And Tate barked and yapped and galloped around in the darkness, almost the only creature who could see without the light, smelling everything that moved and the river and the dust and the sewers, as though they were colours burning in the sun.

In the end, Lyle was amazed by how many people there were down there, who drifted or ran or limped or staggered dazed towards the little group with their torches and yelling. He estimated at least fifty, and those were just the faces he could see in the circle of light – behind the bulks of the capacitors, stretching into the darkness were more faces, grey splotches of slightly paler shadow, who followed like hypnotized children the shouting and the light as the group followed Tate and their instincts, until Lyle felt like a herder, moving around the ever-growing group of people as they shuffled through the hot darkness. He wondered if this was what it was like after a battle – empty faces obeying without question, with no alternative but to obey. He hoped not: it wasn't an image he wanted to dwell on.

They heard the sound of water running past the ladder up from the Machine, before they saw it – the regular splashing sound of a small fountain or ornate waterfall. They then felt it, a lapping of water at their feet, a thin oily sheen over the ground on which they walked. Scuttle muttered, 'Gotta hurry gotta hurry gotta go now!' and hastened towards the noise. Somehow the faster movement of one person encouraged everybody else to accelerate above the dead man's shuffle that had characterized the faces drifting in the gloom. When the torchlight fell on the shaft up to the tunnel, its sides caked with sheets of pouring water, the crowd surged forward without any second thought, people pushing and shoving at each other through the darkness until Lyle elbowed his way to the front, shouting, 'Hey, you lot! Behave! You're not going anywhere up there unless you've got someone who has a bit of light and knows the way, to show you.'

Then, to Scuttle's surprise and horror, he turned and said, 'That's you, lad.'

'Me?' exclaimed Scuttle.

'Sadly, yes,' Lyle told him. 'You look – and smell, may I say – as if you know the tunnels. Get everyone out.'

'Oh, I know that voice . . .' said Tess. 'It's that bathtime kinda voice.'

'Teresa . . .' began Lyle firmly.

'Yes?'

'You go up with Scuttle, Thomas and Tate. You get to the surface, and you make sure everyone gets out.'

'An' I'm guessin' as how you're gonna stay down here till the last person's up so they don't get left behind, right?'

'Something like.'

'Well, that's just *stupid*!' she began.

'Tess!' Lyle looked tired in the torchlight, his skin white, his eyes heavy. 'There's something I need to know.'

She hesitated, mouth moving silently as she worked it out. Then, 'Oh.'

'What . . .' began Thomas.

'Make sure everyone gets out,' repeated Lyle. 'And *hurry*. I'll see you at the top.'

For a moment, Tess thought about arguing. The moment passed, and she was glad it did. 'Right,' she announced, turning to the grey faces in the darkness, 'you heard the mister, get your lazy ars . . . bottoms . . . up the ladder chop chop toot sweet!'

'Tout de suite,' corrected Thomas automatically.

'That too, come *on*!'

And to her surprise, they obeyed, like children, following her instructions and climbing up into the gloom of the sewers.

Thomas had to carry Tate through the sewers, ahead of the shuffling tide of people. The water was too high for Tate to walk through, and it was moving fast. He held Tate under one arm and a burning torch in the other made of chemicals that, if anything, smelt as bad as the sewer itself, while the water tugged and pressed against his knees, and kept rising. He followed the shadow of Scuttle through the dark, and Scuttle followed the rats, an exodus of black bodies scampering and swimming and paddling upwards through the darkness, little black shapes brushing against Thomas's legs as they paddled by him, bodies gleaming with water clinging oily to their skin. Walking through the water was hard, every step an effort, swinging from the hips to get some kind of momentum going against the pressure pushing back at them. Behind him kept coming the tide of people, pushing and scrambling through the shadows in the dark of the tunnels, their faces frightened and angry and dazed and confused; so many, of such variety, all turned dust-white. And still the water kept rising, above the knees now, pushing against his thighs as he waded forward, straining to keep going, the top of the water scummy with dead things and grease driven up from the bottom of the sewer. The ground beneath his feet was unsteady too: Tess kept slipping on patches of slime and pitching into the water. Thomas had to grab her, and pull her along with the same hand that held Tate, while ahead Scuttle whispered in a hushed voice that echoed down the tunnel, 'Gotta get out gotta get out left at the end and run gotta get out!'

Lyle waited at the bottom of the ladder until every last face had climbed up, and watched them all, and examined every feature, and didn't see what he was looking for. He waited thirty seconds longer, staring into the darkness, then he called out, 'If anyone's still down here . . .' and stopped himself. *If anyone's still down here . . . what?*

'I'm sorry,' he whispered, and turned and started to climb the ladder, bowing his head against the weight of water sloshing over the side from the sewer above. When he got to the top he had to climb up through waist-high water, clinging to the side of the tunnel for support, ears filled with the rush of it. He struck a match against the wet stones and watched the phosphorus ignite, casting a dull yellow flame. He staggered through the water, pushing and pulling along those people who were running the risk of falling behind, muttering, 'Come on, just a little bit further,' although in truth he had no idea how much further it was. The water was cold, which was almost a relief after the stifling heat around the Machine; but after a while it was more than cold, it was a numbness that caused him to shiver and made his already tired limbs even heavier as he struggled to wade onwards.

Another match guttered and Lyle fumbled in the darkness, lifting above the water line the scant handful of matches he had in an effort to keep them dry. In that moment of darkness towards the end of the line, he heard a splashing, and a voice call out, 'Can someone help me? Is anyone there?'

'Hold on!' He managed to isolate just one match, struck it, looked in the darkness and saw a shadow that had somehow managed to fall behind him in the dark, half-bowed over, head nearly touching the water, leaning against a wall for support as if at any second it might break under its own weight. Lyle struggled back towards it, took it by the shoulders and murmured, 'Come on, we just need to . . .'

The upward swipe caught him squarely in the throat with the butt of the gun, trailing water as it came up to hit. Lyle, his fall cushioned by the rushing tide, was flung backward, barely managing to keep afloat as his head exploded in pain. His lungs caught fire as every part of his throat tried to constrict all at once. He clawed at his neck and tilted his head back to try to get air, the match falling from his fingers and landing in the water, still burning though beneath its surface, reflecting a dozen strange shimmers on to the walls. Havelock marched down on Lyle, ramming the soaking gun into his chest and hissing, 'I don't know if it'll fire, Horatio, but it will be an interesting test to find out.'

Lyle wheezed and tried to speak and couldn't.

'Is it really worth dying so you can save *them*?' demanded Havelock.

Lyle pressed his head back against the tunnel wall and felt the water cold against his middle, and tried to slow his breathing. 'No,' he whispered.

'Then why do it?' boomed Havelock in the darkness.

'It's not . . . *who* the Tseiqin are,' hissed Lyle, his voice like the dust in his mouth. 'It's who *I* am, who we *want* to be. More than a war, Augustus. More than this.'

'Fool,' hissed Havelock. 'I should let you live so you can see the day that they burn your books.'

'You should let me live for a much better reason than that,' whispered Lyle.

'Tell me.'

'It isn't *necessary* to kill me.' Havelock hesitated, just for a second. Lyle smiled grimly. 'Oh, and because there's someone who'd like to have a word with you.'

Havelock didn't seem to understand. So Lin, standing calmly in the rushing waters, tapped him on the shoulder and said, 'Hello, you nasty evolutionary specimen, you.'

Havelock spun round and pulled the trigger. Nothing happened. Lin's smile widened, her white teeth shining in the dark. 'I do believe that your weapon is soggy. Good word, "soggy"; should be used more often. As for that nasty magnetic field your Machine was giving off . . .' she sighed and shook her head. 'Sometimes I have to remind myself of the beauty of the polka, if I want to recall humanity's good side.'

Havelock swung the gun towards Lin's face. She caught his arm by the wrist and twisted it easily, bending him round and back until his fingers opened and the gun flopped into the water. She looked at Lyle and said, as the match finally guttered out, 'Is there anything in particular you want done, Mister Lyle?'

Lyle shook his head, and felt stupid; but Lin saw well enough. She smiled and turned to Augustus Havelock. 'Now, sir,' she said, 'your death *is* a necessary one. But then . . .' She drew in a long sigh of contemplation. 'All deaths are necessary deaths, all people must age and decay and make stupid mistakes that really are wince-making to contemplate, and die. You will die, Mr Havelock, and I will die, and your people shall die, and my people shall die, and the empire will fade and ideas will fade and in a hundred years people will look back on you, and their strongest impression will be that you wore a funny kind of hat. Your death is necessary, and mine is necessary, and Lyle's is necessary so that, frankly, we can all move on with life and change and learn and be ourselves, unique to our own time and place and ideals and so on and so forth. Wouldn't you agree, Mister Lyle?'

'I wouldn't have put it quite that way, Miss Lin.'

'I imagine you would have used shorter words,' she said nicely.

'You play with thoughts, Miss Lin. It's just a difference.' Lyle's voice, quiet in the darkness, asking a question.

Lin sighed, switching her attention. 'Mr Havelock, you are lucky; perhaps, just for today, life has more to offer than its conclusion.'

And though it was dark, Augustus Havelock looked up and saw nothing but bright green eyes, filling his world, filling his thoughts, and could hear nothing but a voice like wind chimes, and knew only that he would do anything for those eyes, because they were beautiful.

*

In the dead of night, just south of Piccadilly Circus, something goes bump.

A cat squeals and runs away, as much from the smell as anything else.

A grate in the middle of the newly polished street next to the newly polished statue near the newly polished clubs where gentlemen with exceptionally polished manners and often equally shiny skulls sit and play bridge and drink port and discuss yet *another* Reform Act to please the masses. It lifts up on a pair of small, muck-coloured hands. It's pushed to one side. A small, muck-coloured head appears, followed by a small body that is, indeed, covered in muck and a red velvet jacket. This is followed by two more children, one of whom is carrying a dog.

The first child says, 'Is this . . . London?'

The second says, 'This is bigwig land!'

The third says, 'I say – that's my father's club! Oh my . . .'

And behind them are more hands, and more faces, clambering out into the street, nestling under the street lamps and peering in at the windows of the clubs until even the occupants, usually determined not to see anything unless it's out of the eye which has the monocle, are forced to notice. Slowly but surely, the street starts to fill up with people, rising from the darkness out into a cold but clear London evening. Faces drift around each other, lost and dazed. One or two recognize where they are and know the way home, but somehow, it doesn't seem quite right to walk away – everyone appears to be waiting for the police, or for the army, or for someone with some sense of authority, or maybe just for a miraculous sign to say, yes, it is all over, well done, go to bed.

Tess and Thomas are forced away from the grate in the middle of the street by the press of dripping bodies scrambling to get up. Some people simply lie down on the cobbles, too exhausted to move, some sit on the pavement's edge, kicking at old horse droppings left from the day's cabs, some try to convince the men guarding the doors to the aristocrats' clubs that they really, really need a whisky.

Tess, Thomas and Tate sit and wait. More than fifty people, maybe more than a hundred, filthy and wet, fill the street.

Tess says, 'I smell horrid. I wonder if this means I'll 'ave to 'ave a bath?'

Thomas says, 'I do hope Father didn't go to the club today. I wonder how I'd explain this if he saw me?'

Tate rolls over and over and over like a puppy in the mud, and looks contented.

Tess thinks about what Thomas has said. 'Bigwig, this is against my principles an' all, but . . . maybe what you should do with your pa is try the whole truth thing for a while an' see how it works out. An' if it don't work out, then just learn how to fib better, 'cos I gotta say it, you're rubbish at the yarn.' Then as an afterthought, in the middle of a yawn she adds, 'An' you smell too, bigwig. Horrid an' all.'

Eventually, some in the gaggle of faces start to break away, and the clocks strike one in the morning, and Tess finds herself yawning even more, eyes drifting shut and head flopping to one side as she makes Thomas her personal pillow. The faces don't say anything much: no one seems inclined to talk about what happened. They just split off, some heading towards Haymarket, some towards St James's Park, some back down towards the river, some west into the streets behind Piccadilly, some up towards the slums of Soho.

Scuttle stands in front of Tess and says, 'That's my best jacket what you gone an' ruined!'

Tess says through a yawn, 'Bigwig'll buy you a new one.'

'I suppose I could . . .' begins Thomas.

'See?' says Tess. 'It's good 'avin' friends what understand you.'

Scuttle looks suspicious. 'You'll really go an' get me a new jacket?'

'If you like, yes.'

'A really big proper one, what has all the pockets?'

'What do you mean by all the pockets?'

'For the gear, the swag, the goods, the boodle, the booty! All the pockets!'

'Well, if you want, I'm sure my tailor could arrange something.'

Scuttle beams. 'In that case, mister, it's been a pleasure workin' with you an' you know where to find me for next time an' for my payment what I have rightly earned.'

'Uh, yes. Good man,' says Thomas. 'Well done. Carry on.'

'You ain't so rubbish,' agrees Tess sleepily.

Eventually, even Scuttle scuttles off.

'Hello.'

Thomas opened his eyes sleepily, and for a moment didn't know where he was. There was a lamp post on one side, and Tess on the other, and Tate in his lap and he was on the street where he'd been, last time he'd checked.

'Hello,' he said.

'You fell asleep here?'

'I think I must have.'

'You must be tired.'

'No, I mean . . . of course not, I'm ready for anything . . .' Thomas yawned. On his shoulder, Tess snored.

'Past your bedtime, I should think.'

'I don't have a bedtime!' replied Thomas indignantly.

'Careful, lad, you've still got a long way to go before you don't have a bedtime.'

'Are you all right?' asked Thomas, suddenly worried.

'Me? Yes, fine.'

'You sound . . . hurt.'

'I'll be fine.' Horatio Lyle bent down and bundled the sleeping Tess into his arms. The street was long since empty, no one else left. The church clock struck quarter to — but quarter to what, Thomas couldn't tell. Tess stirred, opened one eye, saw Lyle and muttered, 'You smell like poo.'

'Past your bedtime too, lass,' replied Lyle. 'And tomorrow, baths all round.'

'An' a really big breakfast,' added Tess from somewhere in Lyle's shoulder. 'An' a discussion about pocket money.'

'Come on,' said Lyle. 'Let's go home.'

CHAPTER 19

Night time in London.

Many of the best things about the city happen in the night – for a start, there's the lights, which when seen from a hill or tall tower, spread out in glimmering candlelight and gas lamps, turning the city orange-yellow and full of stars. There's the theatre, the music hall, the best of the entertainers, and the costermongers who sell their special sweets and sticky caramels to the customers who indulge in these pleasures – somehow, at night, the city seems to heave a sigh of relief and conclude that whatever the day may bring, this time is for its personal consumption and joy.

Night time by the riverside. A single stub of candle burns down in the bottom of a tin bowl. The mudlarks gather round the bathtub throne and listen in awe to their king in his huge green velvet coat, bulging with pockets.

'So there I was . . . in this *huge* underground place full of machines, an' everyone else was in trouble or captured so I had to save the day, just me, by myself! Well, I went to work, I wasn't gonna let this happen to my friends, so, all on me lonesome I took down three of the guards – bam wham bam! – and raced over to this big banging type device in an iron case, which I exploded by use of these things that sparked what I used to carry round in my old jacket, though I went an' lost my old jacket but now I got this new one, 'cos of how I was *soooo* brave . . .'

And Scuttle, king of the sewers, spins his yarn, and spins it well, for the awestruck listeners, and tells tales of wonders and delights, long into the night.

Night time on Primrose Hill, and a man wearing an iron ring on one finger sits on the wet grass, which feels like cold silk under his fingertips, and stares down at the city, and tries to remember this very, very important thing he had to do.

Something about . . .

. . . a thing that kept the rhythm . . .

. . . being regular . . .

. . . regulated . . .

. . . something about . . .

. . . green. Lots and lots of green.

A footstep on the grass near to him, a tiny sound of disturbed water droplets and the hiss of drifting fog. 'Good evening, sir,' says a polite voice.

The man looks over and sees a very plain gentleman, of

almost no distinguishing feature at all, leaning lightly on a walking cane. 'Good evening, my lord,' he says.

Lord Lincoln smiles nicely at the man and says, 'Tell me, Mr Havelock, do you feel that something's missing in your life?'

Augustus Havelock thinks about it. 'No,' he says finally. 'I feel . . . fine. Just fine.'

'I see. Well, Mr Havelock, should you ever *not* feel fine, may I recommend a brief walk, a pleasant talk, a dip in the hot springs and perhaps some weight lifting of very heavy magnetically charged objects, to refresh your memory? I find nothing clears the brain quite so well. Good evening to you, Mr Havelock.'

'Good evening, my lord.'

Lord Lincoln drifts into the fog. Havelock hesitates, then calls out, 'My lord?'

Lord Lincoln turns. 'Yes, Mr Havelock?'

'I feel as though there's something very important I need to be doing.'

'There is, Mr Havelock, but not for a while. We have plenty of time yet for that sort of thing, and all the resources in the world. There'll be time, and next time, fewer mistakes, I feel. We are, after all, only just beginning to learn. Goodnight, Mr Havelock.'

'My lord.'

Lord Lincoln fades away, into the fog, leaving Havelock alone, his mind full of the colour of laughing green eyes.

Night time in Hammersmith, and all the lamps are burning in the house of Lord Thomas Henry Elwick. Lord Elwick sits in his study in the easy chair, and reads Voltaire.

There is a knock at his door.

'Enter!'

Thomas enters. 'Good evening, Father.'

'Ah, Thomas, you are well?'

'Yes, Father, very.'

'I see you got cleaned up.'

Thomas blushes head to toe. 'Father, I . . .'

'I just want to know you're safe, Thomas. That's all that I care about; that's all that matters to me.'

Thomas hesitates. Then nods. 'I understand, Father.'

'If you think that you can't . . . if you think I won't be . . . open . . . to what you have to say, I apologize. I apologize for . . . many things.'

And Thomas Edward Elwick does something he's never done before. He walks into the room and sits at his father's feet like a child about to be told a story and says, 'There is a lot I need to tell you, Father.'

And Lord Elwick smiles, and feels hot with relief, though he isn't entirely sure why. 'Well . . .' he says. 'We have time.'

Teresa Hatch sits in a bath that she has run herself, from water she boiled in the kettle while Lyle wasn't looking – the second of the day. She won't tell Lyle, of course, even though it's in Lyle's house; that would be admitting defeat, that would be confessing to enjoying the bath thing, which somehow would seem wrong after all the battles they've waged on the subject.

But for tonight, she has a bath, and it is wonderful.

Night time in London. The dead hour between two and three of the morning, and a man walks from Blackfriars Bridge to

Westminster, unafraid of anything that might get in his way. And because his walk is so unafraid, no one does get in his way, the muggers and the thieves concluding that this man probably has a reason to be confident, a reason not to be afraid of the dark, and that therefore they should probably be afraid of him. And tonight, they may not be far wrong.

The lamps are burning on Westminster Bridge, but there is fog too, not too thick, but enough to cut one end of the bridge off from another, so that you may stand in the middle and see nothing but roadway on either side, never ending, no embankments and no water below.

The man walked to the middle of the bridge, where one shadow waited under a lamp. He said, 'Hello, Miss Lin.'

She said, 'Hello, Mister Lyle,' and did a little curtsey.

'I'm surprised you wanted to see me – here, now,' said Lyle, looking into the fog.

'I like it here,' said Lin. 'It seems very private, at this time, but in a public space. That pleases me.'

'You are pleased by odd things, miss.'

'You brought a magnet, though?' she said sweetly. 'Don't you trust me?'

Lyle bit his lip. 'No,' he said finally, in a thoughtful voice. 'I find it hard to trust anyone, right now.'

'You've had a bad few days,' she admitted.

'You could say that.' He smiled grimly. 'On the plus side, I've still got my little finger.'

'That was how we first met!' She clapped her hands together happily. 'That was a nice night.'

'For you, maybe.'

'Don't be so negative.'

'Negative?' he exclaimed. 'I'm talking to a Tseiqin on a bridge where . . .' He hesitated.

'Your friend died?'

'One . . . of my friends died here, yes,' replied Lyle. 'Not too long ago, on this bridge, fighting . . . I want to say monsters, but you'd probably find that offensive.'

'Not at all. It hardly matters what shape the monster is, what colour their blood is, if their actions are, by definition, monstrous.'

'I'm sorry.' Then he asked, 'What do you want, miss?'

She smiled, and held out one hand. 'To dance.'

'Come again?'

'I like dancing, Mister Lyle. I think it's the best thing human-ity has had to offer so far. Dancing and maybe the toffee apple.'

'You like toffee apples?'

'Yes!' Her tone implied that it was stupid and futile to ask anyone if they liked toffee apples. 'Now, you may look at me and see an evil Tseiqin manipulating her scheming way to some foul intent, but that doesn't matter. I look at you and see someone who has had a very bad succession of days, and needs something to take his mind off it. Will you dance, Horatio Lyle?'

He hesitated. 'I'm not sure if it's entirely appropriate for . . .'

'A man to dance with a woman, alone in the night?'

'See, when you put it like that, it sounds downright wrong, all things considered, with all due respect, ma'am.'

'Think of me as . . . less a lady and more . . . something unique.' She raised her hand again, fingers beckoning him towards her.

'I'm very bad . . .' he began.

'Of course you're very bad, you're a scientist with a vague concept of the legal system, this makes you by definition an uncharismatic, unattractive, socially inept baboon of a dancer!'

'Well, when you put it like that . . .'

'But you do have lovely eyes, Mister Lyle.'

He hesitated. Then he said, 'Tell me, Miss Lin, just one thing. I have seen the Machine, I know how it works. I could have built it, if I had had . . . the imagination, I suppose . . . to dream it up. I suppose what I'm asking is . . . am I . . . I mean, would you . . .' He stopped, then grinned. 'Socially inept, wasn't it?'

'I think,' said Lin carefully, 'that the answer is "no". Unless your question was about to take an unexpected and interesting twist, in which case the answer might have been "yes", but I find it unlikely you were going to say anything surprising, so the answer remains "no". You are not my enemy, Horatio Lyle. I don't think that having enemies as such is really the best way to get by. Merely . . . misunderstood acquaintances, yes?'

Lyle thought about this, staring into the fog. Then, without a change on his face, he reached into his pocket, and pulled out a very small, grey magnet. He put it carefully on the balustrade on the side of the bridge, and stepped away from it. He took Lin's out-held hand, looked into her eyes, and said, 'What do we do about music?'

'Notes don't really matter, just the rhythm, the dance.'

'Well, yes, but . . .'

'I can sing?'

'Christ, it's going to be a long night. Ow!'

'Was that your foot, Mister Lyle?'

'I'm really not a very good dancer . . .'

'It's quite simple, you just *step* two three, *step* two three . . .'

'Like this?'

'No.'

'Ouch!'

'Oh, for goodness' sake, swap round.'

'What?'

'I'll be the man, you follow what *I* do, all right?' said Lin impatiently.

'I'm sure this is a sin,' sighed Lyle.

'Atheist,' she replied sweetly.

'Me too, doesn't mean I'm going to covet my neighbour's camel any time soon.'

'You're still not going to see my ankles, although many men would swoon at the suggestion.'

'You aren't like normal people – of any kind – are you, Miss Lin?'

'This from a man who fears green eyes. Now . . . *step* two three, *step* two three, *step* two three . . .'

'Am I going . . .'

'Be quiet and pay attention!'

'Sorry,' mumbled Lyle, and was surprised to find he meant it.

'And *step* two three, *step* two three . . .'

They drifted through the fog. 'You know . . .' Lyle's voice was muffled by the greyness rising from the river, 'I feel I'm getting the knack of this . . .'

'No, I'm merely not pointing out the error of your ways. There are snowmen with carrots for noses who have more elegance and grace than you when it comes to the waltz, Mister Lyle.'

'I could just go home, you know, have a nice night in with the oxides . . .'

'It is more ungentlemanly *not* to dance for a lady's pleasure, Mister Lyle, than it is to dance badly . . .' Lin's voice, like wind chimes, waltzed through the air. 'And *step* two three, *step* two three . . . mind the toes . . .'

And though things might be bad, or have been bad, or may be bad again — as in all probability they will — just for now, in this moment they dance on, into the night.

ABOUT THE AUTHOR

Catherine Webb published her extraordinary debut, *Mirror Dreams*, at the age of 14, garnering comparisons with Terry Pratchett and Philip Pullman. Subsequent books have brought Carnegie Medal longlistings, a *Guardian* Children's Book of the Week, a BBC television appearance and praise from the *Sunday Times* and the *Sunday Telegraph*, amongst many others. Catherine Webb is currently reading History at university but still found time to establish herself as one of the most talented and exciting young writers in the UK. She lives in London – without a cat but she plans to remedy that, soon.

For more information about Catherine Webb and other Atom authors go to www.atombooks.co.uk